Craving: A Willow Creek Vampires Novel

Stephanie Summers

Willow Creek: Craving
© 2014, Stephanie Summers.

Published by: Wicked Dragon Publishing

ISBN-10: 1515313824
ISBN-13: 978-1515313823

Prologue

May 19, 1798: Willow Creek

Screams ricocheted through the still of night as chaos ensued in the burgeoning little town. Deep crimson splattered and pooled on the soft, green earth. The echoes of conversations and laughter dissipated within seconds. An evening of celebration quickly spiraled into a night of terror.

Members of the newly established community of Willow Creek gathered in the center of town for food and camaraderie. Shortly after giving thanks to God for the good fortune that had been bestowed upon them, a blood curdling scream erupted from the outskirts of the community.

Several men ran to the aid of the woman. As they approached her body lying on the ground, people with beast-like teeth and blood dripping from their faces pounced on the men, ripping their throats out in an instant. Pure panic overtook the remaining members as they fled in all directions trying to escape the onslaught. One by one, they fell victim to the evil things lurking in the dark.

Before the villagers' very eyes, one lone man swooped in and took out the rogues, one by one. Bones cracked. Flesh ripped. Blood poured as heads rolled. None of them stood a chance against his strength and speed. Covered in blood and eyes lit up with fury, the man addressed the remaining residents.

"My name is Bastian Florien. I would very much like to speak to whomever is in charge." His powerful voice echoed with an Eastern European accent through the night. Piercing blue eyes scanned the crowd of terrified humans until one hand reluctantly wavered above the crowd.

"Yes, you." Bastian pointed to the man and motioned him closer. "Come forward. What is your name?"

"My n-name is Thomas Crowley."

"Mr. Crowley, do not be afraid. I mean you no harm, but I cannot speak for others of my kind." Bastian rested his hand on the man's shoulder as he spoke.

"What ailed them? What made them attack their fellow man in such a savage way?"

"They, as well as I, are vampire. There is a great power here that draws them and other supernatural creatures into the borders of your town. I wish to make a bargain with you that will help your town and its people flourish for generations to come."

"Go on." Thomas stood tall, trying to stay brave in the face of danger, even though he remained terrified and skeptical of the man's words.

"If you choose to stay, I will protect the residents of Willow Creek from otherworldly outsiders, as well as other humans, if necessary. This is a desirable area—rich in resources—you won't be the only people wishing to settle here."

Thomas glanced down at the ground before looking up to meet Bastian's eyes. "How would this arrangement benefit you?"

"In return, I only wish that I, and a few of my kind, may walk freely, not ever having to hide our true nature."

"I have heard tales of unspeakable evil that lurks in the dark; monsters that attack and drain their victims of blood. This is what you are?" Thomas asked as his eyes studied Bastian.

"Not exactly... I am not evil, nor do I lurk in the shadows waiting for unsuspecting victims. Are there others who do this? Yes, this is true, but you must not only fear the night. Though vampires are weakened in sunlight, you are still vulnerable and far weaker than any of us will ever be. You have witnessed the destruction we are capable of, and more will come. Many more will die until none of your people remain. I have witnessed the total annihilation of four groups of settlers in the last three years. The others would not heed my warnings or enter into any arrangement with me."

"If the stories are true, and from what I've seen here tonight, vampires survive on blood, do they not? How will you feed? I cannot and will not agree to vampires running rampant and drinking the blood of those in our community whenever they please."

"One person per vampire will be paired with me and mine so that we can feed exclusively from the offering. They will reside in my home, and I will provide them with food and shelter until their life comes to its natural end."

Shaking his head, Thomas spoke sternly. "I will not subject my people to such torture. You may walk among us if you so choose, but you must feed on the animals of the forest. We will not be sustenance for demons."

"I am no demon. I started out human and am still flesh and blood, just like you. Would you yourself agree to eat only weeds and berries you had to gather in the forest for the rest of your life when there were plump, juicy turkeys constantly running about? It will be worse to let others of my kind and beyond roam freely," Bastian said, taking a step closer to the settlers. His body, though not overly big, stood tall and strong like a statue. "There is a very strong force of power here." His eyes scanned the group of people, watching the terrified faces peering back at him. "One you could not possibly understand. They will never stop coming. You have only been established a short period of time. You have not been around long enough to witness what I have, but I assure you there will be more. What I offer will guarantee the success and survival of this town's people."

"Why would we agree to this when we could just leave? Yes, we have worked tirelessly to establish ourselves here, but it is not worth the lives of our people."

Bastian looked deep into Thomas' eyes, lulling him into a light trance. "You will not leave. Where else would you go that could provide you the resources you have found here? You can accept my offer, or I will not stop them next time. The choice is yours."

Thomas dragged his hands through his dark hair and closed his eyes. He swallowed hard before speaking.

4

"How would you choose the people who would be taken?"

"I will return tomorrow night to finalize the arrangement and discuss details."

And with that, the vampire was gone.

Chapter 1

May 19: Willow Creek, present day

Sabine Crowley sat under the weeping willow in the side-yard of her parents' home. Her dark hair danced gently in the breeze. Light brown eyes focused on the pad of paper in front of her as her hand sketched a scene of Paris with the Eiffel Tower looming in the background. Drawing always seemed to calm her when she had some sort of crisis she needed to hash out. This particular crisis was the biggest she'd ever faced, and she knew it was coming for as long as she could remember. Time had slipped through her fingers as she hurdled toward a potentially cruel fate, not the one she dreamed of for herself. Studying her drawing, a feeling of despair fell over her as she realized she most likely would never see the Eiffel Tower or Paris in person.

She pondered her future and the two drastically different paths her life could take in exactly three days. If she could manage to get through her eighteenth birthday without being called or summoned or whatever the hell they liked to call it, she'd be free to do what she wanted, when she wanted. After graduation in a few weeks, she could flee and go anywhere in the world she wanted to go. That was all she could hope for.

Sabine was an aspiring artist with dreams of exploring the world for inspiration; not some blood bag destined to rot in seclusion while the world outside went on without her. If fate chose her to be the one, she would be confined to a life of serving some blood-sucking monster, all for the sake of a town she didn't really care much about in the first place.

"Beanie? Are you out here?" Her mother, Vivian, walked outside from the back door and knowingly scanned the yard. Her daughter was nothing if she wasn't predictable. Anytime Sabine was upset or worried, Vivian could always find her under that willow tree. This time was no different.

"Unfortunately, yes," Sabine said with contempt in her voice. She'd tried to avoid her mother all day, and couldn't stand the sight of either of her parents at the moment. If they had waited one more year or gotten pregnant one year earlier, she wouldn't be in this predicament to begin with. Having her was selfish and thoughtless on their part. It was better to avoid them altogether than to point out their mistake. She had no desire to talk about what was expected of her and how it would affect *them* if she was the next chosen one.

She watched her parents over the years treating her sister differently than they did her, and though the differences were subtle, they were still apparent to her. Her parents loved her, without a doubt, but she was only half-heartedly encouraged to do anything that might build a solid foundation for her future. They rarely talked to her about college, and when they did, it was more of a formality to try and make her feel normal. Although she had been interested in sports just briefly a few years earlier, her parents wouldn't shell out the money for uniforms and transportation. As far as her artwork was concerned, she could barely get any response from them at all other than a "that's nice".

Her younger sister, Shay, on the other hand, was already planning on touring college campuses and she wasn't even a freshman in high school yet. She was a star athlete on the track team, and their parents never batted an eye at any expense that arose from her activities. They rode Shay's ass to get straight A's so she could have her choice of any college she wanted to attend. As long as Sabine passed, then all was well.

"May I sit?" Vivian said, smiling sweetly.

Sabine sighed, rolled her eyes, and crossed her arms. The sketch pad slid off her lap and onto the ground beside her. "Yeah. It's your yard... your tree... Do what you want."

"Don't be like that, Beanie." Vivian took a deep breath and fiddled with a loose strand of her hair as she chose her words. "We need to talk. I don't think you know the full extent of what your birthday could mean for you, or for all of us for that matter."

Sabine peered off in the distance, avoiding eye contact with her mother. "Oh, believe me, I'm aware of what it means for everyone else. And for me? If one of those freaks shows up and tells me I'm the one, then it's like I never existed. I'm just gone, never to be seen or heard from again."

"You don't know that for sure. I've never heard of any of the others being shut out altogether."

"Does it really matter? I've pretty much been an outcast in this town for as long as I can remember. Would anyone outside of my friends and you guys really miss me? As long as the assholes living here get to go on with their lives while I waste away up on the hill in that mansion of horrors, then all is well with the world. Willow Creek Manor, my ass. Sounds like a lovely place, except that it isn't. Any place swarming with vampires is not a place I want to be."

"I know it must be tough." Vivian reached out to touch Sabine's shoulder, but she pulled away before her mother's hand could make contact.

"No... You don't know. You were safe from all of this." She threw her hands up in exasperation and let them fall to her lap. "It was never something you ever had to worry about for yourself. You knew you wouldn't be eighteen when they were choosing. Your mother and father had enough sense to know not to have a child at the wrong time."

"I know you're upset, but you will not speak that way to me. You know we love you, and we want for you to not be called more than anything in this world. The fact is that it's a good possibility you *will* be the one this time. I'd love to be able to sugarcoat it for you, but I can't. You've got too many things working in your favor. You're a descendant of Thomas Crowley, and, frankly, I think you're the prettiest one of the contenders."

Sabine's eyebrow arched as she stared at her mother. "Contenders? And I'm pretty? You make it sound as if this is something I should want to win... Lucky me if I do, right?" Her mother's words grated her nerves. She'd never considered herself hard to look at, but for Vivian to say she'd be picked because of her looks pissed her off more than it probably should.

"In a way, you *are* lucky. I know you don't see it, but you wouldn't ever have to worry about supporting yourself or whether or not you'll have a roof over your head or food in your belly." Vivian glanced at Sabine's sketch pad with the drawing of Paris on it. "Who knows? You might even get to go to Paris to see the Eiffel Tower sometime if they let you. I know you'd enjoy that."

"Yes, Mother. I'll just love having a roof over my head and not having to worry about paying bills and having the slim at best possibility of going to Paris while I have my blood painfully sucked out of me by a terrifying monster every night. I will be guaranteed a short and sad life." She leaned back against the rough trunk of the tree, stretching her legs out in front of her. "It's not like anyone ever really sees the other ones. Who knows what the hell goes on up there? And, by the way, I'm glad you're okay with me never having children, because I'm certainly not okay with it. But, I guess as long as track star Shay gets to go on to a normal life, the perfect husband and two-point-five kids with a white picket fence around her house and a brand new minivan in the driveway, you won't really be missing out on anything. One perfect child out of two ain't bad, right?"

"I'm so sorry." Her mother sobbed, fat tears streaming down her cheeks. Vivian hung her head, resting it on the palm of her hand. "I would keep you from it if I could."

"Don't cry, Mother." As much as Sabine hated to admit it, her mother crying was one of the few things that ever made her feel guilty. "I know it isn't what you would choose for me, but I have to sit back and wonder why you even decided to have a child in the first place, knowing what the future held. I never would have had a kid who would be eighteen during a year they'd be choosing. I would have planned it out better than you did. Abortion, or giving me up, would have been a better choice than becoming a vampire's concubine."

"It wasn't a choice. You were a surprise."

"Surprise? Hello? Ever heard of birth control? Condoms? The pill?"

Vivian ignored Sabine's comment. She watched the anger seethe through her daughter's body, almost as visible as steam rising off her. "It was one of the happiest days of my life when I found out you were coming. I never would have considered abortion or adoption. I wanted you from the time I was old enough to understand what having a child meant. When I realized you would be in the group to be chosen, I hoped and prayed there would be other kids your age that would be more desirable to them. So far, my prayers haven't been answered, and I'm terrified it's going to be you. If I could take you away from here without any consequences, I would."

"What would they do, huh? Hunt me down like I'm some kind of animal." She rolled her eyes and looked away from Vivian, feeling like she already knew the answer to the question.

11

"Yes. They would. This is what I wanted to talk to you about. I don't think you understand the magnitude of this whole thing and how far reaching it is."

"Then tell me something I don't already know."

"They've kept this town safe for over two hundred years. They will never go against the deal they made with our ancestors. Time is nothing to them, and it's as if this happened seconds ago. To us, it's an antiquated arrangement that should be updated or modified... or done away with altogether."

"What do they get out of all this? I've been told all my life that they protect the town from all sorts of nasty creatures out there, which, by the way, I'm not convinced is even true, but what do they *really* gain?"

Vivian shook her head slowly as if she were searching for a valid answer. "They don't have to hide."

"Yeah, right. I'm calling bullshit. There's got to be more to it than that. It just doesn't make any sense. You can't tell me they haven't existed amongst humans just fine for thousands of years. And what is it about this Podunk town that draws all these supernatural nasties here anyway?"

"I'm afraid I don't know the answer to that, Beanie."

She shuddered at the mention of the pet name her parents had given her as a child. It normally didn't bother her, but it seemed too juvenile for the situation.

"Just go away." She waved her mother off. "I want to be by myself. I might as well get used to it."

12

"Don't say that. You don't know that you won't still be able to see us, and there's a chance you won't be the one."

"Don't really think they care if we stay in contact. Like I've said before, it's not like any of the previous ones were ever really seen out and about socializing."

"You have to stay positive."

She nodded. "So I can really feel my insides rip apart when it doesn't turn out how I want it to?"

Her mother stood and walked away. Sabine eyed her as she walked back into the house.

Why would they bother to come after me if I leave? Why would they even care? Wouldn't they just pick someone else?

To hell with the consequences. She was getting out. All she had to do was pack a few things in her backpack and head for the bus station. She still had roughly $500 saved from babysitting over the summer. She could easily buy a bus ticket, and she was old enough to get a job wherever she landed. She'd just have to get her GED once she was settled somewhere instead of graduating. It wasn't the ideal plan, but at least it would get her far away from Willow Creek. It would have to do.

Slamming the door as she entered the house, Sabine ran up the stairs to her room, making sure to hit every step a little heavier than need be. If she made a big enough production, neither her parents nor her sister would bother her, and she'd be able to sneak away without them noticing she was gone. It was a tactic she'd employed numerous times before.

She frantically searched through her closet for a few items of clothing she absolutely couldn't leave home without and threw them all in her backpack. The window eased up quietly under the pressure from her fingers. Tossing her backpack out the window, it landed with a soft thud just before she climbed through the window and over to a large tree branch. She'd snuck out so many times over the years that it became second nature to her, and her parents were none the wiser. She always made sure to be home and back in bed before they had a chance to notice. This time they'd notice her absence, but she'd be long gone.

* * *

May 19: London, England

"Remy?"

The door to the large bedroom creaked open as a stocky man peered through the crack. A thin stream of light from the hallway illuminated the darkened room.

Remy dropped the young lady's wrist and licked at the corners of his mouth. "What is it, Mason?" He scowled, never wanting to be interrupted during his dinner.

"This arrived for you just a minute ago." Mason held up his hand, showing Remy a tightly bound roll of paper.

He immediately knew who it was from once he spotted the familiar dark blue ribbon tied around it.

"Thank you," Remy said as he slipped the vampire 100 pounds he'd fetched from the drawer of the night stand. "Take this one away. I'm done with her." He pushed the young red head away from him and into the arms of his assistant, who would undoubtedly have a few drops of her blood and a taste of her flesh as well.

"Anything else for you, Remy?"

"That'll be all. Thank you."

He held the scroll in his hand, hesitating to open it. Whatever was contained within, he'd be forced to comply with, and he wasn't too keen on leaving London. Any correspondence from his maker would more than likely require him to, and he wanted to put a stake through his own heart just to get out of going to that dreadful town in the States. There was nothing exciting or exhilarating to do there, and he'd be forced to eat bunnies or deer for fear he would be reprimanded, or worse, by Bastian.

Reaching over, he flipped on a dimly lit lamp and focused on the paper in front of him. The ribbon slid off the scroll easily under his long, pale fingers. He unrolled it and took a deep breath. Not that he needed to breathe, but some trivial things from his mortal life lingered like a bad habit. He'd been nearly dead for over four hundred years, but things like breathing and occasionally craving the taste of a specific human food had never quite gone away.

Only Bastian would still send me a scroll instead of simply texting or calling. Will he ever move into this century? He scanned the document quickly.

My Dear Remington,

It is time for you to take your place by my side. You will come to me by the 22nd. I trust you will make arrangements for travel accordingly. Do not be late.

15

Regards,
Bastian

"Bollocks," he said aloud to himself.

His worst nightmare appeared to be coming true. Not only would he have to go to that God forsaken place, but he would have to stay indefinitely. The pact was the stupidest thing he'd heard in all the years he'd walked the earth. What vampire in their right mind would want to willingly feed from one person for years or even decades straight?

The hunt for a new donor was part of the thrill of the feed. Stalking unsuspecting prey and pouncing on them gave him a rush that could never be fulfilled from just one lousy human. Of course, the willing ones could be good, too. They weren't as thrilling, but they made up for it in other ways. Sex while feeding could be almost as good as the hunt, but even sex with the same person for decades sounded dreadfully boring.

* * *

Sabine found herself walking out of town, and toward the future *she* would make for herself, not the one that had been mapped out for her two hundred years ago. The closest bus station that still had buses running at that time was over ten miles away, and she was starting to rethink this plan of hers. She wasn't sure she could even make it that far on foot without stopping along the way. Keeping off the main roads had proved challenging at times, and she was convinced she would be caught at any moment. The town had a strict curfew for minors and if someone suspected she was underage, she'd be hauled back to her parents immediately. Funny how the all-important pact wasn't as secure as people liked to let on. When you have vampires walking the streets at night, people aren't as trusting as they are in the daylight.

It was silly, though, really. Vampires could get you whenever—day or night—if they really wanted you. It wasn't completely true that sunlight would kill them. The older ones could go out in the daylight, and most of the ones in Willow Creek were probably older than dirt, if she had to guess. Everyone acted so open and trusting on the surface, yet things like curfews were put in place, and whispers could be heard throughout the town whenever someone went missing. Disappearances were always blamed on the person simply running away or a rogue vampire attack by an outsider, but Sabine couldn't help but wonder if it was the town's own resident vampires who were actually responsible.

She'd wondered to herself so many times over the years why the people here didn't leave. Why didn't her parents just leave? Why cohabitate with a bunch of bloodsuckers that could kill you or coerce you into doing things you would never remember? At least she thought that was one of the things they could do. She wasn't entirely sure. She'd found out some of the popular lore about vampires wasn't true, but how many abilities they truly possessed she did not know and really had no desire to find out.

Maybe they had hypnotized all of the townspeople so they wouldn't leave and wouldn't tell their secrets when they travelled. That would certainly explain why on the rare occasion she traveled with her parents, none of them ever seemed to remember the history the town had with vampires. She even remembered watching a vampire movie once while on vacation and wondering to herself if they really existed. It was only after they returned home that she remembered how silly the thought was when she knew them to be absolutely 100% real.

A mile, or so, into her journey, the huge glass of sweet tea she consumed right before sneaking out of her room began to catch up with her. Trying to get a boost of caffeine had backfired. Maybe she could slip into the restroom at the little fast food restaurant at the edge of town and get out without being seen.

Willow Creek was closely monitored by the vampire lord, Bastian, and no outside chains were ever allowed to set up shop in town, though many had tried over the years. All the restaurants, shops, and convenience stores were locally owned and employed only citizens of Willow Creek. She longed for a *McDonalds*, and aimed to run away to a place that had at least two within its borders.

She approached the side door of the little restaurant and slipped into the restroom. Only two people were seated nearby, and if she was quick, maybe she wouldn't draw any attention to herself. Though she tried not to linger too long, she took the opportunity to freshen up just a little. Her eyelids had grown heavy, so she splashed a little water on her face. The cold liquid on her skin was just what she needed to help wake herself up.

As she emerged from the restaurant several minutes later, a set of flashing, blue lights caught her attention. *Shit!*

"Sabine Crowley?" A tall police officer approached her cautiously.

"No, I'm sorry. My name is Rachael Gifford," she said casually as she tried to keep walking. Thankfully, the name had sprung to mind quickly so she didn't stammer over herself.

The cop looked annoyed, and the tone of his voice only reinforced it. "Let me rephrase that. You're coming with me, Sabine Crowley."

The thought of bolting into the woods and out of there to freedom crossed her mind, but this cop wasn't one of the usual morbidly obese officers in town. This one looked like he was fresh out of the police academy. He could easily run her down and catch her. She reluctantly went with him to the station where her father, Rob, waited for her.

Chapter 2

"I don't know what kind of shit you were trying to pull, but your mother and sister have been worried to death that you were gone and they'd never see you again." Sabine's father's voice dripped with anger.

"They might as well get used to it, don't you think?"

The two didn't speak another word to each other the rest of the way home. She sensed her father wanted to say more, but for whatever reason, he'd chosen to ignore her the rest of the way. Her mother said nothing, and Shay was nowhere to be found as Sabine entered the house and ran up to her room.

A soft knock came at her bedroom door an hour later, just after she'd gotten into bed for the night.

"Come in," she said softly.

Her mother entered the room and sat down beside her on the bed. "I understand why you left, but where did you think you were going to go?"

"Anywhere but here."

"I understand, Sabine. I really do. This is hard on me and Dad, too. Shay is falling apart, though she tries to act like it doesn't bother her. My greatest wish for you is that you get to live your dreams and your life however you see fit. It tears me apart to know that your life might not go the way you want it to. Try as I might to see the positives, I keep failing." Vivian stroked Sabine's dark, wavy hair.

"I know it isn't your fault, Mom. I shouldn't have put the blame on you guys earlier. I'm sorry for worrying you."

"Don't be sorry, Beanie." She put her arms around Sabine and squeezed her. "Just know that if there is a way, Dad and I will find it."

"I know, Mom."

"Promise you won't run again?"

She subtly shook her head. "I can't make a promise I might not be able to keep."

"Fair enough. Get some rest. It's been a long day."

* * *

May 21: Willow Creek

"Remington, my boy," Bastian said, standing up and raising his hand slightly. "So good to see you. It's been, what? A hundred years or more? My how time flies. I trust you know why I have summoned you?"

Remy stood straight with his chin tilted slightly. "I presume it has to do with that ridiculous agreement you have with the daft cows who inhabit this," Remy crinkled his nose as if he'd smelled something putrid, "place."

"Agreement with the people of this town? Yes. Ridiculous? No." Bastian shook his head and smirked.

"But it's beyond ridiculous. It's easier now than ever to find willing donors. So many wish to live out their fantasies of Damon Salvatore and Edward Cullen, and the like. Though, if I'm being honest, I do quite like that Damon. I often wonder who he was based on. Reminds me a little of myself actually."

21

"I know nothing of these characters of whom you speak," Bastian said, waving Remy off.

"Of course you don't. You aren't out in the world like the rest of us. You choose to stay in one place and feed from one human until he or she grows sick and withered. Outside of this town lies a vast world of flavors, some of which are quite willing to play whatever role you wish them to play. We don't have to hide as much as we once did."

"Nonsense... Why would I give up not having to hide *at all* and being in control of Willow Creek and its secrets for a life of seclusion where I must make others forget? I, as well as my fellow vampire companions, am free to come and go as I please, and all I have to do is keep the others out. Quite easy for someone as old as I am."

Remy turned, and subtly rolled his eyes. He was never one to stifle his thoughts and opinions, but there was still a part of him that feared Bastian and what he could do to him if he angered him too much. His maker had mellowed tremendously throughout the years, but he knew what Bastian was capable of, and it wasn't a side he ever wanted to see again. "We will have to agree to disagree on this one, my lord."

"I am afraid not, Remy. There is no room for disagreement. It is your time now to take your place at my side. I have given you close to two centuries to do as you please. Now is the time."

If he were capable of vomiting, he would've just then. His gut twisted into knots at the thought of staying in Willow Creek for the next several decades, at the very least.

"No. I will not stay here like a prisoner. I would rather rot than be monogamous... Unless, of course, you're willing to grant me a few liberties."

"Such as?"

"I can feed from whomever I like, I'll even go out of town if need be, and I want my freedom to travel when I want. As long as I spend most of my time here with you, I don't see why that's not a fair trade."

"No. Your blood mate has already been chosen. When she is procured, she will belong wholly to you. You will be responsible for her well-being, and, in return, she will provide you with the sustenance you require while you are on duty protecting the citizens of this great town. You have a little more time to get used to the idea, but you will stay here with me in the meantime. I need you to familiarize yourself with the rules and what I expect of you."

"Why must you torture me so?"

"Torture? HA." Bastian's hand slapped the edge of an end table loudly as his voice bounced off the walls. Remy flinched as a familiar look in Bastian's eyes took over. "You think serving at my side is torture? Learning everything I know?" His voice grew louder with every question. "Am I not the one who gave you immortality? Am I not the one that took you from the filth you called a life, and gave you the world?"

"Forgive me, my lord." Remy went to one knee and dropped his head. "I did not intend to offend you. I let my tongue get the better of me. My apologies."

Bastian turned away. "Gretchen will show you to your quarters. Get settled, and return to me before morning."

* * *

May 22: Willow Creek—Sabine's 18th Birthday

The couple of days leading up to Sabine's eighteenth birthday had been mostly uneventful. She'd tried to live as normal an existence as possible: hanging out with her friends, listening to angst-filled music by musicians that just seemed to *get* her, and working on her latest art project. She'd continued to work on schoolwork, hoping to get some good grades this term, though she wasn't sure there was much point. Graduation wasn't very far away, and she was happy it would be done and over with soon. A small spark of hope still remained, though it was mostly buried beneath thick layers of pessimism.

The morning of her birthday, she'd awakened to no sign that she'd been chosen. She'd heard, mostly from her two best friends who'd heard it from God only knows who, the dreaded scroll with the dark blue ribbon wrapped around it would arrive during the early hours on the morning of the chosen one's eighteenth birthday. She began to relax by late afternoon, and was even looking forward to spending the night with her two best friends, Delia and Lana. They had nothing too exciting planned, but were looking forward to a horror movie marathon—

though vampires were definitely not going to be featured—popcorn, and plenty of boy talk and gossip.

As she did almost daily when the weather was nice, she found herself sketching under the weeping willow. The wind blew through the swaying branches gently, and the grass rustled all around her. Dogs barked in the distance, and children in the neighborhood yelled and laughed with no care in the world as they played. The sun was bright, and warmed her skin.

As she sat under the tree, planning her future, a fancy, black Lincoln pulled up in front of the house. Her breath caught in her throat, heart skipping a beat. *No, no, no, no, no, please, no.*

A tall, strikingly beautiful woman with flowing blonde hair emerged from the back seat, her gaze instantly focused on Sabine. A split second later, the stranger stood directly in front of her. Saying nothing, the woman looked down at Sabine with cold eyes. A scroll with a dark blue ribbon binding it teetered on the stranger's fingers. Sabine hesitated before reaching out to take it. Just as quickly as the woman had arrived, she was gone.

Sabine struggled to get air to her lungs as she gasped heavily to force oxygen into her body. Collapsing onto her back, she stared straight up into the tree branches. Her world had ended, and it might as well have been her life.

Her mother rushed out to her and fell to her knees at Sabine's side. She wrapped her arms around her daughter and screamed. The realization of what had happened thrust into her gut like a hot knife cutting through butter.

Her firstborn would be ripped away from her, and she was helpless to stop it.

Vivian's scream crashed into the kitchen where Rob was loading the dishwasher. A glass dropped to the floor and shattered as he rushed to find her. He frantically searched the yard, trying to locate where she was. Moments later, he found his wife and daughter in a heap under the tree.

Dropping to his knees, he scooped Sabine into his arms. She sobbed into his chest as his heart shattered into a million pieces. His little girl would be gone, and he'd never get to learn of all the accomplishments she should have made in her life—graduating high school and going off to college, the first real grown-up job, marriage, and children. Even if they were permitted visitation, she would no longer grow as a person. She'd never live beyond the walls of Willow Creek Manor.

After what seemed like hours, but in reality was only minutes, Sabine calmed down enough to open the scroll. She squinted through teary eyes to make out the dreaded words written on the paper. The penmanship was like nothing she'd ever seen. The letters swirled and flowed across the page like a beautiful work of art.

Miss Crowley,

As you know, an arrangement was made long ago that has kept Willow Creek and its citizens safe from evil, otherworldly creatures who have wanted nothing more than to harm the residents of this wonderful town for the last two hundred years. Every ten years, a lucky youth, soon to reach adulthood, is chosen to fulfill the obligations of this arrangement. You, sweet child, have been chosen from a select group of your peers.

You will meet with me tomorrow evening at 8:00. Food and drink will be provided for you and your family while we get to know one another. Though I know a good bit about you already, I look forward to officially meeting you, Miss Crowley.

Regards,

Bastian Florien of Willow Creek Manor

Sabine stood and looked around at her house, her yard, her tree, and the neighborhood that surrounded her. Birds chirped. Bees buzzed. A small child's laughter echoed in the distance. A dog from next door barked. A light breeze caused the branches of her beloved tree to sway and the grass to rustle. The world around her hadn't changed a bit in the last few minutes, but *her* world was over. "I need to go lay down."

Chapter 3

Remy awoke just as the sun melted into the horizon. A pang of hunger hit him, and he knew he would have to feed soon before blood lust set in. The longer a vampire delayed feeding, the more intense and hard to control the desire became. The thought of hunting down some woodland creature was not appealing at all, but it would have to do. Draining a deer or a few rabbits was the only option. Bastian wouldn't agree to let him leave so soon to feed; not when he'd just arrived and made it known he'd rather be anywhere in the world but Willow Creek.

The hunt would have to wait for the time being as he had to meet with Bastian before he went out for the night. He'd agreed to meet with him earlier, before the sun came up, but when Remy went to him, Bastian was nowhere to be found. Sleep seemed to be the better option, and he decided not to wait around all day for Bastian. Being awake during the day or going out in the sun didn't really bother him, but he was more nocturnal by nature and preferred the night.

He sat up and stretched in the huge bed that was adorned with burgundy satin sheets and a plush comforter that reminded him of the color of blood. The accommodations provided were more than suitable. There was a large bedroom, with oversized furniture and a closet the size of a smaller bedroom. Vampires could amass quite the collection of possessions, and he'd have to send for his things soon if he couldn't find a way out of this mess. Not wearing a stitch of clothing, he got out of bed and waltzed across the room. Clothes were optional in bed as far as he was concerned, whether he was alone or not.

Adjacent to the bedroom was a bathroom. As he entered to take a shower, he noticed a toilet sitting off to the side. An oddity for sure. He had no use for one and couldn't fathom why Bastian would even include such a thing in the rooms meant for vampires. Surely there were separate rooms meant for human guests elsewhere, but maybe that wasn't the case. The enormous bathtub that sat against the wall... now that was different. He could definitely see himself occupying it. All he'd need was a warm-blooded woman or two to help him fill it. He stepped into the shower, and turned the water on, not caring that it would be cold for a minute or so before warming up. His flesh was cool most of the time anyway, so it didn't really bother him.

Water cascaded over his back, and his skin warmed with the water as steam collected around him. He turned to let the water flow over his chest and down the rest of his body as he lost himself in thought. *Maybe this won't be so bad. Would Bastian know for sure if I choose to feed on others? I could always make them forget if I have to. Maybe I'll get lucky and she'll die an early death... I could try to get away after she's gone. Surely, Bastian won't want to keep me here against my will when he knows better than anyone what I've endured in my past. It seems ludicrous that he would go through all of this nonsense for two centuries just because he fancies being able to say publicly that he is vampire. I've told numerous humans of my true nature, and I haven't been hunted or staked as of yet. Quite the opposite actually...*

His thoughts turned to the girl he'd been paired with. *Where is she going to stay? Certainly not with me. She better have her own living quarters far away from me. I have no desire to use her for anything other than a bite to eat now and then. I can't imagine ever having anything in common with a mortal teenager. I've been around for over four hundred years. The notion of an eighteen year old being a mature adult suitable as a companion for me is laughable and quite ridiculous.*

Bastian summoning him interrupted his thoughts and his shower. The sensation rushed through him, and he was immediately compelled to get out and to Bastian as soon as possible. He raced into the bedroom, throwing on a pair of dark jeans and a white T-shirt over his wet body. His hair dripped little dots of water onto his shirt as he made his way to his maker.

Bastian sat at a desk writing as Remy entered the office only seconds after being summoned.

"Apologies for being away this morning. I had business with a friend to attend to that could not wait." Bastian continued writing without looking at Remy as he addressed him.

"What kind of business?" Remy moved closer and stood just in front of the desk.

"All in good time, my boy. All in good time." A wolfish smile spread across Bastian's lips as he looked up at Remy.

A feeling of uneasiness rippled through Remy's body. "So what am I doing here? You're running off to take care of top secret issues, yet I'm supposed to be your second in command now."

"You will know everything I know and everywhere I go in due time. I want to catch up with you first and get to know you again. If we didn't have the bond we share you would be almost like a stranger to me. A lot must have happened in the last hundred years or so. Where have you been?"

"You know where I've been. You always know where I've been. You can find me any time you like. Why bother with all the tedious details now?"

"As you wish, Remy, and you are correct. I can *always* find you. It would do you well to remember that should you have the urge or desire to leave." Bastian's expression became serious.

A chill went through Remy's body. It didn't happen often, but when it did, it was always Bastian exerting his power and control over him.

"I won't be running away, but when this girl dies, I want the opportunity to discuss taking my leave."

"Of course, of course... I hope by then you will understand the importance of this place and won't want to leave me, but we can leave the option open. Now, onto business. I trust you want to go out this evening to explore your new surroundings, so I will make this brief. Your blood mate's name is Sabine Crowley. She will not be coming to us until she turns twenty-one, three years from now. I do not really know why Thomas chose that age back when the covenant was established, but it is what it is. Seems rather silly to me. What difference does three years make? I suppose he thought at twenty-one, in those days, the offering may be near the end of their life, and it would be less time they would be trapped here, but I digress. When Sabine comes to us, she will share your living space with you, and you will oversee her day to day life."

"No bloody way! That is preposterous. As big as this place is, and she has to room with me? Put her somewhere else. Are there no other rooms she can live in?"

"This is not up for discussion. She *will* be living with you. She will be safest close to you. On the rare occasion I allow you to leave on business or for pleasure, you must take her with you and return as soon as I say."

Remy understood there was no point in arguing. She might be required to stay in his room, but he didn't have to share his bed with her. *Let the thing sleep on the floor.*

"Forgive me for asking, and I mean no disrespect, but why summon me now? I'm quite familiar with the *rules* you spoke of last night. Why not wait until she turns twenty-one?"

"Because she is your responsibility now. She may not be here with us yet, but it is up to you to ensure she does not run... or die. Once word gets out that the pairing has been made, she may become a target from those who wish us harm or to cause problems for us with the residents of Willow Creek. For all intents and purposes, you are to view her as your wife. There will be a vampire wedding ceremony on her twenty-first birthday to make it known."

His jaw clenched. "May I take my leave now?" He tried hard to cloak the irritation he felt. Bastian could kill him or make him suffer with one look, and if he stayed much longer, he ran the risk of letting his tongue get him into trouble.

"You may go."

Remy turned and began to make his way to the door.

"Oh, and Remy? If you must feed tonight, I suggest you hunt a deer because you are forbidden to feed on anyone from Willow Creek, with the exception of Sabine once she moves in with us. Everyone else is off limits, and I don't want you leaving town right now."

* * *

Her phone rang, jolting her awake. Judging by the ringtone, it was Delia, most likely calling to see if she was ready to come over for her birthday celebration. Though she knew she'd be alone indefinitely, she couldn't stand the thought of being around anyone for very long at that moment. She ignored the call, and tapped out a text instead before heading downstairs to see what her family was up to.

I'm not coming tonight. Bad news. I'm sure I don't have to elaborate. I'm fine, but I'm not in the mood for celebrating. Let Lana know. I'll talk later tomorrow night after I find out more details.

Rob tossed tiny bits of pineapple and ham onto an unbaked pizza while Vivian spread chocolate icing over the tops of yellow cupcakes. Shay haphazardly wrapped a

T-shirt in a sheet of newspaper. Sabine smiled as she walked down the steps and the open kitchen came into view. The aroma of freshly baked cupcakes was almost intoxicating. Every year, her parents did this for her, and it brought back so many happy memories of birthdays past. Just as soon as she'd forgotten how her life had turned to shit a few hours earlier, it came rushing back to her. How could she be excited to eat or celebrate at a time like this?

Shortly after dinner, Shay grabbed the present she'd wrapped earlier and tossed it to Sabine. "Here."

Sabine tore into the paper to find a fitted black T-shirt featuring a photo of Eric Northman from the television show *True Blood*.

Sabine smacked Shay in the arm and chuckled. "You shit-ass! You think you're sooooo funny, don't you?"

"Hey, I wouldn't feel a bit sorry for you if you were paired with that Viking," Shay said, chuckling.

Ignoring her sister's comment, she turned to her mom and dad. "Thanks so much for the dinner, Dad, and these cupcakes look fantastic, Mom," she said as she picked one up and began to peal the paper off the bottom.

"Glad you enjoyed it, Beanie. How are you holding up?"

Sabine looked at her mother, and noticed the huge bags under her eyes and a few grays poking through her normally dyed light brown hair. Her mother appeared to have aged ten years in the short time Sabine had slept.

"I'm okay, I guess. I've decided to go ahead and go tonight after I eat this cupcake, if that's okay. I want to enjoy my birthday while I can."

"I think it'll be good for you to hang out with the girls. Can you help Dad with the dishes first?"

"Yeah."

An hour later, Sabine was out the door and headed to one of her favorite spots in town—not Delia's or Lana's like she'd claimed. She didn't want to lie to her parents, but she couldn't stand being in that house any longer. Now that she knew she couldn't stay, she almost wanted to just go and get it over with already. Maybe the vampires would take her the next night when she met with them. She had no clue what to expect because she was only eight the last time this happened, and she wasn't the least bit interested in all that at the time. She wondered if the boy that'd been chosen last time was still there. *What was his name? Brandon? It's kind of sad that I don't remember, and now I'm headed off to be forgotten by everyone, too.*

She walked for about fifteen minutes to Cleary Park. She'd snuck out God only knows how many times over the past couple of years, and this seemed to be where she would end up—whether she was meeting with her friends or some boy. This might be the last time she could spend time alone in the park, and she was going to enjoy the solitude. Once she moved to Willow Creek Manor she probably wouldn't even be able to pee without some vamp leering at her. It would be past curfew soon, but she no longer had to worry about that. She was officially an adult and was free to come and go as she wanted, for the time being anyway.

Sabine sat on the park bench for close to two hours alone with her thoughts. She managed to clear her head for a good portion of that time and just look at the sky as it darkened and the stars and moon grew brighter.

As she sat there, the feeling of eyes on her chilled her to the bone as someone else's presence enveloped her. She'd experienced a similar feeling so many times throughout her life and now wondered if she'd been watched all along. Maybe they'd known from the moment of her birth that she'd be chosen and had kept tabs on her.

"You shouldn't be alone like this in a place where vampires roam freely."

She jerked her head around and yelped. The stranger stood mere inches away. He hadn't made a noise as he approached her.

She inhaled and placed her hand over her heart. "Jesus Christ! You scared the hell out of me."

"Mm, sounds delicious." He closed his eye to savor the sound of her heart beating rapidly inside her chest.

"Leave me alone. I'm not afraid of you. You can't do anything to me anyway." She stood to face him head on. He moved quickly to stand in front of her. Startled, she fell back onto the bench.

"Nonsense, you little twit. You *should* be afraid of me. I could have you dead before you took your next breath, and you'd be none the wiser. Would you like me to show you?" He flashed his canines at her as they elongated and glistened in the moonlight.

Okay, so maybe she was a little afraid. She hadn't really been that close to a vampire, despite them being so visible at times. Thinking fast, she said, "I know you could hurt me, but you probably shouldn't. You'd be in deep shit with Bastian if you did." She swallowed hard as she tried to figure out how to get away from him.

"Doubtful... Why would he care about some young girl too daft to know not to be alone after dark when it's so easy to be snatched up? Look around you. There are no witnesses."

"He cares because I'm the one he's chosen to feed off of for the rest of my life. You must not be too important if you didn't know that already. Or maybe you're not from here and are going to get an ass whooping regardless." *Why am I being mouthy? He might really kill me.*

"Bloody hell." His brow furrowed as he retracted his fangs.

"Problem?" She arched an eyebrow.

"You'll see soon enough." He said before turning to leave.

She watched him walk away and found herself strangely drawn to the beast. He was mysterious and had a certain air to him, like he'd seen everything there was to see. She envied him if it were true. His Londoner accent echoed in her ears. Her love of rock and roll had made her a fool for men with longer hair, and his flowed gently in the wind as he walked away. Now she wished she'd noticed the color of his eyes, but it'd been so dark and he towered over her which made it difficult for her to see. The fact that she was terrified hadn't helped either.

Chapter 4

Her stomach cramped and muscles in her arms and hands trembled as night began to fall. Fearing this could be the last time they'd see each other, she hugged Shay tighter than she ever had before, and though her sister normally annoyed the crap out of her, she couldn't stand the thought of leaving her. She walked out the front door of her parents' house, not knowing whether or not she would be coming back. Her legs felt like they weighed a ton as she struggled to move.

Vivian, Rob, and Sabine traveled in silence through town, and up the winding road that led to the huge compound overlooking Willow Creek. It looked so out of place in such a small Appalachian mountain town. On the outside, it looked like a beautiful mansion that may have belonged to some kind of celebrity in the Hollywood Hills. Though it was beautiful, it gave her the creeps. The thought of how many people probably met their fate behind the huge oak doors chilled her to the bone. Would she be the next victim?

As they pulled into the circled driveway out front, two men—presumably vampires—and the woman—definitely vampire—who'd given her the scroll, waited for them. A look of indifference was plastered across all three of their faces. Before they could even completely stop the car, the vampires were at their doors quicker than the blink of an eye.

"My name is Gretchen. We met yesterday. Welcome." She opened Sabine's door and slightly bowed as she held out her arm toward the huge house.

"Hello, Gretchen," Sabine said cordially. *Yeah, we met alright, if you call handing someone a life changing scroll without so much as a 'hello', then, yeah, we met, you freak.* Gretchen's gaze turned cold as ice as she peered at Sabine. *Oh shit! I wonder if that mind reading thing is real. Sorry, Gretchen! I'm just stressed. I'm sure you're a lovely vampire.* Gretchen looked away, and the smallest hint of a smile crossed her red lips.

"Please, come with me. Bastian awaits."

They stepped through the front door, and Sabine was in awe of what lay before her. The place was immaculate. It looked as if it'd been snatched out of another time and place. Various paintings and tapestries adorned the tall walls, and an elaborate mural covered the vaulted ceiling in the front room. It reminded her of The Sistine Chapel—yet another place she could forget about ever seeing in person.

A grand staircase sprawled out before them. They followed Gretchen up the stairs and down a long hallway to a formal dining room where a feast had been laid out on a table big enough to easily seat twenty guests.

At the head of the table, sat an ordinary looking man. He had short dirty blonde hair and piercing blue eyes. Looking closer at him, Sabine realized this man was Bastian Florien. She'd seen him at different times from afar in town, but had never been very close. He stood gracefully, and walked toward her and her parents. If she hadn't actually seen his legs moving, she would've thought he was floating for sure. Taking her hand in his, Bastian looked her over.

"Ah, yes. Just as pretty as I thought you would be. Such lovely eyes."

Her hand trembled in his as she struggled to speak.

"Th-thank you, s-sir."

"Do not be afraid, child. You are safe. You will never know any harm from here on out."

Except when you bite me.

The corners of Bastian's mouth turned up. "I assure you, it will not hurt if that is what you are worried about. We choose for it to be painful or not when we feed; so, no harm done." He smiled warmly at her.

Sabine gasped. He'd heard her thoughts; there was no doubt this time. She tried hard to not think of anything when suddenly she heard a voice. But she wasn't hearing this voice with her ears. It was coming from inside her head. *I can hear your thoughts, child, though not all of us possess this special gift. Do not ever be afraid to think. As old as I am, there is nothing you could say or think that would shock, anger, or surprise me. I would not want to stifle your creativity as I hear you are a blossoming artist. You will find anything and everything you desire to nurture your talent when you come here to live. I look forward to adding some of your work to my collection.*

Sabine began to grin as her parents looked at her like she was crazy. At least she'd still be able to do what she loved, and maybe this Bastian guy wasn't so bad. Her nerves began to settle, and she wasn't shaking nearly as much as she had been moments before.

"Please, come in and sit down. Eat all you like. I would like to spend some time getting to know you and your parents. You have a sister, yes? I would like to have met her as well, but another time will be fine."

The small family took their seats close to where Bastian had been sitting moments before. There was a whole turkey, a ham, an assortment of freshly baked breads and pastries, and all kinds of side dishes laid out on the table. It was like Thanksgiving and Christmas dinner all rolled into one.

Bastian spoke at length with Vivian and Rob about their lives. He was interested in learning of their careers and how they'd grown up. He wanted to know details of Sabine and Shay and things they'd experienced. It was all getting a little boring for Sabine as she was more interested in getting to the details of the arrangement. She ate quietly while they finished their conversation.

"Let us get down to business, shall we? Sabine, you must have many questions. Would you prefer I answer them, or would you rather I explain the details?"

"Just tell me, and I'll ask if there's anything else I want to know."

"Very well then. You have been chosen to fulfill the agreement made by your ancestors and myself. I protect Willow Creek from various entities that wish nothing more than to take over and cause harm, and in exchange, one young adult who will provide sustenance is chosen every ten years to be paired with a vampire residing here.

We do not have to hide our nature, and the citizens of this town need not worry about being attacked by outsiders or drained by any of us. You, sweet girl, have been chosen."

"I have a question now."

"Go ahead."

"When do I come here?" Her heart thumped in her chest in anticipation of the answer.

"You will come to live with us on your twenty-first birthday. For now, you will go about your life and live it as you would, with one exception. You cannot leave the borders of Willow Creek without first being granted permission by me. This is so we do not have to worry that you will run and to make sure you stay safe."

"Safe from what?" asked Vivian.

"Others of my kind. There have been those who have tried to harm the offering simply to cause problems for me here in Willow Creek. You see, if the citizens of this town believe I have gone against my promise to protect the person chosen, they could end our agreement, and I may no longer be safe here. I do not wish to be slain while I sleep over a false belief that I have killed someone when I did not."

Sabine shifted uncomfortably in her chair. What if the stranger from the park wanted her dead? Maybe he was playing mind games with her just to kill her later.

"Have they ever succeeded?" asked Sabine.

"Not as of yet, though that has not stopped some from trying," Bastian replied.

"Couldn't you just pick another if she did run?" Rob asked. "I'm sorry, but I'd rather she left than to be hunted or stalked."

"No, I am afraid not. If I let someone leave with no consequences, then everyone would simply do the same. So you see, this is not an option. I assure you, she is in no real danger now that she is under my protection. I can keep her safe with no disruptions to her daily life as long as she stays in Willow Creek."

"Why do you choose every ten years instead of at random times?" Sabine inquired.

"Thomas Crowley put that stipulation into the agreement. He thought it best for the town's people to be prepared. We occasionally share an offering if a blood mate dies before it is time to select another, but more often than not, the lone vampire either leaves until it is time to choose again or they feed from animals in the forest. On the rare occasion a paired vampire is killed, we have released the offering from their duty if there were no others in need of a blood mate, but that has only happened twice."

"Could I see the room I'll be living in?"

"Yes, of course; just as soon as you have had your fill of food and drink."

Vivian cleared her throat and began to speak. "Will we see her after she comes here? That's been one of our concerns. We don't want her taken from us."

"I would not dream of severing a family tie. There may be some planning involved, but she will not be cut off from you completely. Think of it as her being away at college or off living on her own in another city for the first time."

Sabine looked at her mother, and saw her eyes mist over. She didn't know if Vivian was relieved or upset, but she hated to see her cry either way.

Shortly after, Bastian took Sabine and her parents to the room she'd be living in. Though it was beautiful with its ornate four-poster canopied bed that was covered in fancy burgundy bedding, it felt like too much for her. She wasn't sure how the posters of the bands she liked or her pieces of artwork would look on the fancy walls. Her taste in music and style of painting would most definitely clash with the décor. This room was quiet with elegance, while her artwork mostly screamed with rage.

As she looked around the room, she noticed men's clothing slung over the back of a chair and a few bags sitting about. She wondered who the mystery person was and concluded it was most likely a guest or someone that would be moving out before she moved in permanently.

Almost two hours later, their visit was nearing the end. They made their way back down the long hallway and down the stairway while Bastian spoke of the paintings hanging on the walls and the artists who'd created them. She found herself intrigued by what she might learn from him. Maybe he'd even met some of the greats. Though he only looked to be about thirty or so years old, she knew he had to be way older than that. He was at least two hundred, judging by the timeline of the town. *Should I ask him how old he is, or would that be rude? Doesn't really matter. I guess I'll have plenty of time to find out that kind of stuff while he feeds on me.*

"No, no, no, child. I will not be feeding on you. I require very little blood at my age, and though my blood mate grows old, I am still satiated with her."

"Oh... I just thought I'd be with you."

"No, and since you are curious, I will tell you. I am fourteen hundred years old."

"Wow, that's old!" She quickly covered her mouth with one hand, and her eyes widened.

Bastian chuckled, and said, "That I am."

The front door lurched open just then, and a dark figure entered. He stepped into the light, and she saw the familiar strands of hair blowing around his face from the light breeze following him through the door. Her breath caught in her throat as she recognized the vampire.

"Remy... Come, come... I want you to meet Miss Sabine Crowley."

He moved gracefully as his long legs carried him toward where the small group stood. "We've met, last night in the park."

"Yes, unfortunately we did meet already," Sabine said as she tried to look away, but she was mesmerized by the sight of him. "He was kind of rude to me, actually."

Remy's lips parted. Looking down at Sabine, he ran his tongue over the just barely extended sharp point of one of his fangs. "Nonsense. I was only telling you how dangerous it was to be alone at night, what with all the rogue groups of creatures always looking to terrorize the town. I don't think caring about a young girl's wellbeing is being rude at all."

"Sabine, what does he mean you were by yourself?" Vivian asked. "I thought you were at Delia's."

"Thanks—Remy, was it? I needed some time alone to deal." She glanced out of the corner of her eye at her parents but saw nothing that would indicate they were too upset.

"Oops. Mummy and Daddy didn't know you were alone? Even dumber than I thought," he sneered.

Rob's whole body tensed, though he kept still. He might have wanted to defend his little girl, but he knew it best to not add fuel to the fire.

"Remy!" Bastian's voice boomed and echoed through the hall. "You might not have been rude last night, but you are being rude now. Stop."

*

Remy looked at Sabine, only to find her smirking at him. He most certainly was not going to enjoy his time with her, the little brat. The sooner she died, the better. Maybe she'd have a little accident and he could be out of this mess and back to his home in London in no time.

"I apologize for Remy's behavior. He will not be so difficult when you come here to live. He will have three more years to get used to the pairing."

"Wait... *He's* who will be biting me?"

"Yes. You will be sharing his quarters as well."

Sabine threw her head back and glared at the ceiling. "Bloody hell."

"Told you," Remy said with a sly grin.

47

Chapter 5

Cool fingers slid around the back of Sabine's neck, pulling her close to his body. Her head tilted away while his tongue traced the artery that thumped with every beat of her heart. His body was firm pressed up against her own, and the thought of making love to him threatened to ignite her flesh. His skin began to warm more and more with every second he touched her. The tips of his fangs gently pricked her skin as she waited for the euphoria to set in. She longed for the glorious high that was to come.

Euphoria never came. Instead white hot pain ripped at her neck. Balling her fists up, she pulled back and punched him as hard as she could in the side of the head, but it made no difference. He continued taking her blood against her will. Her body instinctively jerked and her fingers scratched at him as she tried desperately to get away. She grew weaker by the second as her life force left her body. Her sight faded until all she could see was a hazy mist and a bloody smile hovering over her.

Sabine jerked in her sleep, and startled herself awake. The dream had seemed so real. She looked around the room half expecting Remy to be hiding somewhere watching her, ready to pounce in an instant. Her hand shot up to her neck, frantically feeling for anything abnormal. She found no wounds and no soreness. *It was just a dream, right?*

As she closed her eyes, she could feel his tongue on her. The euphoria she anticipated turned her on until the pain had hit. How would she even know if it was euphoric or not? Maybe it just simply wouldn't hurt. Would he make it painful? Would that be how it was? Would he be cruel to her and make it hurt every time he bit her? Bastian had assured her no harm would come to her, but this was an ancient vampire capable of Christ only knows what. It's not like Bastian was someone she could fully trust, and she didn't trust Remy at all to not hurt her.

Droplets of sweat formed on her brow and around her hairline. *Yuck. Time for a shower.* Her feet dangled over the edge of the bed as she stretched and tried to shake the dream from her mind. She managed to pull herself completely out of bed and shuffle to the bathroom. While in the shower, flashes of Remy pulling her near and putting his lips and tongue on her danced in her head.

That's it. I'm a nutjob! There's no other explanation. He's a monster, and I'm having dreams about him that turn me on. What kind of person in their right mind does that? Shit, I've had crushes on some shady boys before, but this is just insane. The so called bad boys I know couldn't hold a candle to this guy.

"Sabine? Are you almost done?" her mother asked as she cracked open the door just a little.

Pulled back to reality, she yelled her reply to her mother. "Getting out now, Mom. I'll be down in a few minutes."

"Okay. You have company, so you should probably hurry," she said before pulling the door shut.

It had to be her two best friends, no doubt stopping by since she'd bailed on them the night of her birthday. She'd fallen right into bed without calling either of them after her meeting with Bastian, so they had to be eager to hear the details. She prepared herself for all things vampire, though it was the last topic she wanted to discuss. No way was she telling them about her sick attraction to the vampire she was paired with. She couldn't even think of his name without her stomach doing somersaults.

Since it was her friends visiting, she didn't feel the need to get fancy with her clothes. It was supposed to be warm, so she slipped into some shorts and pulled on a t-shirt of her favorite band, Ferrum.

There were some minor similarities between Remy and the lead singer of Ferrum, Ash London. She began to rationalize that her attraction to Remy was due to the tiny resemblance between the two. Both of them were pretty tall and they both had longer hair. Ash was bigger, though. He was a complete beast of a man, but she thought to herself that even someone like Ash would be no match for a vampire.

She finished the ensemble with her go-to shoes, a pair of Chuck Taylors she'd decorated with various doodles and violet laces to make them uniquely hers.

She hurried down the steps toward the living room. Her friends always made themselves at home, and Sabine knew that's where they'd be. Hell, the girls had probably made a snack or gotten themselves something to drink already.

51

"Sorry it took me so long. I didn't know you were coming by," she said, stopping dead in her tracks as her eyes met Remy's.

He sat slouched on the couch as if he were bored and had waited an eternity for her to appear.

"How could you have known? It's not like you can read minds."

"I was expecting my friends to be here, not you."

"Am I not your friend, Sabine?" He stuck out his bottom lip and furrowed his brow.

"Not at all."

"You're hurting my heart." His hand lingered lazily over his chest.

"You'd have to have a heart in order for me to hurt it."

"But I do have a heart." In an instant, he stood an inch away from her grabbing her hand. He placed it on his chest, and said, "You feel that?"

"No." His chest was every bit as firm as it'd been in her dream, but much colder than she'd imagined.

"Oh… That's right. I have a heart; it just happens to be dead." He looked down at her and laughed, failing to mention that his heart did actually beat. It just didn't beat anywhere near the same speed as a living, breathing human being. "Come walk with me. I suppose I should see if you're as annoying as I think you are."

"I don't think that sounds like a good idea at all. I don't want anything to do with you until I'm forced into it." She turned to walk back upstairs to her room.

He placed his hand on her arm, preventing her from taking another step. "Need I remind you that I could force you now if I wanted?"

She whirled around quickly to face him and to get his hand off of her. "Wow. You really know how to treat a girl, don't you?"

"Actually, yes, I do. I'm quite good at treating a lady, and doing really nice things to her... I mean, for her. However, that kind of treatment is only reserved for the special ones."

"Gross. I don't want to hear about your sexual escapades."

"Too bad. Now, come on. Let's go."

"Fine," she said through gritted teeth.

She yelled to her mother to tell her where she was going. How her mother didn't protest was beyond her. The meeting had gone alright, but her mother couldn't possibly just magically be okay with everything... unless, he made her be okay with it.

"Did you do something her?" she asked, eying him.

"I wouldn't dream of it."

They stepped through the door and into the sun.

"It's a shame you didn't burst into flames just now. I guess you're pretty old."

"That would depend on how you define old, but age has nothing to do with it. We can all go in the sun. The only thing age affects is how well we tolerate it. A new vampire can only stand short periods of time before becoming too weak. They can even sometimes be vulnerable to humans if they're in the sun too long.

That's why you don't see many of our young out and about on a bright day."

"So, it doesn't make you weak if you're older?"

"No, it still weakens us, but the older we get, the more we're able to tolerate it. See, as we get older, our abilities become stronger. Even though the sun weakens me, I am still far superior to a human and could defend myself against other supernatural creatures if need be."

"Can you read minds? Bastian told me not all of you can."

"I've only been able to hear someone's thoughts here and there over the centuries. It's not something I've focused on much. I probably could develop the skill if I wanted, but why? So I can hear even more incessant chatter? No, thank you... Anyway, I don't want to give away all my secrets. So tell me about you."

"There's not much to tell. I've known for a long time that I would probably be the one chosen, and I've felt trapped. Because of that, I live a pretty boring life. There's really been no point in putting much effort into anything; though, for some reason, I've managed to keep my grades up at school. That was a huge waste of time, I guess."

"It's never a waste of time to gain knowledge. If there's anything I've learned, it's that the more knowledge you have, the better you're prepared for whatever you're faced with."

"Gee, thanks, Dad. That was some awesome fatherly advice."

"You have no idea how happy I am that I'm not your father, or anyone's father for that matter."

"You never had kids before you were turned?"

He shook his head. "None that lived. My wife was pregnant twice, but the babies were both stillborn. She died shortly after she birthed the second one."

"I'm sorry to hear that." For the first time since she met him, she saw past the vampire to the man he used to be, and her heart ached for his loss.

He waved her off. "Ancient history. None of those kind of feelings remain."

"If you say so. How old are you, anyway?"

"I was twenty-four when I was turned, and I've walked the earth for four hundred and six years."

"Remind me to hit you up if I need help in my history class."

"That would be cheating, Missy. I'll have no part in that."

"I forgot. Vampires are known for their strong moral and ethical values." Sabine rolled her eyes at him. "The more you talk, the more you sound like my father. You can deny it all you want, but you're giving me paternal vibes."

"Yuck."

"That's what you'll be to me, right? Like a parent or some kind of authority figure telling me what I can and can't do all the time."

"Not quite." He cocked his eyebrow and turned his head slightly toward her as they walked.

"Don't look at me like that. It creeps me out."

"You brought it up. I was told that I am to consider you my wife."

"Yuck." A shudder ran up her spine as she looked away from him.

"Brush up on your skills, my dear. I expect you to be well versed in wifely duties when you bed with me," he said, draping an arm over her shoulder.

"Okay. I'm out." She threw up her hands, and turned around. Not only was he a vampire, but he was also a pig. The attraction she felt toward him dwindled by the second.

*

"Relax. I won't rape you. I'm not a complete monster. But you'll be begging me in no time to show you all the things I've learned over the last four hundred years."

It was too late. She wasn't hearing anymore. Remy laughed to himself, and let her go. *Hello new favorite pastime. I could get used to working her last nerve.*

Chapter 6

The cafeteria of Crowley High bustled with activity. Students crowded around tables, more concerned with social time than eating. The three girls went to their usual table in the back by the auditorium and sat down. So many sets of eyes darted in her direction, but every time she looked up, their gazes shifted away.

"I guess the news is out," Delia said.

"You noticed that, too?" Sabine picked at her food, trying to ignore the attention she was receiving.

"Yeah. Everyone keeps gawking at you and then looking away. You'd think they'd offer a thank you or something." Delia glanced around at their peers.

"That won't happen, but Delia and I do understand the sacrifice you're making. I don't like it at all, and I understand that it isn't easy," Lana said.

"Thanks. I'm just glad you two are still seventeen and safe from it all now. Supposedly, I'll still be able to see my family and you guys. We'll see."

"Doesn't sound like you're too sure about that one." A slight frown appeared on Lana's face.

"I'm not. I don't know how I can ever fully trust anything Bastian says until I'm actually there. I mean, how many times has anyone seen the others after they've gone there to live?"

"Was he scary?" Delia inquired.

"That's the weird thing about all of it. He wasn't scary at all. He seemed pretty interesting. He acted supportive of me being an artist, and told me I'd have

57

access to any supplies I might need so I could keep painting."

"That doesn't sound too bad," said Lana.

"So that's who will be snacking on you?"

"No, Delia, he isn't the one. The one who will be biting me scares the hell out of me. He just…" she said as she inhaled, "makes me feel weird."

"What did he do to you?" Lana asked as she picked up a piece of bread and bit into it.

"He hasn't really done anything to me; he just gives me the creeps. Like yesterday, he made me go for a walk with him, and told me he expected me to have sex with him."

"Is he hot?" Delia leaned in and smiled.

"Delia," Lana exclaimed. "It doesn't matter how hot he is or isn't, he shouldn't say things like that."

"Thank you. He didn't come out and say it like that, though, and he could've been joking. He's very cocky. He thinks he's way above me."

"But, is he hot?"

Sabine looked at Delia, and sighed. "He's not bad, I guess."

"Then, what's the problem?" Delia shrugged as the other two girls stared at her with their mouths hanging open. "Oh, come on! I'm only trying to lighten the mood. You know I don't really think any of this is okay."

"I know."

"What *does* he look like, though?" Lana questioned.

"Well, he's tall. I'd say probably 6'2" or maybe even 6'3". His hair comes to a little below his chin, and it's kind of a dark, chestnut brown. He seems kind of muscular, but not bulky, more on the lean side. Oh, and his eyes are *really* bright green, I think. I tried not to look him right in the eyes too much. I was afraid he'd mind fuck me or something."

"Can they do that?" Lana's eyes widened.

"I think so. I mean I don't know what all they can do, but I'm pretty sure they can control humans if they want. I know some of them can read minds, and the whole super speed thing is definitely true."

"Well, as much as I hate to, I have to go to the library before my next class. Can we get together later, girls?"

"Absolutely, Lana. See you after school. We're still walking home together, right?"

"Yep."

* * *

"You should go buy a lottery ticket now that you're eighteen," Lana said as she laughed.

"Yeah, because it would do me so much good if I won," Sabine quipped with her usual sense of sarcasm.

Lana looked at Sabine with a big, toothy grin, and said, "You could give the jackpot to me if you did."

Sabine and Lana continued to walk down Main Street toward their houses. They'd grown up a few blocks away from each other, and had been friends for as long as either one of them could remember. Walking home together was a daily ritual where they would gossip about everything that happened during the day, and stop at the little convenience store on the corner to grab snacks to eat while they continued their gab fests at one of their homes. Today, it was Sabine's house they'd chosen. The sun was bright, and the breeze was warm, so they elected to sit on the swing on the back porch until it was time for Lana to head home for dinner.

They'd been sitting for close to a half an hour when Lana looked over at the small picnic table on the porch.

"What's that over there? Did your mom leave you a note or something?"

Sabine crinkled her brow and walked over to the table. "I don't think so. She usually just texts me if she needs to tell me anything." Sabine picked the letter up, and carefully opened it. She pulled a piece of paper out and began to read to herself.

Are you ready for me to show you those things I've learned?

She immediately wadded the paper up and threw it in the garbage can that sat at the edge of the porch.

"What did it say?"

"It was from that jerk that I'm supposed to spend the rest of my life with. He asked me if I was ready for him to show me the things he's learned."

"What the heck does that mean?"

Sabine arched her right eyebrow and crinkled her nose. "He told me he expected me to act like a wife. Apparently, that's the sort of relationship I'm supposed to have with him, and I got grossed out and left. He told me I'd be begging him in no time to show me all the things he's learned about sex. That's what he meant. He's such a pig."

"He's probably just messing with you. I mean, is he happy about this arrangement?"

Sabine erupted with a sarcastic laugh. "Yeah... That'd be a big fat no, I'm sure."

"Maybe he thinks he can get out of it somehow if he messes with you enough."

"Maybe, but unless I die, I think he's pretty much stuck. Even if something happened to me, he'd probably be paired with whoever the runner up might've been."

"Well, if he's hot, you know Delia is all in to be a runner up on her birthday. She's so crazy sometimes. I still think he's probably just trying to get a rise out of you, though."

"Maybe, but he's over four hundred years old. His views on women can't be that great. Think about it."

"Maybe he's evolved."

They both laughed.

"Yeah, right. That's why he's leaving me pervy notes, because he's so evolved."

"Geez, Sabine. What are you going to do if he tries to force you to have sex with him?"

"He won't try. If he wants to, he will. What could I do to stop him? The only thing that might help me is Bastian, if what he says is true about no one hurting me."

"Hey, look at it this way. Maybe he'll end up being the love of your life."

"Kill me now." Though she was disgusted on the outside, she pondered the possibility for a split second.

"You could be like all those movies and TV shows where the vampire guy ends up being dreamy, and you can't live without him and he would die for you." Lana sighed as she smiled dreamily at the notion.

"You want me to vomit, don't you?"

"Maybe that stuff was based on real stories. We know vamps are real, even though the rest of the world doesn't seem to. Maybe there are other people out there who know about them, too, and had some kind of sexy rendezvous with one."

"Possible, I guess, but I'm pretty sure they weren't based on Remy. He's too creepy."

"Remy? That's a sexy name."

"You're getting to be as bad as Delia."

*

Remy sat out of sight on the roof above them. He'd positioned himself so they couldn't see him when they'd approached the house, and he stayed still so he wouldn't be heard. Listening to the two girls talk almost made him laugh. The thought of him being the romantic hero they thought he might be who would fall deeply in love with her was ridiculous. He hadn't been in love in centuries, and didn't even know what love felt like anymore or if he was still capable of such a thing.

When his wife, Beatrix, died, it almost destroyed him. His father tried to arrange another marriage for him almost immediately, but Remy was having none of it. When he refused, he was forced into hard labor and stripped of the few luxuries he had. His father didn't understand why he wouldn't marry another since his marriage to Beatrix had been arranged as well. He'd grown to love her almost immediately, despite the fact that he'd resented her at first.

I suppose this situation is similar. Bastian has arranged our marriage, so to speak. Even if we aren't officially together yet, we might as well be. We won't fall in love, though. Lust, maybe. She is cute, even if she is a twit.

He briefly considered jumping down from where he sat just to scare the hell out of them. It would be quite amusing, but he decided against it. Maybe next time.

* * *

Sabine and Delia sat outside a little café in downtown Willow Creek, sipping iced cappuccinos. They often met there on Saturday evenings to chat and to kill time when they were bored.

"Don't make it obvious, but you need to look at that table over there," Delia said, glancing to her left. "There is a really hot guy sitting there looking at us."

"Oh no." Sabine closed her eyes for a second before opening them again. "What does he look like?"

"Just look. You'll know as soon as you see him. He's practically staring a hole right through you."

"I really don't want to."

"Why not? You've never passed up the opportunity to look at man candy before."

"Because I know when I look, I'm going to see Remy looking back at me."

"Sweetheart, if that's Remy, then I don't feel one bit bad for you anymore. That guy's body is practically smoking he's so hot. I'd let him bite me right now."

Sabine slowly turned her head to the right. It *was* him, just as she suspected. Just as she turned her head to the left to look away from him, he was sitting in the chair beside her. Both Sabine and Delia jumped and screeched.

"Why do you *do* that?"

"Because I can. Now, who is your lovely friend?" Remy turned to Delia and smiled as he took her hand and kissed it.

"Delia, Remy. Remy, Delia. Now, what do you want?"

"Can I not just visit with my beloved and her beautiful friend?"

Delia blushed.

"I am not your beloved, and I'd rather you didn't. Just leave me the hell alone until I turn twenty-one." If he left her alone, maybe she could get over her strange attraction to him.

"If only it were that easy. You see, I'm stuck in this shitty little town from now until you cease to exist. So, why not mess with you when I get bored?"

Delia began to giggle. Sabine glared at her.

"I'm sorry, Sabine! He is kind of funny, though."

"No, he's not. Not at all. He's a prick, and I think it's time for me to go home now."

"Come on, Sabine… I'm sorry. Do you want me to come with you?" Delia asked.

"It's fine, and no. I'm going home and going to bed. I'll text you later."

She stood up and picked up her bag. Remy also stood, and she hoped that he wouldn't follow. She walked away quickly, but felt him right behind her. Stopping suddenly, she crossed her arms and turned to face him.

"*What* are you doing? Leave me alone," she said, her voice raising a pitch in the process.

"I'm only seeing you home safely."

"Well, since I know where I live and how to get there, I don't need or want your help. Please, just go away." Tears began to well up in her eyes, and she hoped he wouldn't notice. She didn't want him to get some kind of pleasure out of making her cry.

"It's nothing to cry over. Why are you getting upset?" He placed a hand on her shoulder, and watched her intently.

Fire raged through every piece of her body. She dropped her bag and shoved his hand away from her shoulder as she looked up at him.

"*Why do you think I'm upset?*" she yelled. "I'm going to be your slave in less than three years, and all I want is to be free to live my life right now without you being around me! Is that too much to ask for?"

He peered down at her seriously. A chill shot up her back as she met his eyes. "You won't be a slave. I promise you that."

And just like that, he was gone.

Chapter 7

May 17: Willow Creek—Two Years Later

The week of Sabine's twentieth birthday left her with the perfect opportunity. Her favorite band in the whole world was playing a show only an hour and a half away from Willow Creek two days after her birthday. She'd been obsessed with them and Ash, the lead singer, for the last six years, and hadn't had the chance to see them live. This very well could be the only opportunity she'd ever have. All she had to do was get permission to go.

She hadn't asked to leave town at all in two years. Hopefully, she would be granted permission as a treat for her birthday. Once she was allowed, she could plan her escape. She hadn't attempted to run since before she was chosen. Maybe they wouldn't suspect she was going to bolt. The only way she could pull it off was if they'd let her out of town. Otherwise, she was doomed to spend the rest of her life with that jerk.

She'd only seen him from a distance a couple of times since she'd blown up at him shortly after her eighteenth birthday, though he still made regular appearances in her dreams; so much for getting over her attraction to him. He never acknowledged that he knew her, and hadn't even looked at her when she did see him anywhere. Surprisingly, so far he had granted her the one thing she wanted from him, which was to be rid of him until she turned twenty-one.

She drove up the driveway, and parked the old red Toyota her parents had given her for her nineteenth birthday. It wasn't quite sunset when she knocked on the door.

No one answered at first. Not knowing if anyone would even open the door at all, she knocked again. A moment later, the door creaked open. Gretchen, as stunningly gorgeous as she had been the last time she saw her two years before, stood before her.

"Sabine. To what do we owe the pleasure?" Gretchen smiled a warm, friendly smile at her.

"I hope it's not a bad time, but I'd like to speak to Bastian. I need to ask him if it's okay if I go to a concert out of town next week. I haven't asked to leave before, so I wasn't sure really how to go about it, and I didn't know how to get ahold of him other than to just stop by."

"Come in. I'll see if Bastian is busy. If he can't see you right now, I'll ask him when a good time will be for you to meet with him. Please, have a seat in the sitting room."

"Thank you."

Several minutes later, Bastian appeared. His looks hadn't changed at all, though she didn't really expect them to.

"Sweet child. It's so good to see you. What can I do for you?"

"Hi, Bastian. I hope I'm not bothering you."

"Not at all."

"I haven't asked for permission to leave before, but there's this concert coming up, and I'd really like to go for my birthday. I've been a huge fan of this band for years now, and this is the closest they've ever played. So would it be okay if I go?" she asked as her smiled beamed at him.

Bastian was silent as he thought about her question. His eyes softened when he began to speak. "I do not see why not. Go. Have fun, but make sure you return quickly."

"Oh, thank you so much! I really appreciate it." She made sure to think to herself that she'd never get away without being caught just in case he was listening in on her thoughts.

"You are most welcome. Who will you be going with?"

"Probably my two best friends. One for sure. The other has to see if she can get the night off from work."

"It sounds like you will have an excellent time. Now, do you mind staying and speaking with me a little?"

"I have some plans with my family in about an hour, but I can stay for a few minutes."

"What is the name of this musical group you are going to see play?"

"Ferrum."

"Hmmm. Ferrum? I think that might be one that Remy listens to on occasion. The name seems familiar to me, and I am sure that is how I have come to know it. I do not take to modern music very often. I prefer the classics."

Remy has good taste in music. That's a shocker. I wonder if he's here. Not that I want to see him. I don't. Hopefully he isn't.

"Remy is out at the moment. No need to worry about running into him, but I am curious. What has he done to make you despise him so much?"

"Nothing—recently. Right after I turned eighteen, I felt like he was harassing me at times."

"How so?"

"He would say rude things to me, and pop up out of nowhere to bother me when all I wanted was to be far away from all of this."

"I see. What made him stop?"

"I kind of yelled at him, and he just stopped. I don't know why he actually listened to me."

"That does not sound like my Remy at all. I hate to speak ill of my progeny, but he has always had a habit of being rather obnoxious. He has never let up just because someone told him to stop. You must have said something that resonated with him."

"If he's always been so obnoxious, why did you turn him in the first place? I can't imagine wanting to spend an eternity with the guy." *I don't even want to spend a minute with him, and yet I'm stuck with him anyway.*

"I will leave that to him to decide to tell you or not, but I will say he has always been a fighter, and he has been surprisingly loyal to me since he arrived two years ago. I know it was the last thing he wanted to do when I summoned him here, but still he has stayed."

Sabine smiled and nodded. She had nothing nice to say, so she kept her mouth, and her mind, shut.

"Would you like a drink or something to eat?"

"No, I'm okay. Thank you. I'm supposed to have dinner with my parents."

"Oh, yes, of course. I will let you get back to the rest of your evening."

"Thank you, again!"

"I expect you to be back in Willow Creek no later than the morning after the concert." With that, he turned and left her sitting alone.

While driving home, she devised a plan.

* * *

The band was every bit as great as Sabine thought they would be, and she didn't want to leave. Though she hadn't seen them perform before, she knew they always played her favorite song last, but she had to get moving now in case anyone was following her.

"Delia," she shouted over the crowd. "I'll be right back! I have to pee!"

"Now? I think they're almost done!" Delia's arms swayed above her head as she danced along with the music.

"Yes, now! I'll be quick."

"Okay! Meet me by my car if you get lost or can't find me when you're done."

She pushed her way through the crowd, hoping to blend in and not be noticed. She pulled out her cell phone after looking at the note she had scrawled on the back of her hand, and opened the app that would allow her to get a taxi. It was really convenient, and she didn't even have to talk to anyone so she wouldn't have to worry about being overheard. She could touch the screen a couple of times, and a taxi would be on its way. A confirmation flashed on her screen that she'd be picked up in about five minutes.

She had to keep reading the notes she'd left for herself in her purse and on her hand so that she would remember why exactly she was leaving. Once anyone left the borders of Willow Creek, they magically seemed to forget the vampire population that resided there. If she didn't keep reminding herself, she might give up altogether and go back. She would regret losing the one chance she had to escape.

Now, all she had to do was to get out unnoticed. Then, she'd be on her way to the airport, which was only a fifteen minute drive if traffic wasn't bad. If she could get through security and board the plane, she'd be free. Luckily for her, she'd managed to find a late flight that would accommodate her. New York City was where she was headed, and if she couldn't blend in there, then she had no chance of escaping anywhere.

Her heart pounded, and her palms began to sweat as she trembled. She expected to be stopped any second, and it came to her as a total surprise when she had not only been able to get in the taxi, but also to the airport and through security without anyone stopping her. She stood anxiously at the gate, waiting to board the plane.

While waiting, she began to think of ways to stretch the money she had until she could get a job. She'd squirreled away almost every penny she'd made over the last two years. Willow Creek was small, but her customers tipped well. Maybe it was their strange way of thanking her for what she would be forced to do. Her saving had allowed her to not only buy a plane ticket, but also afford a cheap hotel for at least a couple of weeks once she got there. Finding a job was priority number one so she could find a more permanent place to live.

Finally, the announcement to board arrived. She breathed a sigh of relief once she was seated at the window seat she'd chosen when the ticket was reserved. It had been ages since she'd been on an airplane, but she loved sitting by the window so she could look out at the land and lights below.

The plane filled up quickly with passengers. She opened the book she bought at the airport, and settled into her seat. The flight would only take an hour or so, and reading would make the time pass quickly. She was anxious to get off the ground and to her new life.

Something moved beside her, and she quickly realized the passenger in the aisle seat had finally shown up. She didn't look up from her book because she was never one to gawk at people. It was something she felt was incredibly rude, and she tried not to do it. But when the man sat down and leaned into her personal space, staring right at her, she was forced. She slowly looked over. To her horror, Remy stared back at her with the right corner of his mouth turned up.

"Going somewhere fun?"

"I was... Now, not so much."

"Did you really think you could get away so easily?"

"No, but I had to try."

"I certainly can't blame you for trying," he said as he tapped one long index finger against his chin.

"How did you find me, and how the hell do I remember everything now that you're here? I've had to keep reminding myself why I was leaving." She held up her hand, exposing the words she'd written before she left Willow Creek.

He turned to face her full on and spoke just loud enough for her to hear. "You remember because I'm here. It's weird, I know, but apparently if you see one of us you know from Willow Creek, then the fog is lifted from your mind. And as for finding you... Funny thing about those of my species, we can see really well from really far away. I could easily read your computer screen from where I sat in that old willow tree outside your bedroom. I saw the exact reservations you made for this flight, even down to the seat you chose, and, now," he sat back and laced his fingers together, "here I am."

Her mouth dropped open. "You spied on me?"

"Yes. I was ordered to watch you."

"But I thought you left me alone after I freaked out on you."

"I decided not to bug you, but I was always near."

"You make me sick. Watching me like a deranged psycho. All the times I got dressed in my room, not knowing someone was watching me. I want to vomit." Her skin turned ghostly white, and her stomach did flips.

"Nothing I haven't seen before."

"I don't care how many women you've seen naked. You had no right to watch me like that."

"Oh, but I did. It was my responsibility to make sure you didn't run and to keep you safe from those who would try to hurt you because of who you are. I had to watch for signs that you were planning something, and I had to make sure no outside vampires were stalking you. How else could I do that, other than watch you when you were alone in your room?"

"So you ended up being the one to stalk me. You disgust me."

"I've heard worse. You'll get over it, and you should be thanking me. To date, I've taken care of six vampires who would've devoured you before you knew what hit you."

"I don't believe you."

"You can choose to believe I'm lying to you, but that doesn't make what I'm saying not true."

"Wait, if you knew I was leaving, why didn't you stop me before I left the concert? Or before I even left my house?"

"Because I've been stuck in Willow Creek for two years. If I let you get this far, then I could at least get a trip to New York for my troubles. I've spoken to Bastian already. He knows you're with me, and that we will be taking our time getting back."

"He knows I tried to run. Great. Now I'll probably be locked up in that room for the rest of my life."

"Oh, no, he doesn't know you tried to run. I told him that I had some business to tend to that would take some time, and that I planned to bring you with me after the concert."

Her eyes widened as her gaze darted away from him. She didn't know he was capable of being nice. "Thanks for not telling him, I guess. What happens once we get to New York?"

"We'll go to my apartment tonight. I suppose I can get you something to eat, and you'll stay there while I go out and get myself a bite to eat. We'll be in Manhattan for a few days until it's time to move on."

"I'm a little impressed that you have an apartment in New York. How long has it been since you were there last if you've been in Willow Creek for two years?"

"Ten, maybe fifteen years…"

She raised her eyebrows in disbelief. "You have an apartment in New York City, and you haven't even been there in over a decade? Don't you think that's a huge waste of money?"

"No. I have a place in London, too, that I haven't been to in two years. It doesn't mean I won't ever go back, and I like things the way I have them."

"Alright, then. I don't see the point in paying the outrageous cost of an apartment and not living there full-time."

"I have more money than I know what to do with. I pay a man to stay there and take care of it. He knows I'm on my way, and he'll stay gone while I'm there. I put him up in a 5-star hotel in the meantime. It's really quite a nice set up for him."

"I bet it is." She shook her head and watched the ground get further and further away.

They were mostly quiet during the flight. She was sure he could hear her just fine if she spoke, but she wasn't so lucky. She could barely hear anything over the sound of the engines.

They landed at JFK not long after they'd taken off and were soon on their way into Manhattan.

"I need to get some things before we go to your apartment."

"Such as?"

"I didn't bring anything with me. I have to get some personal care stuff and preferably a set of pajamas or something comfortable to sleep in. I'll have to get some clothes somewhere, too."

"Why don't you wait until we get there, and see what I have? The guy that looks after the place is supposed to keep it well stocked in case I ever show up unexpectedly or allow someone to use the place while they're in the city."

"Alright, but I don't want to sleep in what I've got on. Just sayin'."

"Sleeping in the nude is always an option."

"Swine," she whispered.

Her breath caught in her throat as she saw the skyline lighting up the night. She and her parents had visited the city a few times when she was younger, but this was the first time she was there as an adult. Whether or not she got to actually enjoy the city this time was a whole other subject. She doubted she'd be seeing much other than what she could maybe see from a window.

The taxi pulled up to a building directly across from Central Park on the Upper East Side. She followed Remy inside and onto the elevator where he pulled out a key. He inserted the key into a keyhole at the top of the buttons and pushed the one next to "PH." *Holy shit. This guy is unbelievable. Not only does he have an apartment in Manhattan he hasn't been to in over a decade, but his apartment is on the friggin' top floor.*

She followed him off the elevator to a small hallway leading to a double door that he promptly opened. Stepping through the doors, she was astonished by the sprawling living room with windows overlooking the park. It was breathtaking and much nicer than any flea bag hotel room she would have been staying in. At least she wouldn't be sharing a bathroom with complete strangers here either.

"Come with me, and I'll show you where you'll be sleeping."

She followed him down a narrow hallway until they reached a closed door on the left. He opened it, reached in, and flipped on a light. The room, much larger than she expected, also overlooked the park.

"The bathroom is right across the hall, and my room is right next door. You might as well make yourself at home, because we'll be here at least a few days. You can look in the bathroom to see if I have the things you require. I'll look in the closet in here and see what I have in the way of something for you to sleep in, since you've objected to sleeping naked."

She waited until he left the room to check out the bathroom. It was immaculate. Her fingers glided over the cool marble countertops as she looked around. She opened the closet to find a stockpile of tooth brushes, toothpaste, shampoo, conditioner, body wash, moisturizer, razors, and really anything else you could possibly need to achieve the highest quality of hygiene.

She walked back to the room that was to be hers and flopped down on the bed. She was exhausted and needed to sleep soon.

Remy walked in a few moments later, and she sat up. Her eyes immediately landed on his well-defined chest and abs, and she quickly looked away. He tossed her the black T-shirt he'd been wearing only minutes before.

"I don't have anything for you to sleep in, but you can sleep in that. It might not cover your ass all the way, but then I've already seen it, so…"

It was strange to her that instead of being warm from just leaving his body, the black T-shirt was oddly cool.

"You're so hilarious. You know I have to go somewhere and get some clothes to wear, though, right?"

"Yes. We'll get you something tomorrow. What should I get you for dinner?"

"Nothing. I'm not hungry. I just want to go to sleep."

"Suit yourself." He walked out of the room, and a second later, she heard his bedroom door shut.

Sabine pulled the blanket and top sheet back. Just before she got into bed, she stripped off her jeans and the form fitting Ferrum T-shirt she'd been wearing. She pulled on Remy's black V-neck T-shirt. The soft material caressed her skin and hung comfortably just below her bottom.

A hint of something masculine smelling tickled her nose. It was a scent she had never smelled before, and she wondered if it was some exotic cologne from some exotic land she'd never see. Under normal circumstances, the thought of sleeping in a man's shirt and being bathed in his scent would have been one of the hottest things she could imagine. She would not let herself be intoxicated by anything Remy, though, even if he did invade her dreams a few, or fifty, times too many.

Just as she got under the covers, the bedroom door cracked open, and he stepped through. He was now dressed in a dark button down shirt, dark jeans, and a leather jacket that looked like it cost a couple grand. His hair was pulled back, exposing the angular cut of his face. His green eyes almost looked as if they were glowing at her. The sight of him made her feel something stirring deep inside that she tried like hell to ignore.

"I'm headed out for a bite to eat. Don't try to leave. It'll do you no good. I'll be back in less than an hour. Not enough time for the scent of your trail to disappear, so stay put. Before I go, would you like me to tuck you in?"

"Just get out, you perv." She yanked the blankets up over her and rolled to her side away from him.

Leaving had crossed her mind, but it would only be a matter of time before he caught her. Maybe he wouldn't be so accommodating next time, so she decided not to press her luck. Settling down into bed, she fell asleep quickly.

He moved swiftly down 7th Avenue toward Times Square. It wasn't the most discreet place to feed, but he could work around that. He'd found a pretty, young girl to flatter in Times Square so many times he couldn't remember them all. Tourists were all the same. So caught up in the moment that they let their inhibitions go, and would inevitably follow him wherever he asked them to. He didn't even have to use his gift of influence to coerce them into going away with a complete stranger.

He was drawn to a certain type this night, and it wouldn't take him long to choose. Petite and pale, with dark, wavy hair was what he craved. On the rare occasion Bastian allowed him to leave Willow Creek to feed, he usually tried to avoid anyone that resembled her, knowing he'd be stuck with her indefinitely. Why tonight was different he did not know.

He scanned the crowd until he found a suitable woman, and easily caught her eye from the opposite side of the street. Never looking away from her, he crossed the busy intersection to where she stood. Walking right up to her, he smiled and her face flushed pale red. She was mesmerized by him instantly.

"First time in New York?" he asked, flashing a devilish grin down at her. His gums ached in anticipation of releasing his fangs. It took all of his will to keep them in their place and not suck her dry right there at the corner of Broadway and 7th.

"No. This is the third time I've been here."

"Surely you're not alone?"

"No. I'm here with some friends, but I got separated from them in the crowd. I thought maybe if I stayed here, I'd be able to spot them. You sound European. Are you visiting, too, or do you live here?"

"I have an apartment uptown. It's really too bad you're busy. I was on my way to a party, and I don't have a plus one."

"Oh... Well, if I could maybe borrow a cell phone, I could just text one of my friends and let them know. My battery died, and we haven't been back to our hotel all day."

"Of course, but let's get out of this crowd first. I don't like pulling out my phone with so many people around. You never know who is waiting to steal it right out of your hands."

She looked at him, unsure if she should trust him or not. "Wow. I never would have thought someone would steal right out in the open like this. So many people around to see them."

"Believe me when I say thieves can be ruthless."

She nodded and smiled. "I can wait. Which way are we going?"

He took her hand and led her back toward Central Park. "It's uptown. As soon as we get a block or two up, I'll let you use my phone and we can grab a taxi if you like."

"Your hand is so cold. It's not even that chilly tonight. Did you have them in a freezer or something?" The girl chuckled. "Kind of overkill with that jacket, too, isn't it?"

"I tend to be cold most of the time. Always have been, but… You can warm them, and me, if you like."

She took his hand and slid it into the back pocket of her jeans and wrapped her arm around his back. They continued to walk away from Times Square.

"You're really attractive. I can't believe you don't have anyone to go to a party with you."

"I know. Mind blowing, isn't it?"

"I don't think I got your name."

"You didn't get it, because I didn't offer it."

"Well, what is it? Mine is Sasha."

He stopped to face her. Something about looking into a lust stricken woman's eyes gave him great pleasure, especially when he was about to go in for the kill. Figuratively, of course. Killing was too much of a mess to clean up in today's society where someone would inevitably notice a missing person right away. It was much easier to make them forget.

"My name is Joseph. Do you really want to go to a lame party, or would you rather have a bit fun?" Remy rarely gave his real name when he was about to feed, just in case his coercion didn't hold up long term.

"What do you mean by fun?" she purred.

"I think you know what I mean." He moved closer to her, bending down to brush his lips against her neck.

"Is your apartment close?"

"No. Let's be adventurous. It's quite thrilling with the possibility of getting caught in public."

"I'm down for anything you want. This is turning out to be the best vacation I've ever taken."

His hand slid around her body and pulled her to a secluded area between buildings.

"I think this will do."

Pressing her against a brick wall, he smashed his body against hers. His tongue explored the softness of her mouth, and the familiar ache in his gums returned quickly. She dug her nails into his leather jacket as she tried to pull him closer. He grabbed her hair, pulling her head to the side, and ran his tongue along her neck, savoring every beat of her heart. So she wouldn't scream when he bit her, he exerted his power over her to lull her into a state of euphoria. His fangs descended and he sunk his teeth into her neck, letting her blood flow over his tongue and down his throat. She gasped as he drank deeply from her. Visions of Sabine in his embrace flashed through his mind, and he ravaged the girl even more.

Careful not to take too much, he pulled himself away from her after only a minute or so. He nicked his fingertip with one fang and rubbed the two tiny holes on her neck. As they began to close, he caught her gaze and put her in a trance as he spoke to her.

"I did not bite you or drink your blood. All you know is that you got separated from your group of friends and tried to find them. Some nice guy named Joseph helped you, but you got separated from him, too. You will return to the corner where you were standing in Times Square, and stay there until your friends find you."

The girl blinked, and looked around her. Not recognizing her surroundings and Joseph nowhere to be found, she headed for Times Square.

Chapter 8

"It's about time you got up." Remy's gaze did not lift from the newspaper he was reading.

"I didn't realize I was on a schedule," said Sabine. "I'm starving, and I still need clothes."

"Yes, I am aware. That happens to be one of my favorite shirts, and I'd like it back. We'll go shopping in a little while. I took the liberty of ordering you a cheese omelet and a side of bacon. It's already set up for you in the dining room."

"Thank you, though I do find it extremely creepy that you know what my favorite breakfast is. Oh, and I'm not giving you this shirt back until after we go shopping. It's bad enough I had to wear my jeans again, but I'm not wearing my shirt until it's washed."

Luckily, she had thrown a couple pairs of underwear in her handbag before she left for the concert, knowing it might be a day or so before she could buy more.

He flippantly waved his hand in her direction. "Whatever. I could take it back easily enough if I wanted."

"Yes, I get it. You're an all-powerful, supernatural being. Enough already."

"Enjoy your breakfast."

* * *

They arrived at the entrance of Barney's shortly before 2pm.

Looking at the door with a confused look on her face, Sabine said, "I can't afford to shop at Barney's. Are you crazy? Anything I buy here will eat up most, if not all of the money I have."

"I already told you I have more money than I know what to do with. Don't worry about how much you have. Pick whatever you like."

"Oh, no... No." She shook her head and pointed her index finger at him. "I'm not having you buy my clothes. You'll think I owe you, and I'm not having you hold it over my head anytime you want something from me."

"Listen to me. I told you I had some things I had to do before we go back to that mind numbingly boring town. You have to look like someone who I'd be traveling with. I can't have you showing up in some cheap rags you got from a tourist shop. So, shut up, and go shopping already."

She glared at him for telling her to shut up, but bit her tongue. There was no use in arguing right there in the middle of the sidewalk. "Where are we going that I have to be all decked out in designer clothing?"

"We'll discuss it later. This isn't the place."

"Fine, but for the record, I don't like it one bit, and I'm only getting a couple things. I'm heading for the nearest tourist shop as soon as we leave. I can at least buy my own pajamas. They don't have to be designer, do they?" She walked by him, glaring all the way.

She entered the store with Remy close behind, and tried to pretend he wasn't there, though it was a lost cause. Every time she picked something up, he had to provide commentary on whether or not he liked the garment or if it would look good on her or not. She sighed loudly, and turned to face him.

"How about you just pick whatever it is that you think I should wear? That's what you want, isn't it?" She crossed her arms and cocked her head to the side.

Throwing his hands up in the air, he exclaimed, "Finally."

Remy left her standing there alone as he went in search of what he thought would complement her. Sales people and other customers began to eye her as she drew attention to herself by standing alone in the middle of the main aisle. She reluctantly hurried after him.

Sabine soon caught up to Remy, and to her surprise, he already held an armful of things he'd picked off various racks.

"I seriously would like to punch you in the nose right now."

"No need for violence, Sabine. It's never the answer... except for when it is, of course. Anyway, go try this stuff on." He handed her the clothes and gently pushed her toward the nearest dressing room. "Run along, now."

"I don't want this stuff. I just want you to leave me alone long enough to pick out things for myself."

"Go try them on. I guarantee you will like some of it, and if you hate all of it, then we'll do things your way."

Gritting her teeth, she was determined to hate it all no matter what. To her dismay, she liked most of what he picked. It was almost as if he'd really paid attention to her usual style, and tried to find things that she would be comfortable in. As much as she hated to admit it, she had to give him credit.

She took her time in the dressing room, hoping maybe he'd think she ran again. The thought of making him nervous gave her a minute amount of joy.

He was waiting outside the main door to the dressing room when she came out.

"Well?"

"I like the stuff. Now can we go, please?"

"Not yet. You need shoes."

"What's wrong with these?" she asked as she looked down at the old Chuck Taylors she'd had for years.

"What's right with them should be the question. I guess they're fine for ambling around town, but you need something with a bit more class if you're going to be seen with me."

Off they went to the fourth floor where all the designer shoes lived. Sabine was overwhelmed with all the choices, and when she looked at the price tags, she almost passed out. The shoes were absolutely fabulous, but she couldn't fathom paying $600, or a lot more, for a pair of shoes she'd probably wear once. She watched Remy circle around the showroom, and that's what it was for sure—a showroom. Shoes of all colors and styles were artfully arranged with just the perfect amount of lighting above and behind them.

He ordered her to try on two different pairs of heels, and a pair of ballet flats. She liked them all, but fell in love with the simple black sling backs with the red soles. She'd never heard of Christian Louboutin before, but recognized the infamous red sole from all the times she'd seen pictures of celebrities wearing them on the red carpet.

"You look pleased. Did I do something right again?"

Her face lit up as she spoke, almost forgetting who she was talking to. "I love these! I like them all, but I don't know that I could ever take these off if I had them. They're too expensive, though. With everything you picked out already, I can't ask you to buy these, too."

"You didn't ask me to buy any of the other stuff either, if you recall. Who am I to say no to something that makes you smile like that? You might annoy the shit out of me, but you have a beautiful smile."

She blushed and looked away. There was no way she would let him see what he said had any effect on her.

"Thank you," was all she could muster.

* * *

"What do you want for dinner tonight? Should I order in, or do you want to go out to get something?"

"I don't really care, but I would like a big slice of pizza. Maybe I could go to Famous Original Ray's Pizza, or was it just Ray's Pizza? I think I saw a couple places on our way here last night."

"We can go whenever you're ready. Are you going to wear those new heels of yours?"

"Um, no. I don't think walking through the streets of Manhattan to find a pizza joint is the best time to break in a new pair of shoes. I have no desire to fall in the middle of the street or trip on one of those giant grates in the sidewalk and end up on my face."

"You have no faith in my ability to keep you safe, do you?"

She rolled her eyes. "I'm sure you can, but would you give yourself away just to keep me from falling?"

Remy was silent as he flashed a cocky grin in her direction.

"Yeah, I didn't think so. Falling on my ass is a better alternative than an angry mob chasing you with pitch forks and torches."

"Pitch forks and torches? In Manhattan? You've lost your mind, woman."

"You know what I mean. Will you be dining out tonight as well?"

"No. I fed last night. I should be fine for a few days at least."

"I thought you fed every day." What a relief to know she might not be bitten every night.

"I don't need much to sustain myself. Sure, I like to gorge myself sometimes, much like a human will stuff themselves with sweets and junk food, but I generally only feed once or twice a week."

"Good to know."

"I wouldn't be so happy to hear that if I were you. I know what it can feel like for you, and you'll be begging me to suck you dry every night."

"You're so gross! Can't we have a conversation that doesn't involve your stupid innuendos? I don't want to hear that I'm gonna be some kind of junkie jonesing for you to bite me. Christ, Remy. Enough already. And I wouldn't willingly have sex with you if you were the last thing on this earth that had a penis."

He erupted in raucous laughter. "Only in your dreams, right?" He laughed so hard that he fell to the floor. A bloody tear ran down his face and dripped onto his white shirt. "Look what you've done to me," he exclaimed as he pointed to the red dot on his chest. "You've made me ruin my shirt…"

He only laughed harder as she turned and stomped down the hallway, slamming the door behind her.

I guess I haven't done a very good job of hiding that little fact. Has it been so obvious that I dream about him because I think he's hot even if he is a dick?

She slipped into her shoes—not the heels—and debated on trying to leave on her own. Spending another second with him seemed like torture, but her stomach was starting to hurt because she was so hungry. Breakfast had been hours ago, and she wasn't in the mood for lunch after they finished up shopping. She swallowed her pride, and walked back out to where he still sat in the middle of the floor.

He stopped laughing and looked at her with a grin on his face.

"I'm hungry. Let's go," Sabine said.

"I have to change my shirt first," he said with a chuckle. "Be back in a second." And he was, quite literally, back in a second.

I will never get used to that speed thing.

Sabine followed just behind Remy as they walked down the street looking for a place to get her some food.

She tried to look *anywhere* but his ass, but she found herself stealing a glance here and there.

A block from the apartment, Remy stopped suddenly, causing her to almost run into him. He turned, and just as she was about to ask him what the hell was going on, he wrapped his fingers around her wrist. His body stiffened as he looked toward the tops of buildings, up and down the street, and all around them. His gaze finally settled on her.

Leaning down, he spoke softly, but sternly, into her ear. "Follow my lead, and do not resist me." His cool breath tickled her neck as he spoke.

She nodded in agreement. He never acted that way around her before, and it frightened her. His demeanor had changed so suddenly that it had given her a sense that she was in real danger. Gone was the sarcastic prick she was accustomed to, and his place was a vampire on high alert. They continued on in silence.

A block later, his hand slid behind her back and around her waist. Pulling her near, he looked down into her eyes as if to remind her of what he'd said a few minutes before.

She swallowed hard and nodded her head once just before a voice caught her attention.

"Remy... How long has it been? I haven't seen you in New York in ten years or more." A man of average height and average build with dark hair stepped out of the shadow of a nearby building and walked toward them. He stopped a few feet away from Remy and Sabine.

Remy stood tall and unmoving as he addressed the man. "It has been a long time, Timothy. How have you been?"

"Can't complain," he said as he took a step back and looked Sabine over from head toe and back.

"Timothy, this is my companion, Sabine." His grip on her tightened.

"Pleased to meet you, Sabine. You must be something if you got this one to settle down," he said, pointing at Remy with his thumb.

Sabine smiled politely and clung to Remy. It didn't take her long to figure out this guy might be a threat by the way Remy acted before he showed up. She looked past her contempt for her vampire "husband" because, at that moment, he was the lesser of two evils.

"Are you going next week?" Timothy asked

"Doubtful, but I'll consider it if I'm bored."

"We haven't seen you at one of Martin's gatherings in decades, but we can catch up then if you make it. It was nice meeting you, Sabine." Timothy brought her hand to his lips, and kissed gently.

"You, too." She again smiled politely.

The man disappeared into the shadows again, and she wondered if he would follow them. They picked up the pace and were back at the apartment with food in hand in no time.

"Okay, so may I ask what that was all about? That guy seemed nice enough."

"I sensed another vampire, but I didn't know who it might be or if it was someone I was familiar with."

She pulled a chair out at the table and sat down. "I'm glad you knew him. I thought the guy was some big, bad threat or something by the way you acted before you saw him."

Remy placed one hand on the table and leaned against it, peering down at her with a serious look about him. "Every vampire is a big, bad threat. The sooner you embrace that, the better."

"Oh, believe me. I'm aware. I just meant I was a little scared until I saw that he was your friend."

"He's no friend. He would've snatched you away from me in a heartbeat if he thought he could. The only thing keeping him from it was that I'm older than him, and it is forbidden to take another vampire's companion."

"Oh... well, I thought the way you talked to each other seemed like you were on good terms."

"Never trust a vampire, Sabine. We have friendly relationships with others of our kind, but we prefer to keep them at arm's length when we can."

Remy pulled out a chair and sat down. Leaning back, he placed an elbow on the table. He glanced at her before turning his face away.

"What was he talking about? Where did he think you might be going?"

"One of the few vampires I actually am friendly with is having a gathering next week, which he does every couple of years. You and I are going because I have business with someone who will be in attendance, and I didn't want him to relay to certain people that I will be there. If I don't take the chance now, I may not have another chance until… well, until you're dead."

"I bet you can't wait until that happens," she muttered.

Pretending he didn't hear her or just simply choosing not to respond, he continued on with the original subject. "I'm only dragging you along because you're here, and I have to," he said as he stood up and started to walk away. After only a few paces, he turned back. "Now is as good a time as any to talk about this… I have to keep you safe by claiming you. Otherwise, you'll be fair game to anyone who wants you. I've already told you it's forbidden to harm another vampire's human companion, and in order for them to leave you alone, they have to believe we are truly together. I might as well tell you now that it may involve some uncomfortable things for you. I assure you it will be fun for me, though."

She dropped her pizza in mid-bite. "Please don't tell me you're going to bite me in front of a bunch of blood suckers."

"No, most likely I can claim that I've fed already to avoid that if you wish, but vampires can be rather amorous at times, and I have a reputation for being a little more amorous than others. We think nothing of showing our affection in front of others," he said as he sat back down at the table.

"You're going to rape me in front of them, aren't you?" she asked. The color drained from her skin and her hands began to tremble.

"Sabine, don't be ridiculous. I may be a vampire, but I'm not a rapist. There will be no public sexual acts, but I can't guarantee that I won't kiss you or caress you like a lover would do while we're in front of the others."

A shiver ran down her spine at the thought of his lips touching hers and his hands all over her body. She craved his touch, though she'd never known it outside of her dreams before. She fought to push the images from her dreams from her mind.

She pushed her chair away and stood up, leaving her pizza there. "Just take me back to Willow Creek."

Remy watched her as she started to head toward her bedroom. He said, "I can't. If you go back, I go back."

She stopped and faced him. "I don't understand what's so important that you have to go right now. Let's just go home. My mom keeps texting me wanting to know when I'm going to be back."

"You don't need to know what's so important either. It's none of your concern. All you need to concern yourself with is keeping quiet and being obedient."

"Obedient and quiet? You really have no clue. That's why you don't have a *companion*. It has nothing to do with you not wanting to be tied down, or whatever it was that guy said."

"Please," he scoffed. "I could have anyone I wanted. I just don't want anyone. Why be tied down when I don't need to be?"

"Why not me? I mean, you're stuck with me until I die. Why not try to really get to know me, or at least pretend and try to make things enjoyable for me? Maybe you'd actually like me if you gave me half a shot." She smiled brightly at him, hoping to get some sort of pleasant reaction from him. "I don't think I'm too bad to look at, and it's not like I'm going to get to experience romance any other way." It was a shot in the dark. She almost wished she hadn't said anything once it was out in the open.

"I have nothing in common with a twit like you. I've seen every nook and cranny of this world, and lived through so much of what you would consider ancient history. You've not been any further from Willow Creek than you are right now, and if it didn't happen in the last twenty years, you probably have no interest in it."

His words stung. They were just another reminder of her cruel destiny and how she would be utterly alone for the rest of her life. Tears began to form, and she fought to keep them from falling as she looked down at the floor. She would not let him see her cry again.

She raised her head and looked at him square in the eye. "I've had no freedom to see the world or experience the things I want to experience. How dare you assume you know anything about me or what interests me?" Walking quickly toward her room, she closed the door behind her. She didn't even bother to change her clothes before crawling into bed. As she lay down, she wept softly.

Shortly after, he knocked on her door. "Sabine? You didn't finish your food," he said from the other side. "Do you still want it? I'm going to throw it out if you don't. It stinks already. Can't imagine how putrid it will smell when it goes bad."

Burying her face in the pillow, she ignored him. If he wanted her to be quiet, that's what he would get. She was embarrassed that she'd put herself out there like that, only for him to shoot her down. He didn't care about her and never would. She was only a nuisance to him and was right to dislike him from the start.

"Sabine? Are you alright?"

Silence.

"Sabine, answer me."

More silence.

"I'm going to come in there if you don't answer me."

Let him come.

*

He opened the door and marched into the room. Expecting to see her familiar glare looking back at him, he was taken aback at how he found her. He never expected to find her in such a broken down state, and instead had prepared himself to face her head on in an argument.

Looking at her for a few long seconds, he tried to figure out if he could fix her somehow and then wondered why it even mattered to him. *This is pointless. If she wants to ignore me, then let her. Maybe I'll get a little peace and quiet now... Is she crying?*

An overwhelming feeling of hopelessness enveloped him and invaded his senses. The despair she felt was palpable, and it almost knocked him back a step. He moved to the side of the bed and had an overwhelming urge to reach out and touch her... to comfort her.

Memories of a time when he felt such despair came rushing to him. He had been broken and hopeless, so much so that he gladly accepted Bastian's offer to turn him so that he could escape his life and detach himself from human emotion. Seeing Sabine that way reminded him of everything he'd once felt, and he began to worry about her for just a moment. He almost cared.

Just as quickly as the feelings started, he pushed them away and pulled his hand back before touching her.

No... I won't do this. I will not allow myself to care, especially for a girl that I'll have to watch grow old and die. I can't go through that loss again.

He left her alone, and didn't speak to her again until later in the week when they were due to leave New York.

* * *

He yelled through the door to her. "Get all your stuff packed up. It's time to go."

Knowing he couldn't see her, she stuck up her middle finger at the door. *I see he's talking to me again. Yay for me.* She turned off the Ferrum song that had been quietly playing on her phone and quickly threw all her new clothes into a duffle bag she found tucked into the closet. *I'm so going to burn these clothes when I get home. Well, maybe I'll donate them instead. I can't burn things that others could actually use. Maybe I'll keep the shoes...*

She emerged from her room, closed the door behind her, and plopped down into a lounge chair in the living room. She sure wouldn't miss being in New York with him, but she would miss the apartment itself and actually getting to go out without him over the last few days. They hadn't spoken in over three days, and when she first left the building on her own after finding an extra set of keys, she expected him to follow, but if he did, he never revealed himself.

Staying gone from the time she woke up until the time she went to bed, she only stopped in occasionally to freshen up or use the bathroom. A public restroom in New York City was almost as rare as a unicorn, and she found herself desperate enough to trek all the way back to the apartment and deal with him just to find some relief.

He came out of his bedroom in a rush with a scowl on his face. "Get your things and go downstairs. Wait out front for me."

She stood and picked up her purse, slinging it over her shoulder, before picking up the duffle bag she'd packed all of her clothes in. "Yes, master." Her free hand went to her forehead, military style, as he walked away from her.

Reaching for the door knob, he stopped dead in his tracks. His body stiffened, head cocking slightly to the side.

Her heart pounded rapidly until he continued out the front door a few seconds later. *He's still a vampire. I probably should try not to piss him off anymore.*

She followed him onto the elevator where they rode in silence until they got to the lobby. Exiting quickly, she found herself outside within a few seconds. He disappeared around the corner, leaving her standing alone.

A few minutes later, a silver BMW pulled up to the curb. Expecting to see a yuppie stock broker exit the car, she looked away to avoid eye contact. In an instant, Remy stood beside her, grabbing the bag from her hand. Her mouth dropped open as she realized this was his car and really eyeballed the gorgeous machine. Then she felt bad, like she was cheating on her Toyota.

Before she could ask when he'd had time to buy a car without her knowing, he slammed the trunk and walked to the driver's side.

"Why are you just standing there? Get in already. We've got somewhere to be," he said as he disappeared into the car.

Part of her wished he'd been a gentlemen and opened the door for her. She always swooned over men in movies that did that for their woman. No one had ever done something so chivalrous for her, but then her experience had been limited to high school boys, so what could she really expect? The realization that he would also never do anything like that for her settled over her. Maybe there was someone out there who had been meant for her—a prince charming who would've done all of those romantic hero acts of kindness for her. That fairytale dream was dead now.

She climbed in the car while Remy gripped the steering wheel and waited. As soon as her door was shut, he revved the engine and took off faster than she'd expected. She scrambled to buckle her seatbelt as he weaved in and out of traffic at breakneck speed. Her stomach flipped every time they had a near collision with another vehicle or a pedestrian. Traveling through the Lincoln Tunnel was horrifying and she was sure she wouldn't make it out alive. *Look on the bright side, if he gets you killed now, you're free.*

Her right hand clung to the arm rest as her left hand latched onto the seatbelt. Her stomach churned as what little she'd had for breakfast threatened to reappear.

"Could you slow down a little, please?" Her body jerked as he swerved into the adjacent lane, nearly missing a delivery truck.

"No," he said, clenching his jaw and never taking his eyes off the road.

"Remy, you're scaring me," she said as her voice quivered. "Please, slow down. I know you want me dead, but this isn't the way to go about it."

He relaxed his tense muscles, and eased off the gas a little.

"You wouldn't die even if we did crash."

"Glad you're confident about that, because I sure as shit am not." Her grip on the armrest loosened just a little as the car continued forward at a less terrifying speed.

"I would shield you from impact if we crashed, but we wouldn't." After a few minutes of silence, he spoke again. "I don't want to be your master." His head tilted slightly toward her as he spoke.

"Yes, I'm aware. You don't have to keep rubbing it in that you don't want to be around me. If it's all the same to you, I'd rather you stay away once we get home."

"I meant I don't want you to think of me that way. I have no desire to rule over you."

"So why do you? If you don't want to, then don't do it."

"I can't stop. Bastian has commanded me to watch you and keep you secure. I physically can't disobey."

"You have to do everything he says? I can't imagine you taking orders from anyone."

"He sired me, which means I have to obey him. If I don't, the pain of defying him is excruciating, and I don't always have control over my actions once he's commanded me. It just depends on how much power he uses."

"That sounds kind of sucky," she said, slouching a little in her seat and looking out toward the city getting further away.

"It isn't an issue most of the time."

"What about the past few days when I went out alone?" she asked as she looked over at him.

"You're sure you were alone?"

She shifted in her seat, and peered back out the window. "Sorry I've been such an inconvenience for you."

Silence then fell over the vehicle en route to where ever the hell they were going.

Chapter 9

"Are we stopping soon?" She shifted uncomfortably and crossed her legs.

"I don't plan on stopping until we get there."

"Can we please stop?"

"I don't see the point. We'll be there in a couple more hours."

"We've been on the road for six hours, and I NEED TO PEE!"

A disgusted groan rumbled in his throat. "Like I said, we're almost there. You should've gone when we stopped for gas. I don't have time for your biological functions. You're a big girl. You can hold it."

"Almost there? Two more hours is not almost there," she said, raising her voice.

Glancing at her out of the corner of his eye, he said, "Calm down. Two hours isn't that long. Nothing to go off your trolley over."

"I will calm down after I pee. Now, you can either stop somewhere that has a restroom, or I can piss all over this seat. Your choice." Her eyebrows raised as she looked at him.

He said nothing, but only a few minutes later, they stopped at a *Burger King* that sat right off the highway.

"Be quick about it."

"Don't worry about me. Once again, sorry I'm such an inconvenience," she said, grabbing her purse and exiting the car.

She walked a little slower than usual toward the restaurant and could feel his gaze cutting through her like daggers.

When she finished, she decided it was of the utmost importance to finger comb her hair, touch up her make-up, and thoroughly wash and dry her hands—twice. *Might as well get something to eat while I'm here, too.*

All in all, it had taken her over twenty minutes from the time she got out of the car until she got back in. As she approached the door to the restaurant, she looked through the glass toward the car. The tinted windows obstructed her view, but she knew Remy was most likely seething with anger. *I should be terrified to make him so mad, but screw him. I know for sure he's not going to hurt me now. He's not allowed.*

His nose crinkled, and his hand quickly pinched his nostrils together after she got in the car. "That smells horrid. Get rid of the bloody stuff. I don't want it stinking up my new car."

"No. I have to eat, and this is where you stopped. It isn't horrid at all. It's the best food I've ever tasted in my entire life." She smirked at him in his discomfort as she unwrapped her sandwich and took a big bite. It was her turn to play the jerk. Let him see how it feels.

Two hours later, they finally pulled up to a rather plain looking two story home. It sat on a huge plot of land an hour away from the nearest city. Several vehicles varying from clunkers to top of the line luxury vehicles were parked all around the front and side of the house.

Remy pulled the car into the large driveway, and put it in park.

They hadn't said a word to each other since their pit stop. Now was not the time for the silent treatment. He had to explain to her what was going on, how she needed to act, and why she shouldn't resist him.

Turning toward her, he rested his arm on the headrest of her seat. She leaned away before any part of him accidentally touched her.

"I need to tell you some things before we get in there. Once we're inside, we can't have any slip ups or someone will have you for dinner. Clear?"

She nodded. She wasn't ready to speak just yet, but for her own safety, she listened.

"Everyone in there has to believe we fancy one another. They have to believe that you've tamed the beast, so to speak. If you act like you hate me, they'll see right through it, and we will both be in trouble."

"What would they do to you?"

"Nothing, but I'm not too fond of finding out what I would face if I go back to Willow Creek without you. I'm not worried about my safety here, only yours. You have to trust me."

"Okay, but I will never trust you ever again if someone tries to eat me."

"Stay where you are. I'm going to come around and open your door. I expect a smile from you waiting for me when I do."

It was just the kind of thing she wanted to happen, but it wasn't sincere so it didn't matter. He strolled around to her side and opened the door. Taking her hand in his, he helped her out of the car. He walked beside her up the steps and onto the front porch, never once letting go of her. Before either one of them had the chance to ring the bell, a tall man with a goatee and dark eyes opened the door.

The two vampires stared at each other, growls rumbling in their throats as their eyes lit up with rage. Remy stepped to the other vampire. She squeezed Remy's hand, hoping to pull him out of whatever state of mind he was in. That's all she needed was for him to get in a fight with another vampire and leave her vulnerable for the picking.

He dropped her hand, and she prepared for impact. The other vampire threw his arms around Remy as they both laughed from their bellies while embracing each other. It was the strangest greeting she'd ever seen.

"Who is your lovely guest?"

"This," he paused to take her hand once again and brought it to his lips, "is my Sabine." His lips softly skimmed over the skin on her hand and sent tingles up her arm. She wanted to hate him. She tried to hate him. Even though she knew it was all an act, she still couldn't shake how good that small amount of attention made her feel.

Shit, shit, shit! What if this guy can hear me? I can't do this. I'll never be able to keep up this charade.

"Sabine, this is my friend, Martin. We've known each other for over three hundred years now. He's really more of a brother to me than a friend."

"Nice to meet you, Martin." She smiled politely.

"Likewise. I look forward to getting to know you. Please, come in. I'm sorry I don't have many refreshments for you, Sabine. Is there something you might like? I could send someone out to get anything you'd like."

"No, thank you. I'm fine. I ate a little while ago, and I have a bottle of water in my purse."

"Very well, then. The others are all inside. They've been quite anxious to hear what you've been up to. No one has seen you in such a long time. We'd begun to think you had perished."

"Still alive, though I didn't feel like I was until I met this one. I spent a lot of time around Europe by myself until recently. I happened to be visiting Bastian when I met Sabine, and I've been hooked on her ever since." He smiled sweetly and pulled her close.

"I'm glad you found someone to make you happy. I never thought I'd see the day."

"It feels good to love."

He sounded so sincere. If she let herself, she could easily fall in love with him acting like she was the love of his life. She figured she might as well enjoy it while she could. The contempt he held for her would return soon enough.

"I trust she hasn't quelled your thirst for vengeance?"

"Never."

"The one you seek has not yet arrived, but I have it on good authority that he will be here, none the wiser, after sundown. He usually shows up when we have our gatherings, and I have no reason to believe he won't this time."

"We'll return later tonight. I have no desire to scare him off if he realizes I'm here before he arrives. Give my regards to the others until I return."

Martin nodded his head and returned inside the house as Remy and Sabine made their way back to the car.

* * *

An hour later, they pulled into the parking lot of a hotel. Remy left Sabine waiting as he got them checked into a room. It seemed nice enough from the exterior, but it wouldn't compare to Remy's apartment in Manhattan. Sabine yawned and stretched once she was out of the car.

"I hope you aren't too tired. You'll have to be ready to go back to Martin's in just a bit."

"Can I please just rest my eyes for a few minutes? It's been a long day, and it looks like it's going to be a long night. I don't get why you can't leave me here while you go do your thing. You know I'm not going to leave."

"I don't know that you won't, therefore you have to come with me. Your scent would be long gone by the time I return. You don't have much time, but I suppose you could nap for an hour or so before you have to make yourself presentable again."

As luck would have it, they were parked close to the room they were to share. Sabine waited by the door as he retrieved the bags from the trunk of the car. He unlocked the door, and they stepped into the room.

She followed him inside and peered around the room, though her eyes instantly stopped at the bed.

"One bed? Seriously? One bed? You couldn't get a double with your endless supply of money you like to throw around?"

"I didn't think it was a big deal. You can easily sleep on the floor. There's an extra pillow, and I don't really *need* a blanket, so I suppose you could have the one on the bed."

"Why do you hate me so much?"

"I don't hate you. You're just too easy to rile. You take things too seriously."

"Well, it's not like you've ever really been all that nice to me. How else would I take it?"

"I have been nice to you. Need I remind you of the clothes I purchased for you, or the fact that I didn't tell Bastian you tried to run away? I even fetched you your favorite breakfast once."

He had a point, even though she protested him buying the clothes for that very reason. She didn't want it thrown in her face every time he saw the opportunity. Rather than escalate the conversation, she decided it was time to rest.

"May I lie down now, master?"

"You have no idea what a master really is, but yes, go ahead."

She pulled the bedspread back, kicked off her fancy shoes, and slid in between the sheets, falling asleep only a little while later.

* * *

110

The room was quiet, save for the soft, steady breath and beat of a heart coming from across the room. She seemed so peaceful, and in that moment, the feelings he worked so hard to repress came bubbling to the surface again. The more he studied her, the harder it was to deny he cared about her and her well-being, but he could never be what she wanted him to be. He wasn't capable of it anymore even if he wanted to try. Those days were long behind him.

He quickly pushed her to the back of his mind and focused on his mission. Despite keeping most vampires at arm's length, there was only one vampire in the world he longed to kill—Jackson Carter. The thought of him almost made his blood boil. He was the only one who'd ever managed to steal something so precious to him and get away with it. Being a thief was bad enough, but Jackson took something Remy held dear to his heart that could never be replaced.

The item wasn't just some random, meaningless trinket or even cash he had lying around. Jackson took the last bit Remy had of his mother—a necklace given to him shortly before he was married. It was the only thing his father hadn't managed to strip Remy of before he was forced into slavery under his father's command.

Jackson would pay for taking the only thing in the world that mattered to Remy. What made it worse was that he knew Jackson carried the necklace with him to flaunt it as a trophy. It would be a bonus to get the jewelry back because he understood there was a chance Jackson might not have it on him at the gathering. The true prize, and the one he was looking most forward to, would be thrashing the despicable excuse for a vampire until he was obliterated.

For over one hundred and fifty years, Jackson managed to elude him, but not this time. This time, Remy was one step ahead of him.

A quiet vibration coming from his pocket caught his attention. He reached in and pulled his phone out without bothering to see who was calling.

"Hello?"

"Jackson isn't coming tonight. He phoned a few minutes ago and said he's been held up by a personal matter, but that he intends to be here tomorrow afternoon sometime."

Remy sat straight up in his chair. Rage ran through his veins. "Do you think he knows?" His jaws clenched.

"No, I'm certain he does not."

"You're sure the others haven't alerted him?"

"I'm sure. I've been watching them closely."

"Very well, then, Martin. I will see you tomorrow."

He placed the phone on the table beside him before the urge to throw it across the room had the chance to take over. Had Jackson eluded him once more? The thought of Jackson slipping away once again pissed him off to the point he wanted to break or kill something.

Knowing it would calm him, he turned and focused on her. What was it about her that made him so calm? No human had ever had much influence over him accept making him hungry or annoyed and occasionally horny. He couldn't help but think of all the times he'd watched her sleep—all the times he influenced her to dream of him. It was just another way he tried to convince himself that she was nothing more than a plaything and to get under her skin.

Sabine stirred. Walking quietly to her bedside, he reached out with his mind and quickly pulled back. He would let her be free to dream of whatever and whomever she wanted. The lids of his eyes grew heavy as he watched her sleep. He stripped off his clothes—all of them—and crawled into bed beside her. He smirked to himself as he thought of her face seeing him lying naked next to her. That would be far more entertaining than making her dream of him.

* * *

Her eyes fluttered open. Looking at the clock on the nightstand, she squinted, but the red light from the numbers hurt her eyes. Finally, she was able to focus enough to see that it was 4:30 in the morning.

Why didn't he wake me up hours ago? Maybe he left without me. I could only be so lucky.

She stretched her legs and rolled to her back. A streetlight sent a faint glow into the room from a crack in the curtains. Debating on whether or not to get up and close them the rest of the way, something beside her in the bed caught her eye. She looked over, surprised to see Remy sound asleep. *I can't believe he actually got in bed with me. I thought for sure he'd make me sleep on the floor.*

Then, she looked down and saw him. Really saw him—all of him.

"Oh my god," she exclaimed as she jumped out of the bed and flipped the bedspread over his most private of parts.

Without opening his eyes or otherwise moving, he spoke calmly. "What are you yelling about? Can't you see I'm sleeping?"

"Put some pants on! Underwear... something," She covered her eyes with her hands. "I don't want to see that!"

He smirked and draped his forearm over his eyes. "What's the matter? You've never seen a real man with a real knob before?"

"I have, but I don't want to see yours!"

"I hadn't intended to be so exposed. You must have stolen the covers away from me, but you better get used to it, sweetheart. This is what you'll be seeing every day, especially if you don't learn how to share a blanket. I'm just not comfortable sleeping in clothes; too binding."

"Have I told you lately that you're such a pervert?"

"I think you might have mentioned it once or twice recently. Now, you might as well get back into bed, love. We aren't going anywhere for a few more hours."

"I am not getting back in that bed with you being all naked like you are."

"Suit yourself." He propped himself up on one elbow and eyed her. "I am getting a little hungry, though. Don't suppose you'd mind coming over here and letting me have a bite to eat? It would only be a quick nibble."

"Yuck! I will never let you bite me." She turned away from him. "You'll have to force me to let you every single time. I won't submit. Ever."

"Sounds delightful for me. The more you resist, the better you taste."

She ran into the bathroom and slammed the door. Remy stood and pulled on his jeans. He left the room for just a few minutes to pay a visit to the front desk clerk.

Chapter 10

The sensation of non-existent bugs running up and down her skin unnerved her. Sabine trembled ever so slightly as she looked around the large living room at all of the abnormally bright eyes leering at her. The air was thick and warm with little circulation. Sweat beaded in various places all over her body. *Did that guy just lick his lips?*

A familiar chilled hand rested on the small of her back, guiding her to an empty seat. His fingers grasped her hips firmly, pulling her onto his lap as they sat down. The coolness of his body helped her to not be quite so hot. She might have dreamt about it, but it was the only time she seriously considered ripping both of their clothes off and pressing her body against him. The heat was getting to her already, and she thought she might burst into flames at any second if someone didn't open a window or turn on a fan.

"He has arrived, yes?" Remy turned his attention to the vampire from the day before, Martin.

"Yes. He's chained in the basement and awaits your punishment."

"Good. Let him suffer with anticipation for a little while longer."

"Do you intend to kill him?" Martin stiffened, and his eyes flashed with excitement.

Remy nodded once. Though Sabine couldn't see his response, she was pretty sure she knew what it was. Heart pounding against her chest, her breath quickened.

"Perhaps you should calm your lover, Remy? She sounds terrified, and is drawing a lot of attention. Many of our colleagues haven't eaten in a few days. A pounding heart won't help matters any."

His lips brushed softly against her ear. Cool breath caressed her as he whispered to her. "Sabine, you must try and stay calm. You are in no danger with me right here beside you. I am older than anyone in this room by at least seventy-five years, but I don't fancy having to deal with any of them trying to get to you. I'll finish my business soon, and we'll leave. Remember, I love you, and I would die before I let anything happen to you."

His last sentence sent shivers up her spine. No boy, or man, ever told her they loved her like that. Her heart sank because it was all an act for the others in the room. How was he so confident they wouldn't hear her thoughts and know he wasn't sincere? Maybe he didn't really care if they knew. Maybe he was convinced he could take on any who might challenge him. If that was the case, why put on this charade in the first place?

*

Remy pulled her close, guiding her head back to rest against his chest. He gently stroked her hair as he assessed the situation. There were twenty other vampires there, and at least half of them looked ready to pounce. The only thing stopping them was the belief that she belonged to him. He had to take care of Jackson fast if he hoped to get out without putting her in any danger. It was true he could take any of them down, but it wouldn't be so easy to take all of them at once. One vampire acting out against him would be all it would take for most of the others to join and start a killing frenzy.

*

The door to the outside flung open. In marched a line of scantily clad men and women. Fangs grew. Noises resembling snarling or growling emanated from deep within some of the vampires. These people were definitely human and definitely dinner. She averted her eyes away from them, afraid she'd see them meet their deaths.

A vampire she couldn't see yelled out. "Food's here! Have at it!"

With that, the vampires descended on the humans. She sat up quickly on Remy's lap. Blurs of light and wind raced past her. As she looked around, all the vampires, each one with a newly acquired human, had returned to where they were seated only a second before. Groans of ecstasy erupted from almost every human in the room as the vampires bared their teeth. Some of the couples kissed, some of them rubbed and caressed one another, and others had already begun feeding from their human donors. It was apparent that feeding and sex went together naturally in the vampire world. The whole thing gave Sabine the creeps, and she had no desire to watch some bloodlust fueled orgy.

Remy pulled her back into his arms. His lips touched her nape softly. He ran his hand up her spine and cradled her neck as he bent her head away from him and ran his tongue along her jawline before moving onto her throat.

Is he going to bite me? He said he wouldn't!

Just then, he grabbed her, and before she felt any movement at all, she sat in the chair with him on his knees before her. Leaning forward, he wedged himself between her thighs. He looked deep into her eyes, and nodded in an attempt to remind her to play along. Moving even closer, he brought her hands to his lips and kissed her wrists before draping her arms around his neck.

His mouth inched toward hers slowly. When he finally met her lips, he kissed her fervently, pushing her back in the chair as the weight of his body caused her breath to leave. His tongue explored the warm softness of the inside of her mouth. The sharp points of his teeth descended and teased her lip before their tongues intertwined.

She knew this was all for show, but deep down in her core, she *wanted* him to bite her. She wanted to feel what every other person in the room was feeling when a vampire sunk their teeth into flesh.

His hand slid under her shirt and over her ribs, stopping just short of her breast. She screamed to him in her mind to keep going, but her cries went unheard. She didn't know whether to be thankful or pissed that he couldn't hear her thoughts. He pulled away, looking her deep in the eyes once more before tilting his head and moving to place his mouth over her jugular.

*

He did not bite, though the urge almost overwhelmed him. Her flesh tasted just as he imagined it, and he knew her blood would be just as sweet. His promise to not bite her echoed through his mind. If he placed his mouth in

119

just the right spot and sucked gently, he could fool those around him into thinking he was drinking her blood.

He could feel some of the others with their gaze glued to them, just waiting for him to slip up. It was in some vampires' nature to covet what belonged to another despite the possibility of death, and in a group as large as this one, there had to be at least a couple that desired Sabine simply because she was his.

He sucked at the flesh on her neck while his hand wound in her hair, keeping her head in place. He couldn't afford for her to move and someone see that he hadn't really bitten her. Pulling away, he pretended to swallow. He palmed her neck where two bite wounds should have been to hide the lack of evidence and discreetly bit the inside of his own mouth so that the blood would begin to flow. Before returning to the sweet spot on her neck, he flashed a bloody smile at her.

*

She couldn't believe he'd bitten her, and she hadn't even felt it. The evidence was there, though. Blood dripped from his teeth and ran down his chin. Despite being horrified that he'd bitten her, she longed for him to kiss her again. She fought against the feeling with all she had. She glanced around to see most of the vampires had finished feeding and were starting to move around the room. The sound of new conversations sprang up all around them.

*

Remy took his mouth off her neck and stuck his finger to the point of his fang. He gently rubbed the spot he'd pretended to bite. It was the only way to explain why she didn't have puncture wounds. He leaned back and looked at her longingly while he wiped away the blood on his face.

He whispered, "Thank you, my love," and leaned in for one final passionate kiss.

*

Remy stood and announced that he was ready to take care of the vampire in the basement. He held out his hand to her, and she took it as he helped her out of the chair. She walked just behind him as close as she could through the house and down the stairs as the others followed.

A man with shaggy, dirty-blonde hair stood with his arms and legs all separately chained to the walls. By the looks of it, he appeared to be slightly taller than Remy and just as muscular, if not more so. A female vampire who was half their size stood guard in front of him.

Remy dropped Sabine's hand and moved quickly to stand in front of the chained vamp. He stared into the prisoner's eyes as he sneered back at Remy.

"Where is it, Jackson? I hear you like to brag that you've bested me."

"It is here, but I will never give it back to you. You'll have to rip it from my dead body."

"As you wish." Remy turned to the vamp on guard and motioned for her to unchain Jackson. The other vampires backed away and spread out around the room, forming a circle around them. "I *will* kill you, but I won't do it with you chained and unable to fight back. I'll give you that much."

Remy stepped back, waiting for Jackson to attack him. Jackson rubbed his wrists, and paced back and forth. His teeth were bared as he glanced at Sabine for a split second before attempting to pounce on her.

Remy intercepted Jackson and threw him against the wall. He landed with a loud thud, concrete crumbling upon impact.

Sabine startled and raised her hands to her cheeks. Her heart tried to beat right out of her chest as her knees went weak. She braced her back against the wall to keep from falling. Martin gently grasped her elbow to help steady her.

*

Jackson lay crumpled on the floor, trying to regain his composure. Remy stood over him. He knelt down and began to punch the vampire repeatedly in the face. Blood flew from Jackson's mouth and nose. He tried desperately to push Remy off of him, but he was no match. Remy stood above the battered vampire. He lifted his boot and buried his heel in Jackson's skull, crushing it under the impact. Bending down, he easily removed what remained of Jackson's head from his body and tossed it aside.

Bloodied hands searched the dead vampire's pockets. He hung his head and closed his eyes as his fingers felt the fragile chain. He pulled out the necklace he'd lost so long ago and stared at it as if it weren't real. Savoring the feel of the golden chain and purple stone in his hand, he held back tears of satisfaction.

*

Sabine held her breath for what seemed like an eternity. Taking deep breaths, she forced air into her lungs. The whole thing was the bloodiest, most brutal thing she had seen in her whole life, and it had only lasted a few seconds. It made her fear Remy and what he was capable of that much more. She watched closely as he pulled a necklace from the dead thing's jacket pocket. She wasn't sure, but she thought she could see Remy's eyes turning red with bloody tears. As he turned back toward her, his eyes were clear, if only a little darker than they normally were.

He marched over to her and grabbed her around the waist with his bloody hands, then kissed her—long and deep.

* * *

The silence in the car on the way back to the hotel was deafening. She had so many thoughts and questions running through her head, and couldn't focus on just one thing to talk to him about, so she stayed quiet. She was torn in two different directions. He'd left her feeling like she was missing out on something great with all the physical attention he'd paid her, yet she wanted to get as far away from him as she could when she remembered how violent he could be. His true nature had shown itself, and the thought of it chilled her to the bone.

Once they arrived back at the hotel, he unlocked the door to their room and held it open for her before he stepped in.

"Would you like something to eat? I can order you a pizza or something."

"I don't know. I don't have much of an appetite. Let me just sit for a few minutes and figure it out." She avoided eye contact as she spoke to him.

"Are you alright? That must've been a lot for you to take in. I doubt you see a slaughter like that very often."

"I don't know if I am or not."

"I assure you, he deserved what he got."

"Help me understand." Her eyes raised to meet his. "Because what I saw was a one-sided blood bath. That guy didn't have a chance, did he?"

"No, he didn't." He lowered himself into a chair and sat quietly for a minute. "He didn't deserve to have a chance either."

Standing up and walking to the bathroom, she needed to be by herself for a moment, and this was the only place she could do that. Sitting on the edge of the tub, she tried to process everything running through her mind. She closed her eyes to try and ease the pounding sensation developing around her temples.

She could see him ripping the head off that vampire at the same time she could feel his lips on her. She recalled the blood—her blood—dripping from his teeth at the same time she felt his arms around her and his hands tangled in her hair. She still wore the stains from the blood on his hands as her lips ached from the sweet sting of his kiss. Fearing him and lusting after him was the strange dichotomy she'd found herself in.

After a long while, she returned to the bedroom. He stood looking out the window at nothing.

Not turning toward her, he spoke. "You were never in any real danger. You know that, right?"

"I get that, but that's not what I'm having issues with... that's not what scares me."

"What is it then?"

"You."

*

His body stiffened as he heard the fear in her voice. His head turned slightly in her direction.

"You scared me before, but I'm absolutely terrified of you now. You bit me when you said you wouldn't, and I've never seen someone be as violent as you were. I've never seen someone die right in front of me, let alone such a violent death."

"I didn't bite you." He continued looking out the window again, and his body relaxed.

"I saw my blood dripping off your teeth and running down your chin. Now you're going to lie about it?"

"It wasn't your blood. It was mine. I meant it when I said I wouldn't feed on you in front of all them."

"Oh... I saw the blood, and I thought," she trailed off in mid-sentence. "I guess that's why it didn't hurt. I thought maybe you just made it so I didn't feel it."

"I wanted them to believe I was feeding from you, so I bit the inside of my lip. That's why I kept my mouth on your neck for so long. I knew some of them were watching us. If I hadn't pretended to feed on you, things could have turned sour fast, and it's not like I could tell you my intentions without alerting everyone else."

He turned to face her just as she reached up and placed her hand on the spot his mouth had been focused on. He saw lust flash briefly in her eyes. Though he would never admit it to her, he enjoyed being close to her. He planned to tease her about kissing her and sucking on her neck, and he was going to act like he was the pig she thought he was, but he would never tell her how much he enjoyed being so close to her. His lips ached to kiss her again.

"Then what was with killing that guy? All for a necklace?" Sabine shook her head and looked at him incredulously. "You could just buy another."

He looked down at the floor. He couldn't stand making eye contact with her while he revealed the story so close to his heart. "It isn't just a necklace. It's my mother's, and later belonged to my wife. That necklace is the only item I possessed that belonged to either of them, and he stole it from me."

"I didn't realize you still had feelings like that. You made it seem like you don't care about anything," she said, moving to the side of the bed closest to him and sat down.

"I do care about a few things. I may put on a tough exterior, but some feelings linger."

"So, it has sentimental value... couldn't you just take it back? Did you have to kill him?"

"Yes, I did. Everything I owned as a human was stripped from me by my father when I refused him. I managed to hide the necklace in a place he never suspected, and I retrieved it later. So, you see, it wasn't

126

just that it was theirs, but it was the only thing I had left from my mortal life. The necklace was the last bit of myself that I could still hold on to. I helped Jackson after he was first made vampire. His maker abandoned him, and he needed someone to guide him."

She sat on the edge of the bed, quietly listening to him.

"I tried to teach him how to blend in with society and make those he fed on forget instead of killing them. He grew angry with me over time for not allowing him to kill freely, and he knew that was the only way to hurt me. I've searched for him for one hundred and fifty years; all the while he flaunted the necklace to every vampire he could about how he had stolen from me the only thing I cared about. In vampire culture, tolerance and forgiveness are not given easily. He deserved what he got."

"What did your father do to you?"

He shook his head. "Not today."

She nodded her head in agreement and changed the subject.

"I think I want that pizza now."

* * *

"Are we going home tonight or tomorrow?"

"Tomorrow."

"How far away are we? I want to let my parents know when we'll be back, and I need to go talk to Delia and make it up to her for worrying her so much when I left the concert."

"It's only three hours. We'll leave as soon as you're ready in the morning. Sleep in if you like."

She texted her friends and her parents to let them know when she'd be back. It was only 11pm, but she felt like she hadn't slept in days. The fact that she'd been awake since 4:30am or that she'd experienced the most horrific thing and the most pleasurable thing in her life all in the same evening probably didn't help any.

She'd been with boys before. Not that she was promiscuous, but she was no angel. She'd always had a thing for bad boys, and they seemed to know exactly what to say to her to get her clothes off. Maybe she'd been dumb for believing they wanted more from her than sex, or maybe she wasn't all that different than most girls at that age; since before she graduated from high school, she hadn't been with anyone at all. Maybe it was the situation she'd found herself in on her eighteenth birthday. She didn't want to start something with a guy, only for it to go nowhere when she moved to Willow Creek Manor.

Remy was the first man that had paid her that kind of attention. The way he made her feel was nothing she'd experienced before with the boys she'd been with. His kisses and touches felt like they were meant only for her pleasure instead of having an ulterior motive hidden in them like so many of the boys she'd kissed.

He was so good at playing the part of her lover that she began to wonder about how many women he had seduced in four hundred years. How many of them did he ever really have feelings for? Just what had he learned in all that time that he liked to boast about? She shook the thoughts away and prepared for bed.

As she climbed into bed, Remy stood looking out the window at nothing again. "I won't sleep tonight. Don't worry about finding me naked beside you in the morning." He smirked as he glanced in her direction.

"What a relief." She turned on her side so that her back was facing him. After a few minutes, she gathered the courage to ask something that had been bugging her since the day before. "How did you know they wouldn't hear my thoughts?"

"None of them, except Martin, were old enough, and he doesn't possess it. That's an ability that comes with age. Even then most can't do it. I've been able to do it when I really tried only because it is a gift Bastian possesses. Our makers greatly influence the abilities we have. I've just never bothered to hone my skills."

"I was worried someone would know I wasn't really with you romantically. I kept trying not to think about it, but it was really hard not to."

"I think we did a damn fine job of convincing them we bang on a regular basis. Wouldn't you agree?"

"I guess so." She wanted to scream that he'd made *her* almost believe they were together. She fought the urge to invite him into bed with her and finish what they started earlier.

*

He laughed to himself as the quickening beat of her heart gave her feelings away once again. He concentrated on her, trying to hear, but there was nothing. He never really liked listening in on thoughts before, but he was curious to hear exactly what she was thinking in that moment.

"Do you mind if I lie beside you and watch TV? I can turn the volume down so I don't disturb you."

"As long as you keep your pants on, it's fine."

"Good, I can lose the shirt then." He smirked and pulled the shirt over his head, tossing it over the back of the chair.

She sighed heavily, but smiled to herself.

* * *

Hours had passed, and there was nothing on but infomercials. He turned off the TV and continued to lie there bored. Sabine slept facing him now, and he caught himself looking at her again. He studied her face, memorizing every tiny pore of her skin, every strand of her hair, and every curve of her face. He watched the artery in her neck thump with every beat of her heart and longed to taste her. The more he looked at her, the more he wanted her.

He'd started out loathing her and the idea of spending the rest of her life together. He couldn't wait for the day to come when she would die and maybe he would be free again. Feeding off only her was revolting to him. He'd enjoyed countless types, both women and men, for feeding in the past, and he couldn't imagine giving that up. But, now… now, he realized that he hadn't desired anyone but her since he got on the plane only a week before. The girl from Times Square even resembled her, and she was the only one he'd specifically chosen to feed from during that time.

The past two years were spent watching over her, and although Bastian ordered him to keep her safe, he quickly grew to enjoy being around her, even if she never suspected that he was there. He'd learned things about her that made him see who she really was. He knew she cried every time she watched *The Color Purple*, laughed hysterically when she watched *The Big Bang Theory*, and was so invested in the characters on *The Walking Dead* that she spoke about them like she knew them personally. He also knew she was obsessed with the band Ferrum and its lead singer, Ash London. He'd even checked the band out, and found that he enjoyed their music, all because of her.

He knew she loved to read and wished to have her own personal library. Ironically, the one place she would do anything to get away from was the one place where her wish would be fulfilled. He'd had the room adjacent to his remodeled with large shelves and a big, plush chair that had a little table attached to it by a bay window where she could lounge and read to her heart's content. A door had been installed between his bedroom and the library for easy access. All the room needed was the books of her choosing.

He'd even made sure to include an area in that library where she could paint if she wanted. And oh how he loved to watch her paint. It had quickly become one of his favorite things to do. The passion coursing through her when she created a work of art exhilarated him in a way he hadn't felt in centuries.

The way he kissed her earlier in the day was only a small sample of what he wanted to do to her. He couldn't help but feel she would warm up to him if he changed how he treated her. A little respect could go a long way to building a bond between them. Sabine longed to be romanced, and he could do that for her easily.

No. This wasn't what he really wanted. She would die in the blink of an eye in comparison to his long life. The only way he could be with her would be to turn her into one of his kind. She would never go for that, and he wouldn't turn her against her will. He had to bury those feelings deep inside himself before they got out of hand.

He continued to study Sabine, trying hard not to feel anything for her. Drifting off to sleep, her face haunted him as he began to dream—something he hadn't done in over a century.

* * *

Sabine began to wake in the early morning hours of the next day. Her mind, fuzzy and still full of sleep, tried desperately to slip back into oblivion before she opened her eyes. Once they were open, that would be it; she would be wide awake. Keeping her eyes closed, she couldn't help but notice the crick in her neck. She realized then that her head was positioned at an odd angle and her face rested against something firm and smooth.

That doesn't feel like my pillow. Peeping one eye open, the flesh of his unmoving chest stretched out before her. Feeling something heavy around her, she looked down to find his arm firmly holding her body.

She wanted to stay there, pressed against him. His exotic scent tickled her nose, and with her lips so close to his skin, she longed to run her tongue over his nipple so she could taste him. But she couldn't. As soon as he saw her there, he'd make some pervy comment and ruin the mood completely. Plus, this was Remy... the same Remy she was trying hard to convince herself that she didn't have feelings for.

Trying to free herself was no use. His arm was too heavy to move with the grip he had on her. Looking up at his face, she saw him sleeping peacefully with the slightest hint of a smile on his lips. He looked like a happy man for once, instead of his usual asshole-ish vampire self. She pondered for a second if he was really asleep or if he was messing with her again.

*

As if on cue, his eyes opened, and he looked down at her looking up at him. Instead of moving his arm or pushing her away, he stayed still. It was a make or break moment for them. If he moved her away, he would be back to pretending he didn't have feelings for her, but if he stayed where he was, maybe she would see him for who he longed to be, and not the monster she thought he was.

"I'm sorry. I must've rolled over onto you in the middle of the night. I'll get up now."

"No... Stay. You're not bothering me. It's nice to cuddle sometimes. I like the warmth."

His grip tightened a little, gently squeezing her as he remembered her nuzzling up to him only a few hours before. Her movement had awakened him from the wonderful dream he'd been having of her. He'd pulled her up to his chest and wrapped his arm around her as he relished the feeling of his cool skin warming beneath her. It had been his intention to move before she woke up, but having her in his arms had lulled him back to a peaceful sleep.

*

She laughed loud, unable to control herself. "You like to cuddle? Or are you just fucking with me again?"

"There's so much you don't know about me, Sabine. You think you've got me figured out, but you have no idea." He let go of her and slid out from underneath her.

She felt bad for laughing. She didn't mean to offend him, and was just shocked that this evil vampire, who'd portrayed himself as such an ass up to that point, wanted to *cuddle* with her.

"I'm sorry, Remy. I shouldn't have laughed. You caught me off guard, and I thought you were messing with me."

"You might as well get dressed so we can go." He stood up and grabbed his shirt, pulling it quickly over his body.

"Remy..."

"Go on, now. Get to it. I'm sure your parents are anxious for you to come home."

In that moment, she realized the opportunity she had longed for was gone. She had caused him to slam shut the door he'd cracked open to his soul.

Chapter 11

"Anymore hot hook ups between you two I should know about?" Delia questioned.

They sat in their usual spot at the café where they liked to spend Saturday evenings, though their routine of meeting up every Saturday wasn't quite so routine anymore with both of the girls having jobs at different times. They still managed to keep up the tradition when they were both free.

Sabine dropped her head and sighed. "Are you ever going to let that go?" she asked, peeking up at her friend. "It was a one-time thing, and apparently it didn't really mean much to him, anyway."

"I just wondered if he wanted to cuddle again." Delia giggled and lightly tapped Sabine on the arm. She couldn't hold back the laughter any longer, and she let loose.

She took a sip of her drink, and sat back in her chair. "You know, I do feel really bad for laughing at him. It was horrible of me. He was so vulnerable right then, and I kicked him right in the balls." She took another sip her iced coffee. "I really thought he was fucking with me."

"Has he been around at all?" Delia asked as she glanced around at the other patrons.

"More than likely, but I haven't seen him. I'm sure he's close by now, if you want to know the truth. He probably heard everything we just said."

"Seriously? He's around you all the time?" Delia crinkled her brow and leaned forward.

"I don't know if it's all the time. Maybe not much during the day, but he knew I was planning on running. He told me he just quit bothering me, but was never far away. So I'm guessing he's somewhere close by now, since it's almost dark. Maybe he's trying not to bother me again."

Delia grinned and said, "Remy? Come out, come out wherever you are! I will cuddle with you anytime you want!"

"Shut your mouth, Delia," Sabine exclaimed as she reached across and lightly smacked the back of her friend's hand. "I don't really want another scene here like the last time he crashed our Saturday ritual. You do remember how I blew up at him two years ago, don't you?"

"Alright, alright. I'll stop," Delia said, waving her hand.

*

He *was* there, seated at a park bench just out of sight, and he *did* hear every word the two girls had said. He almost made an appearance just to startle them, but decided against it. He and Sabine parted ways awkwardly before, and he wasn't sure he wanted to be face to face with her just yet.

He watched as a young man, appearing to be their age, approached the two girls. There was no way to tell for sure, but he sensed the boy was a vampire. In a town with a healthy vampire population, it was hard to distinguish who exactly was and who wasn't.

This young man was not one he was familiar with if he was a vampire, but then Bastian had so many guests at times it was hard for him to keep up with them all, especially when he was on Sabine watch. He rarely paid any mind to the ones who stopped in for a night or two at the manor and was only mildly familiar with the ones who actually lived there. He was more concerned with those lurking around the edge of town or close to her house because they were the ones who posed a threat.

*

"I just wanted to say I really like your shoes. They're awesome." The young man smiled at Sabine with the straightest, whitest teeth she'd ever seen. His deep brown eyes mesmerized her instantly.

"Thanks! I love my Chucks," she said, glancing down at her shoes, "but I had to make them my own."

"I'm Joshua, but you can call me Josh. I don't think I've seen you ladies around here before. I just moved here a couple of weeks ago."

"I'm Delia, and this is Sabine."

"Mind if I join you? I don't really know anyone yet, and you two look like you might be fun."

They looked at each other and shrugged. "Sure, why not?"

"Thanks. I heard you laughing over here, and I thought to myself, 'That's where I need to be'," he said as he pulled out a chair and sat down next to Sabine.

The three of them talked about common interests for close to an hour before Delia announced she had to get home for the evening.

"Yeah, I should be getting home, too."

Josh stood up, and walked with them until they got to the point where Delia went one way and Sabine went the other.

"Hey, Sabine. Could I walk you home?"

She shifted her weight nervously from one leg to the other. What would Remy think? What would he do if—no, when—he saw them alone together? Delia stood behind Josh nodding her approval with a huge grin spreading across her face.

"Umm, I guess."

"You don't sound so sure." He chuckled.

Snickering in response to him, she said, "No, it's fine."

Let him see me with someone else. Why not? She'd felt very frustrated since her encounter with Remy earlier in the month and had worked her nerves into a tizzy thinking about him and the things she wanted to do to him. She hadn't even seen his face since they returned, which made it clear to her that he wanted no part of her.

Josh walked her up to the front door, and lingered for a second. Turning toward her, he asked, "I know we just met, but can we hang out again sometime?"

She nodded, and said, "I'm free most of the time."

She'd quit her job, or rather she lost her job when she failed to show up for a week straight, and there was no point in getting another one when her parents showered her with anything she wanted. They felt horrible about her being the chosen one, and constantly tried to make up for it with an outpouring of love and gifts. She could probably murder someone. and they'd be okay with it. They never stopped her from going anywhere or doing anything anymore. Her relationship with them had changed drastically from the one of indifference she'd had with them before.

*

Perched like a statue, stoic and unmoving, Remy sat just above them on the roof. He was convinced this one was vampire now that he was close. *I should jump down and tear out his throat before he has a chance to say another word. She's* mine. *She's not open for anyone else to claim. He's too young to even sense that I'm right here. He could never take care of her like I can.* He hesitated just before jumping down.

What was he doing? She wasn't really his, not yet anyway. She would be officially in eleven months whether she liked it or not, but right now, she was free to do as she pleased.

*

"I could just stop by sometime. Would that be okay?" Josh asked.

"Yes."

"Alright… Have a good night."

"You, too," she said as she watched him walk away.

Opening the door, she entered her home and stopped in the living room to let her parents know she was home before heading up to her bedroom.

She went to her closet and tried to decide what she wanted to sleep in. Her heart jumped into her throat at the sound of a soft peck on her bedroom window behind her.

140

She walked across the room cautiously and raised the glass. Before she could stick her head out and see what was going on, a rush of air blew past her.

"How about you use the front door next time?" she said, whirling around to face him.

"Dull."

"I prefer dull," she said.

"Don't lie to me, Sabine. I know better." Stepping closer to her, he looked down into her eyes. His hand skimmed across her cheek before settling just behind her ear. Excitement stirred inside her.

"And just how would you know what I like?" She spoke in a sultry tone, and looked back up at him, deep into his eyes, ready to receive whatever physical goody he wanted to give her.

"I just do." Smirking, he stepped back out of her personal space. "By the way, you are aware your little friend from today is a vampire, right?" He plopped himself down in the chair by the window.

"No, he's not. I don't believe you." *Josh was so sweet. He couldn't have been a vampire.* "You'll say anything to annoy me," she said, moving to her vanity and picking up a brush.

"Would I lie to you?"

"Yes."

"Okay, so maybe I would, but I'm not lying to you now. Don't trust him. Never trust a vampire."

"Using that logic, I shouldn't believe you," she quipped, pointing the brush in his direction, "and I've been stupid to trust you before this."

"You can trust me, just not any other vampire."

"Nope. No, you said never." She ran the brush through her wavy hair and turned away from him.

"Fine. See for yourself, and when he rips your throat out I don't want you crawling to me, begging for me to heal you." He stood up from the chair and turned, blowing her a kiss before disappearing.

She tried desperately to remember if there was anything about Josh that would indicate he was one of them. He seemed like any other guy her age. He dressed like a twenty-year-old. He was into the same things a twenty-year-old would be into. Though none of those things could completely rule out that he was a vampire. She would proceed with caution, but she wasn't too worried. If he was, he couldn't do anything to hurt her anyway. Bastian wouldn't allow it.

* * *

Once he was confident the vampire from earlier was nowhere near Sabine, he returned to Willow Creek Manor. Remy entered through the large doors, and headed up the stairs toward his room. As he got to the top of the staircase, there stood Josh standing off to the side, admiring some artwork.

"Who are you?" He was not threatened by the young vampire at all, and he wanted him to know that, especially after seeing him with Sabine.

"Hey... I'm Josh," he said, holding his hand out to shake Remy's.

Remy left him hanging as he assessed him. "Why are you here?" he asked, lacing his fingers together behind his back.

"I was looking to settle down somewhere for a little bit and heard from a friend of mine about this town. He contacted Bastian to see if I could crash here awhile, and here I am."

"Hmm." Remy was gone in a flash, knocking on Bastian's door a moment later.

"Come in. It is open." Bastian looked up from a dusty old book he was reading as Remy entered the room. "To what do I owe the pleasure of this visit? I thought you would still be watching her, or has she gone to sleep for the night?"

"She's fine." Remy crossed his arms as he began to question Bastian. "Who is Josh, and why is he here?"

Setting the book on the table beside his chair, Bastian said, "Young Josh is here as my guest. I am trying to determine whether or not I should take him under my wing. He shows great potential, and his maker has abandoned him."

"Why didn't I know about him? You should've told me."

"You are never interested in who comes and goes through our home. Why should he be any different?"

"I don't like him. You should send him away."

"No. I will not until *I* decide he needs to go. You sound as if you have something personal against him. Come out with it."

Remy dragged his hand through his hair and looked toward the wall, avoiding eye contact with Bastian. "He's shown an interest in her," he said softly.

"And this bothers you?" Eyebrows raising, Bastian sat back in his seat and laced his fingers together. "My how things have changed."

"It bothers me that he has no regard for our rules here. He shouldn't be seen in public trying to canoodle with her. She belongs to me... She is mine."

Bastian smirked, laughing from his belly. "Remy. Let it go for now. He is harming no one, and he will not harm her. So what if he takes a liking to her? That is one more vampire ensuring her survival for the next year. Now, go. I do not wish to hear any more of this nonsense."

He left Bastian's room, making his way back down the hallway where he last saw Josh. He wasn't there. Fury tore through his body as he thought of where the young vampire might have gone.

Sabine.

Chapter 12

She settled in under the covers while contemplating her future. One more day down, three hundred and thirty to go. She would miss her room and her bed. She'd miss all of the things she collected over the years. Not knowing how much she could take, she constantly added to the mental list of things she couldn't live without.

As desperate as she was to rest, sleep still managed to evade her. The possibility of Josh being one of them was disturbing the peace she tried so hard to attain. Not that there was anything between them or that there ever would be. Still, she couldn't shake him from her thoughts. Maybe she would see him again and could either ask him flat out or observe him and gather enough evidence on her own to decide.

She absolutely believed Remy would lie to her, but she also wholeheartedly knew he wouldn't let anything or anyone hurt her. He couldn't control that. She knew now he was compelled to keep her safe. But how could she trust what he'd said about Josh?

I'm probably jumping to conclusions about Josh's intentions. I doubt he really wants to get to know me. He was just being nice to get in my pants. It's not like we could have a future anyway.

The space around her began to distort, causing her eyes to strain. Waves of nothing swirled just above her. The charged air threw off zings of what looked like electricity leaping about in front of her eyes. *Am I getting a migraine now? Just what I fucking need.* She blinked and rolled to her side, determined to fall asleep before her impending headache could set in.

Sabine startled at the sight of Remy lying next to her, face to face.

"How did you do that?" she asked, clutching at her chest.

"Another perk of being a vampire." Remy cocked one corner of his mouth up in a seductive smirk and propped his head up on his hand. "Why? Not happy to see me?"

"Well you scared me half to death." She rolled her eyes and turned away from him. "How come you haven't done that before?"

"You want me to start magically appearing in your bed more often?"

No response from Sabine.

"Okay. I'll let you in on a little secret." He scooted against her, his front melded to her back, hand sliding over her belly as he spoke against her neck. "It takes too much power and energy to do it all the time. Leaves me—" Voice lowering to a whisper, his cool breath grazed her ear now, sending shivers down her back and goose bumps over her arms. "Vulnerable."

Her body wanted to cry out to his, wanted him to touch her all over; wanted to be as close to him as she could get, but her brain wanted no part of it.

"Please, don't do that. I don't like it."

"Oh, but I think you do. Nonetheless, I don't want an unwilling partner. Takes the fun out of it." He scooted a few inches away, but continued to lie beside her.

"Seriously?" she asked and sat up to face him. Looking down at him, she said, "You like a person to be terrified when you feed on them because their blood supposedly tastes *so* much better, but you want me to believe you're not into an unwilling sexual partner? You're such a confusing man."

"I don't see why it's so hard to understand. Shagging is an act that requires at least two partners interacting with one another for it to be enjoyable. When I feed, I don't need my prey to do anything but stay still. I don't want a lover who just lays there and does nothing." He crossed his arms behind his head and looked up at the ceiling.

"Why are you here?" She had no desire to continue that discussion, and a subject change was sorely needed.

He shrugged. "Boredom."

"Okay... Then go have fun somewhere else. I'm trying to go to sleep." She yawned and laid on her back.

"There is nowhere else that's fun in this fucking town."

"Oh, so you think I'm fun then? Good to know."

"No. You're just the least dull thing around. I like taking the piss out of you. It's one of the only pastimes I've had since I got sentenced to the next however many years with you."

"What the hell are you talking about? Taking my piss? That's gross!"

"Bloody hell, love. You really haven't had much exposure to the world, have you? It means I like bothering you," he said, glancing at her before looking back up at the ceiling. "But if you recall, in an effort to be nice, I left you alone for a good long while. You know, until you tried to run away, so you have only yourself to blame for me being here right now. I'm just catching up on all of the time I missed out on. Since I'm stuck here, I might as well try and entertain myself."

"I'm never going to be good enough, am I?"

"I haven't had your blood. I suppose there is a chance you'll be extra tasty."

"That's not what I meant. Never mind." She waved him off.

"For what it's worth, you're not a bad kisser. I'm up for a good slap and tickle anytime you'd like."

"There you go again…"

"What? What did I do now?"

"Using your weird words when you could've just said you'd kiss me, or whatever you meant, anytime I wanted."

"Sorry, love. I'll try and remember to change the way I've spoken for centuries next time we converse."

"I'm curious about something. It's been bugging me for the last couple of years… What's your last name?"

"Don't have one." He laced his fingers and placed his hands on his stomach.

"I see. You're Remy, like 'Cher' or 'Madonna'."

"You mean 'Cher', like Remy… She's a witch, you know." He cocked an eyebrow and smirked at her.

"Get out of here! I don't believe you." She rolled over to her side to face him.

"How do you think she manages to stay so fabulous after all these years?"

"Madonna, too?"

"No. Madonna is just a hag. I never cared for her the times I was around her, the twat."

She sat up in her bed again, looking straight down at him as if she could bore a hole through him. "Are you going to hurt me? When you bite me?"

"I won't do that to you," he said, reaching over and placing his hand on hers. "I wouldn't hurt you."

The look in his eye assured her that he was telling the truth. Relief washed over her, but there was still a trace of fear.

"I'm so worried... about everything."

"No need to worry about that."

"It's not just that. It's everything."

"What's bothering you? Tell me."

"I worry about the things I'll miss out on. I worry that I'm never going to travel like I've always wanted. I'm worried that I'll never be loved. I worry that you'll always hate me. I worry that—"

"Shhh."

She hadn't noticed him move until he was sitting just in front of her with his index finger touching her lips.

"I don't hate you," he said, dropping his hand to his side. "I might not like being stuck here, but that's not your fault. I blame Bastian and the nitwit who made this arrangement in the first place, not you." He looked away as if he were pondering something before he spoke again. "Let me do something for you."

"I'm listening."

"Let me take one of your worries away."

"Oh, no… I don't want you making me forget or some shit like that."

"I promise this is something I want you to remember."

Curiosity got the better of her, and she couldn't make herself blindly decline him when she didn't know what it was he was offering, and deep down in her gut, she trusted him.

"What do you mean then?"

"Let me show you what it will feel like to be bitten by me."

"I don't want you to bite me." Holding back tears, she looked down at her hands, busy fidgeting with a string on her quilt, for distraction.

"I won't bite you until you're ready for that to happen, but I can show you what it will feel like when I do. I can use the same power now that I will use in the future. How you feel does not come from the bite itself, unless of course, no power is used, then you do feel the bite."

"I don't know." She searched his face, looking for any sign of deceit.

"Trust me." He took her hands into his and brought them close to his chest.

She nodded in agreement. Keeping ahold of one of her hands, he slid his other hand around to the back of her neck and pulled her close to him. Comforting warmth, like a hot bubble bath on a cold winter night spread throughout her body as he bent his head to her. The warmth soon turned to arousal as his lips neared her throat.

She wanted to panic, but she couldn't. He was in complete and absolute control of her. The sensation of his power drowned out all of her flight instincts and everything else but the two of them. His face brushed against hers, cheek to cheek. When their skin touched, pleasure rippled all through her body. He kissed her neck softly before scraping his teeth against the sensitive flesh of her throat. The sensation consumed her. All she could think about was fucking him, and if she could move her body, she would have been all over him. Her own voice in the back of her mind tried to tell her this wasn't reality, and that it was all just a mind fuck, but she shoved it off to the side and ignored it.

He pulled back from her slowly, the euphoria following him. As he did, she wanted to grab him and pull him to her again. No, he couldn't leave her, not like that. Not while she was still high on him.

Just as quickly as the sensation had taken her, it was gone. She blinked rapidly. Her breath heavy as she fought to get air to her lungs. She felt like she'd taken a lethal dose of ecstasy when he exerted his power over her. She was addicted it and what he could do to her instantly.

"Do it again. Please?" she begged, clutching his shoulder. Her body needed more of him, and her mind begged for that beautiful release from reality. For those few seconds, there was no worry or fear of what her future held for her. There was only the two of them.

He pricked his tongue with one still extended fang as he looked sleepily at her. "I think that's enough for now. You're no longer worried?"

"Fuck, no! Not about that. Is that what it will be like every time?"

"Pretty much, though it could be more intense."

"More intense?" Her eyes widened as she contemplated how what she'd just experienced could be amplified. "How is that even possible?"

"Just add sex." He stood, ready to leave.

"Don't go."

"I'm not doing that again tonight."

"You're no fun."

He moved to the side of her bed, guiding her to lay down as he pulled the quilt up over her and brushed the hair from her eyes. "Good night, Beanie."

"My mother calls me that."

"I know." He moved effortlessly to the window.

"Remy?"

He stopped, and tilted his head toward her.

"Why were you really here tonight?"

"Stay away from Josh. He *is* a vampire, whether you want to believe me or not. I've seen him at Bastian's. He's staying there."

*

Remy slipped out of the window and landed on the ground with barely a sound. He looked back up to her bedroom window once more before leaving. The restraint he held in those last few minutes stunned him. He wanted to bite her. *Needed* to bite her and *only* her. The thirst had subsided now that he'd left and his mind had a moment to clear. When he was that close to her and that close to biting her, he was thirstier than he had ever been in his entire immortal life.

When she begged him to do it again, he almost gave into her. Fulfilling all of her wishes and dreams consumed him in that moment. He wanted to give her everything she was worried she'd never have or experience. He wanted to show her the world... He wanted to love her.

Having her writhe in pleasure beneath him had almost driven him over the edge. He'd been mere seconds away from throwing her back and ripping her clothes off. His mouth yearned to taste her again. His cock ached to be deep inside her.

As much as he wanted her, he wouldn't take her like that. She had to want him of her own volition, not because of the control he had over her in that moment. Until she made it clear that she wanted him, he wouldn't touch her.

He hadn't felt that kind of emotion since the first and only time he'd been in love, over four centuries before. *How has she done this to me? The last thing I ever wanted to do was love her.*

Chapter 13

The only place other than her bed he wanted to be was his own bed. He crashed onto the mattress as soon as he returned home. Teleporting to her had taken a lot of energy, and he really overdid it when he made her feel his power without taking her blood. Blood was the ultimate energy shot for a vampire. Instead of hunting in the woods for subpar animal blood, he opted to sleep it off and let his energy and power rebuild naturally.

Before he closed his eyes, he couldn't help but think about his actions. Why had he insisted on teleporting? Josh was nowhere to be found, and he certainly had not been anywhere near her. He could have just as easily ran and been there only a couple minutes later.

He better stay away from her. I will beat him within an inch of his life if he tries to hurt her. I don't trust the little shit. And just who is this friend of Bastian's he claims to know? I need to speak to Bastian again about this, but not tonight. Tonight, I must sleep.

* * *

Sabine sat watching TV alone in the living room when a knock came at the front door. She got up and cautiously approached, wondering if it would be Remy. After their encounter three nights before, she hadn't had any interaction with him, though she knew he probably lurking in the shadows at some point. He was not far from her mind either. The urge to go to him or seek him out had been unbearably strong.

She desperately needed a distraction. Opening the door, Josh's smiling face greeted her. *Hello, distraction.*

"I hope I'm not bothering you, but I wanted to see if you might want to hang out for a while."

"Yeah, sure. What do you want to do?" There was no other way to determine if he really was a vampire like Remy claimed. She had to figure it out for herself.

"Do you want to go to the park and maybe go for a walk or just talk?"

"Let me go tell my mom where I'm going, then I'll be out. Okay?"

"I'll be here." He beamed at her with the sweetest smile.

He can't be a vampire. He's too nice.

A few moments later, they were on their way toward Cleary Park, making small talk as they went. When they passed the spot where she'd met Remy, she pictured herself sitting there looking up at the stars. She thought of how sexy he looked, even though he terrified her. His voice, so velvety and… British, echoed in her ears. *I could have you dead before you took your next breath, and you'd be none the wiser. Would you like me to show you?* How could she be so drawn to someone who could kill her in less than a blink of an eye and had no qualms over making it known?

"Sabine? Are you okay?" Josh touched her shoulder lightly.

"Sorry. I zoned out for a second. What were you saying?"

"I asked you if we could go to dinner sometime, but if I bore you so much you have to zone out, maybe it wasn't meant to be." He playfully crossed his arms and threw his head back.

"I'm sorry! It's not you at all. I was just... It was déjà vu."

"So weird when that happens. What do you think you were reliving?"

She didn't want to admit that it wasn't so much a déjà vu moment as it was an actual memory. She smiled and chuckled. "I don't know. It just felt weird. So, anyway, where did you want to have dinner?"

"Wherever you want. Maybe we could go over to Morgantown. There are a lot of good places to eat there, and it's only an hour or so from here, isn't it?"

"Yeah that's about right, maybe a little less... I don't know. We should probably stay in town."

"Of course. I understand. Might be kind of weird to go too far with a guy you don't know that well. Smart girl."

She laughed playfully again. "Thanks for the compliment, but I kind of have to stick close to Willow Creek for reasons I'd rather not get into right now."

He nodded to show her he wouldn't push for details, but she could see the curiosity on his face. "So where then? And when? Do you want to go tonight?"

"We could go to the steak place over on Robertson Road. It's pretty good, and they have a chocolate peanut butter pie that is to die for. I should be able to go tonight.

I just have to check and make sure my parents don't have any plans for us already."

"Do you want to head back now? Should I meet you there, or at your house later?"

"Come to my house around 8."

* * *

Please don't show up. If he ruins my plans tonight I am going to kill him... I don't want to hear about how stupid I am for going against his warning and seeing Josh. He's not a vampire, but even if he is, who cares? I'll be surrounded by vampires for the rest of my life, what's one more? Maybe he'll be someone I can really talk to or connect with. Remy isn't going to be that for me. At best, I can feel good when he bites me, but there will never be any emotional connection. He's made that pretty clear. And why would Josh take me to dinner if he's a vamp? They don't eat food. It'll be a dead giveaway if he chows down or not.

She paced the porch, waiting for Josh to meet her. Nervously scanning the yard and street, she strained to hear any movement. Remy must be somewhere close, but she hoped maybe something came up and he wasn't there. She could only be so lucky.

Headlights illuminated the street as a dark blue Chevy Cavalier pulled into the driveway. Josh got out of the car, and the sight of him in the light from the garage made her gasp. His hair was perfectly disheveled, and this was the first time she really noticed his body. He'd worn loose T-shirts and baggy jeans with old beat up Vans when she saw him before, but tonight he wore a

157

more form-fitting hunter green Henley with just tight enough dark jeans and black leather boots. He was positively mouth-watering. *Remy who?*

"Ready to go?"

She nodded nervously. It almost felt like she was about to go on a blind date because of his drastic change in appearance. "Yep. I was just waiting for you. Let's go."

He took her hand in his as they descended the five steps to the ground. *Warm. Definitely not a vampire.* Opening the door for her, he waited until she was seated inside before closing her in. The restaurant was only a short drive across town. They arrived and got seated quickly, which wasn't unusual for a Wednesday night.

Sabine nibbled on some bread while they waited for their food to arrive. She ordered a T-bone steak with a baked sweet potato and a salad. He ordered a medium rare sirloin steak with fries; another clue that he wasn't a vampire. Wouldn't he have some kind of excuse to not eat if he was one?

He had no issues with being in the sun, which didn't really mean anything other than he was old enough it didn't affect him too much if he was, but he also had a tan. *Pretty sure vampires don't tan.* All the ones she had ever seen were ghostly pale. Even Remy didn't have much color to his perfect skin. There she went again, thinking about Remy when she should be focusing on Josh.

"Are you getting that pie?" Josh asked as he flipped through the dessert menu that had been left on the table.

"If I don't stuff myself, I will."

"We could get it to go and eat it later, if you want. You don't have to rush home when we're done, do you?"

"That sounds like a good idea to me. Where do you want to go?"

"Not to sound presumptuous, but we could hang out at my place. Could watch a movie or something. I swear I'm not trying to do anything scandalous. There just aren't too many places to go around here."

The corners of her mouth turned up. "Sounds like fun."

"How long have you lived in Willow Creek?"

"Born and raised… and destined to die here."

"Way to be morbid." He threw two thumbs up and laughed.

"It's true," she said, tucking a strand of hair behind her ear. "I won't ever leave this place."

"Don't say that. You can do anything you want in life. You don't have to be trapped here. Why? Because your parents are here?"

The words were on the tip of her tongue and were on the verge of spilling out of her mouth, threatening to pollute their lovely evening together. But, where could this possibly go if she didn't tell him?

"No, it isn't my parents." She paused to take a deep breath before speaking again. "Have you heard anything weird about Willow Creek since you moved here?"

"Oh, you mean the fact that the neighbors up on the hill are vampires?"

Her eyes widened. She blinked rapidly for a second or two. "How did you know that?"

"My uncle lives here, and I've been here several times throughout the years. I used to stay with them during the summer sometimes when my parents would travel."

"I'm sorry I'm so shocked. I didn't think you would know anything about it. No one is supposed to talk about it to outsiders."

"You look more relieved than shocked, but what does that have to do with you not being able to leave?"

"I have been promised to a vampire when I turn twenty-one. I don't know if you know all of the details of why they're allowed to walk free without any repercussions."

"Yeah, I do. So you're the one? I'm... sorry."

"No, I'm sorry. I should never have come here with you. I've just led you on."

"It's okay. Maybe we can get you out of it somehow."

"Not possible. No one has ever gotten out of it. There are no loop holes. The only way out of it is death—either his or mine."

"Doesn't matter. I like you, and I'm not giving up." He reached across the table and touched the back of her hand. "Please don't feel bad for not telling me to begin with. How could you have known that I even knew about any of that stuff?"

"I have something I need to ask you," she said and quickly took a sip of her sweet tea. "I don't want to, but I have to."

"Shoot." He stuffed a piece of bread in his mouth and began to chew.

She shifted in her chair, and swallowed hard. Glancing down at the floor and back up at him, she asked, "Are you a vampire?"

He swallowed the bread he'd been chewing and burst into laughter. "Me? Why would you think that?"

"Someone told me you were. I thought maybe he was lying, but I didn't know for sure. I've been watching you and trying to pick up clues about whether you were or not."

"What do *you* think about me? Did I pass the test or not?"

"I was pretty sure you weren't. Your hands are warm, you just ate some bread, and you look like you have a tan."

"My knowledge may be limited, but I think those are all traits of the living."

Their food came shortly and they enjoyed each other's company as they ate. An hour and a half later, Sabine and Josh sat cozied up on the couch in his living room watching television instead of a movie. His arm draped over her shoulder, and she leaned her head against him as his scent, heady and masculine, enveloped her. It was nothing like the exotic scent Remy wore.

"I probably should go home soon." Thoughts of Remy bursting through the door and killing Josh ripped through her mind. If she wasn't home soon, he would come looking for her if he wasn't already perched somewhere outside.

"No problem. I can take you whenever... But..."

She leaned away from him and looked at him with a hint of a smile blossoming on her lips.

"There's just one thing... and I hope you don't mind..."

He bent his head and brushed his lips against hers, and then kissed her deeply. Resting her hand on his cheek, she kissed him back. Her lips parted slightly as he licked at the tip of her tongue, hands fisting in her hair.

He backed away from her slowly. She tried to follow, closing the distance between them.

"You didn't have to stop."

"I know, but I want to take our time with the physical stuff. You're an awesome kisser. I can't wait to kiss you again... next time."

The second compliment I've ever received about kissing and both less than a week apart.

Twenty minutes later, they were outside her house. Exiting the car, he hurried around to open her door. He grabbed her hand and walked her to the porch. "Good night, Sabine. Talk tomorrow?"

"Yeah. I'd like that."

He bent down slightly to plant a chaste kiss on her cheek and then left. She went inside, practically floating on air as she climbed the stairs to her room. Yawning, she stopped in the bathroom. Stripping her clothes off, she slipped into her touristy New York T-shirt and comfy sleep pants that were still lying in a pile on the floor where she'd left them earlier in the day. She washed her face, brushed her teeth, and dabbed on some moisturizer before heading off to bed.

Flipping on the light and entering her room, she flopped down on her bed, not noticing the man sitting in the chair.

"I told you to stay away from him." His tone was firm and even.

She practically jumped out of her skin and sat straight up. "Don't do that! And don't tell me what I can and cannot do. You don't own me, at least not yet."

"When it comes to your safety, I can tell you whatever I like."

"By the way, he is so not a vampire." She shook her head in derision.

"Oh? Care to enlighten me on how you are so certain of this revelation?"

"He isn't cold as death, and he ate real food right in front of me. He also has a tan. You're wrong, and you lied. He isn't staying at Bastian's because he has his own place. I was there tonight." She watched the muscles in his jaw bounce as he clenched.

He shook his head and smirked as he looked down at the floor. "I guess you have it all figured out." Standing, he stretched his arms out before letting them drop to his side. "So I guess I don't have to tell you that his warm skin just means he's fed recently. I don't have to tell you that vampires can eat human food, we just don't like to. It really has nowhere to go, so it ends up rotting inside until

163

it is gone if we are unable to forcefully expel it. And I don't have to tell you that human beings naturally are of all kinds of skin tones. If he were tanned or had a darker complexion when he was turned, he would remain that way for eternity. And I'm almost certain he got a place because he wanted to stay off my radar."

"I still don't believe you. I asked him if he was and he said he wasn't."

"Oh, well that settles it, doesn't it? He couldn't possibly be lying."

"Maybe he is, but I'm more inclined to believe that you are the liar."

"Don't make me prove he's a vampire. You won't like it. Stay away from him."

She blinked, and he was gone. She went to the window and slammed it shut.

He is such a jerk. Why did I ever think he was attractive? I don't care how good he can make me feel, I will never feel anything else for him but hate. I'm not going to stop seeing Josh just because he says I can't. If he keeps this shit up, I'll talk to Bastian about it. I bet he would make him stop.

I'll talk to Remy tomorrow when I'm not so irritated and give him one more chance to back off.

* * *

She texted Josh the next afternoon.

I can't wait to see you again. I'm busy tonight, but how about I come over tomorrow?

A minute or so later, she received a reply.

That'd be great! See you tomorrow.

She found her spot under the willow tree, and waited patiently. She knew he wasn't around much during the day, or at least she didn't think he was. He had to sleep sometime, and it seemed like most vamps slept during the day since they didn't usually like being in the sun too much. If he didn't back off after she had this talk with him, she would just see Josh during the day.

Two hours went by as she sketched in her drawing pad and enjoyed the warmth on her skin and the fresh air in her lungs. Foot-steps came toward her from the other side of the tree just before dusk. She didn't have to look up to know exactly who it was. She knew he would show himself eventually.

"Good evening."

"Yeah."

"Still annoyed with me? You know I only say to stay away from him for your own good."

"Really? Seems to me like it might not look too good for you if I'm hanging around with some other guy… or vampire, as you claim."

"That has nothing to do with anything. I could not care less what anyone thinks of me. Other than Bastian, I am the oldest vampire in town. I care not."

His words were so strange to her. He sounded modern most of the time, but every once in a while, he sounded so… formal. She wondered if that was how he'd spoken when he was human.

"Yeah, well, I want to talk to you about some things. I've been waiting out here for you."

"Afraid we might get a little too close in your room, Little Miss Do It Again?"

She sighed and crossed her arms. He disgusted her. At least she was trying hard to convince herself that he did.

"No. I want you to back off. Josh is a nice guy, and I want to have fun while I'm still free to do so."

"He isn't good. He lied to you."

"So what if he is a vampire? He doesn't try to control me. He likes me, and I like him."

"If you cannot see how dangerous he is, then I give up," he said, widening his eyes.

"You're dangerous, and you don't seem to have any issues with me being around you."

Remy shook his head. "Let him kill you. Maybe then I can get the fuck out of here and back to London. I'm done."

"So you're done watching me? I can do what I want until I turn twenty-one?"

"Whatever, Sabine." He threw one hand up in the air. "You mean *nothing* to me. I don't give a fuck about what you do. I don't care about you or what he will inevitably do to you. I'll still be around because I have to be, but I won't interfere, even when he attacks you, and he *will* attack you. The pain of disobeying Bastian's order to keep you safe will nearly kill me, but to hell with it. If you're still alive on your birthday, I don't care if you bang him and he feeds from you right in front of me. I'm done." He skulked away.

At a time when she should have been ecstatic that he was going to leave her alone, his words stung her. *I don't care about you.* She knew he didn't, but it still hurt to hear it.

Chapter 14

Two weeks later...

Sabine continued to see Josh, and things were going really well between them. She introduced him to her family, and she had even started spending the night with him, though they hadn't had sex yet. She hadn't seen Remy in two weeks, though she knew he was around, and the thought of him watching or hearing them weirded her out too much. She knew eventually he would be distracted, and they'd agreed to wait until then.

Life had become blissfully peaceful without Remy outright bothering her. It reminded her of the two years he stayed away from her, and she remembered her attempt at running away was why he had been thrust back into her life. Maybe if she had returned home that night after the concert, her life would've continued to be peaceful and drama free without him.

Though she was happy to be rid of him for the time being, some part of her wondered if he was alright. Maybe she really hurt his feelings when she refused to believe him. Josh still hadn't given her any reason to doubt he was human.

Just stop! Stop thinking about Remy. This damn craving I have for him is going to drive me nuts if I don't figure out a way to smash it.

Almost as if he knew she was thinking of him, Remy appeared out of nowhere. This was only the second time she ever saw him teleport, and it was still an awesome, yet scary thing to witness.

"I thought you didn't like to do that."

"I don't, but I could only spare a few minutes, and I needed to talk to you. I can't keep an eye on you tonight. I have to accompany Bastian outside of town, and by the time we get back, I'll need to sleep."

"Why are you telling me this? You made it pretty clear you wouldn't step in to save me if I was in trouble."

He looked away from her. "I was angry, Sabine."

"You still meant every word you said."

"Perhaps, but perhaps anger controlled my actions, and I blurted it all out without thinking first. It's in the past and doesn't matter now." Moving to her and placing his hands on her upper arms, he looked down into her eyes with a look of concern on his face. "I would ask you to stay home tonight. Please?"

"Josh is busy anyway. I have no plans on leaving."

"Good. I shall check in tomorrow night." The air shimmered and distorted as he disappeared.

Yes! This is it!

* * *

"I can't wait to get you in my bed. I've been waiting for this since the first time I saw you." Josh reached over and stroked the hair on the back of Sabine's head.

She smiled coyly at him, and ran her hand along his thigh, grazing his forming erection. "I'm looking forward to it, too."

The car pulled into the driveway of his house, and they exited quickly. Stopping to kiss and paw at each other every few steps, they could barely keep their hands off one another as they made their way to the front door.

Josh stiffened just before a loud swoosh of air rushed past them, blowing her hair into her eyes and pulling Josh away from her arms. The force of the air had caused her to stumble.

She pushed her hair out of her face and regained her footing. Frantically, she scanned the area, searching for Josh, only to find him several feet away in Remy's grip. He held Josh by the neck with his arms and legs flailing wildly as he tried to free himself. Remy looked at her coldly, his lips set in a straight line.

Never once taking his gaze off her, he spoke. "Tell her what you are." His green eyes grew brighter and more intense by the second.

Josh sputtered and choked, trying to speak. Sabine ran to them, and stopped just in front of Remy.

"Stop this, Remy! Let him go! You'll kill him!"

His grip only tightened that much more. "Tell her what you are." He continued to stare down at her, never blinking. "And you can stop with the choking. You don't need to breathe, and I know you can take in enough air to speak. I haven't completely crushed your wind pipe."

Josh only struggled more.

"Let him go!" She clawed at Remy's arm and chest to no avail before slapping him hard in the face.

His lips parted, showing her a glimpse of his descending fangs. "Tell her what you are," he roared.

She wouldn't have believed the booming voice erupted from Remy if she didn't see his mouth move with her own eyes. His body was still, and he hadn't lifted his icy gaze from her.

"Okay! Okay! Sabine, I'm a vampire. I'm sorry I didn't tell you the truth."

"Now you believe me?" he asked her with his eyebrow arched up as smugness settled on his face.

She walked several paces away from them and dropped to her knees, staring at the ground. Remy let go of Josh, and he landed on his feet with a soft thud. Rushing to her side, Josh knelt beside her and tried to take her hand, but she pulled away from him.

"Sabine, you have to believe me. I would never hurt you. I didn't tell you because I could see that you were very anti-vampire, and I wanted you to like me for who I am, not hate me because of my curse."

Remy stood back, scoffing in the background. He observed Josh groveling before her and rolled his eyes at the ridiculousness of the bullshit spewing out of Josh's mouth.

"Remy, take me home."

He walked to her, picked her up, and put her on her feet. His arm slid around her back, gripping her waist. Looking Josh dead in the eyes, he said, "Stay away." Scooping her up with his other arm, he took off with her.

Everything was a blur to her as he raced toward her house. She clung tightly to him, even though she barely felt any movement. Just as she closed her eyes, they stopped abruptly. She was surprised to find herself at home that fast. *Why does he even own a car when he can travel like that?*

Setting her down on her feet, his hand lingered on the small of her back. "I'll see you inside before I go."

He followed her through the door and up the stairs to her bedroom. Thankfully, her parents and sister had long been in bed and were sound asleep. She closed the door behind them.

"You asshole!" She turned and placed her hands on his back, shoving him as hard as she could, but it didn't move him one bit.

Turning to face her, he said, "*I'm* the asshole?" His eyes widened as he pointed to himself. "You can't be serious."

"You couldn't leave well enough alone, could you? You lied to me just to prove a point. You knew I would take advantage of you being gone tonight, and you manipulated me."

"You are a real piece of work, you know that? Calm down, for fuck's sake. You're going to wake your parents. You deserved to know the truth, and you wouldn't believe me when I told you, so I had to show you. It's not my fault you're so predictable."

She fell to her butt and began to cry. Everything that had been building inside her since her eighteenth birthday came flooding out.

He knelt beside her and put his hand on her back. "Don't do that. I don't like it."

"So sorry about *your* discomfort," she said, wiping tears off her cheeks. "Why don't you just leave?"

"I only did it so you would be safe. You had to see that he was dangerous, not to mention a liar."

"But I didn't see that at all. He didn't do anything that screamed 'dangerous' to me."

"Really, Sabine? You don't see it? How is that even possible?" he asked, standing turning his back.

"He's no different than you, except for the fact that he actually cares about me. No, I take that back. I've seen you do *waaaaaay* worse than anything he's ever done around me."

"You're going to see him again, aren't you?"

"I… I don't know. Maybe."

He shook his head, and paced in front of her. "Fine. But at least now you know. I hope he is as noble as you seem to think he is, because if he isn't, it'll be your life."

Her phone rang, and she looked down at the screen to see that it was Josh. She raised her head to face whatever smart-ass thing Remy was going to say to her, but he was gone. She took a deep breath and answered.

"Hello?"

"I'm sorry I didn't tell you. I'm not proud of what I am, and if I could change it, I would. I just didn't want you to hate me from the start because of something I didn't want and cannot change."

"I get it. Really, I do, but I need some time to work things out in my head."

"Sure. Take however long you need. I'll be here when you're ready to talk."

* * *

"So what is this about exactly?" Delia questioned as she plopped down in a chair at the café.

"It's about Sabine." Remy watched her take a sip of her drink. "She's seeing a vampire, and I don't trust him, but she won't listen to me. I want you to talk to her and

173

tell her she should stay away from him. I think she'd be more likely to listen if it comes from you."

Delia placed her cup on the table and sat back in her chair, knitting her eyebrows together. "I don't know about all that. She's my best friend. I just don't want her to think I'm on your side when she figures it out. She'll be pissed."

"Delia, please? It's important that she stay away from him." He leaned forward, knowing he could *make* her do as he asked. All he'd have to do is exert his influence over her, and it would be done. Just as he started to reach out with his power, he pulled it back. *More trouble than it's worth.*

"Why? You say you don't trust him, but why? What has he done?"

"His sudden appearance... and interest in her..." He struggled to find a way to explain just how much he distrusted Josh and why, but the truth was, he hadn't done anything in particular to make Remy distrust him. It was only a gut feeling he had.

"So, you're jealous? That's no reason for me to risk her being pissed at me. Sorry."

"I am *not* jealous. I don't feel those kind of emotions."

"Could've fooled me, because I see a jealous man sitting in front of me. Word of advice, if you're into her, just tell her. Show her that you care."

"I'm not into her, as you say. I have a job to do, and that job is to keep her safe and alive. Josh is a threat."

"Whatever. I don't see it. Sorry."

174

"Fine. I need to talk to the other one then… Lana. Do you know where she is?"

"No. I haven't talked to her for a couple of days. She's been busy getting ready to go on vacation with her parents. They might have left already."

* * *

Remy stalked through the trees surrounding the little white house. He peered through the darkness, and caught sight of several newspapers littering the porch and mail crowding the mailbox.

Damn. Lana isn't here. How am I going to make Sabine see what I see without her friends' help? I could talk to her parents, but it would probably go about as well as it had with Delia. Shay has always been terrified of me, so that's out. Against my better judgement, I could influence someone to talk to her, but God help me if she ever found out. Definitely more trouble than it's worth.

As he stood there contemplating his next move, a thought plowed right through him.

What if I'm wrong? What if he isn't a threat at all? She has a pull over me that I cannot explain. I crave her, though I've not tasted her blood. Have I allowed my feelings for her to cloud my judgment?

* * *

Sabine held her breath as she entered her bedroom after a successful date with Josh. She glanced around the room, fully expecting to see Remy sitting there with a smug look on his face. She relaxed her body once she knew she was alone. A week had passed since the incident with Remy, and she hadn't seen him at all. Part

175

of her wanted him to be there, but she knew it was for the best that he wasn't.

As she went to sit on the edge of her bed, an envelope resting against her pillow caught her attention. Her breath caught in her throat. He *had* been there, just like she originally expected. Not knowing what to expect, she carefully unfolded the paper and began to read.

Sabine,

I have decided I will not stand in your way. If you want to see Josh, I won't stop you. Bastian has allowed me to stop looking after you. I've been tasked with patrolling the edges of town for intruders instead. Apparently, Bastian trusts Josh as well. Maybe I've been wrong all along, but please be careful and cautious as I won't be there to intervene should any trouble arise.

Remy

Her chin hung low as she read over the note again. *I can't believe he's leaving me completely alone.*

* * *

"What's wrong, Babe?" Josh busied himself by sweeping the kitchen floor.

"I miss Lana. I didn't get to see her before she left with her parents last month. They went on some big vacation in Europe." She couldn't help the pang of jealousy she felt when she thought of how much she longed to travel to Europe.

"At least you have Delia."

"Yeah, but they are completely different. I almost feel like I'm missing one-third of myself, if that makes sense."

176

"It does. You girls have been friends for a long time. Have you at least talked to her?"

"She called a couple times and texts me when she gets the chance. I keep trying to get her to Skype with me, but we haven't been able to be around a computer at the same time with the time difference."

"When is she supposed to be home?"

"I think in a couple more weeks. I don't know for sure."

"I've been meaning to ask you, has Remy been around at all?"

"Not since he left that note, or at least I haven't seen him if he has been. You don't sense him, do you?"

"It's hard to pinpoint just one vampire in this town, but I haven't felt any close to us for a while.

"I'm thinking about asking Bastian if we can continue seeing each other after you go to live there. It's pretty obvious—I think, anyway—that Remy has no desire to be paired with you. Maybe he'll let me trade places with him."

"That'd be so awesome… Maybe Remy would get to go back to London. I know he misses it."

"I'm sure he does." Josh looked away from her.

"But I don't want you to give up anything for me." She touched his forearm.

He looked at her once more and took her hand. "I would do it for you. I think I love you, Sabine."

She beamed. "I don't know what to say! It's so fast. I do care about you… I mean, I think I love you, too!" She threw her arms around him. "I'm sorry that came out so weird. I'm such a dork."

"It's okay. Let's celebrate... Let me cook you dinner tonight, and maybe later we can..." His arms wrapped around her waist and pulled her close against his body.

"I'd like that." They hadn't risked doing anything more physical than kissing for fear that Remy would interrupt. It certainly wouldn't have been the first time he pretended to leave her alone, only to destroy her time with Josh later.

"Can you wear those heels with the red soles? I love you in those."

The memory of how she got those shoes flashed in her mind. They would always be linked to Remy as far as she was concerned. She wanted to tell him no, but she had no desire to disappoint him either. "I can." She stood on her tip toes and kissed him on the tip of his nose.

* * *

"I don't know what you're cooking, but it smells divine. I can't wait to eat."

"I'm glad you brought your appetite." He bent down to hug her and kissed her quickly on the lips before getting back to the food.

"How do you even know how to cook if you don't really eat food?"

"I used to work as a chef when I was human. It just kind of stuck with me." He shut off the heat under the pots. "Can you do me a favor? Could you go downstairs and pick out a bottle of wine while I get things finished up and put on the table?"

"You criminal, you. It's illegal to serve alcohol to someone under twenty-one, you know?"

He cocked an eyebrow and moved his head back and forth scanning the room. "I don't see any cops here, do you?"

"Nope. Be right back."

She opened the door to the basement and felt around in the dark for a light. Her fingers found the switch easily enough and flipped it on before descending the stairs to an open room with finished walls and floors. "Do you have a man cave down here?"

"Yeah, something like that," he replied.

The wine rack sat in front of her at the bottom of the steps. There were so many bottles to choose from, and she had no clue on which one to pick.

"Why do you have so much wine?" she yelled up to him.

"I cook with it occasionally when I have guests. I like having a good variety."

As she pulled out bottles one by one before placing them back on the rack, something moved to her right. She looked instinctively, expecting to see a mouse or maybe a cat that Josh hadn't told her about.

The glass bottle of wine dropped to the floor and shattered at her feet. There, sitting at a small table, gagged and bound, was Lana. Sabine ran over to her, and dropped to her knees beside her. She raced to untie her. Lana shook her head violently. Tears gushed from her eyes and she whimpered through the cloth stretching so tight across her mouth that it dug into her lips.

179

Cold hands yanked Sabine up by the waist and threw her into a chair beside Lana. Within seconds her legs and back were bound to the chair. Her arms were free, though she couldn't untie herself with him so close. He stalked around them menacingly as he sat plates and silverware in front of them.

"I thought you might like a dinner guest. You've been whining incessantly over missing this one. I've been keeping her as a surprise for you. It's just too bad you didn't figure it out before now, or you could've been reunited much sooner."

Sabine opened her mouth to speak, only to have Josh's hand firmly around her throat.

"Keep your mouth shut. You're not allowed to speak or question me, do you understand?"

She nodded as he loosened his grip, but kept his hand in place.

"I thought I'd be nice and give you a farewell dinner before I kill you... This was never about you, Sabine. You were only a pawn in my game." He took his hand from her throat and returned to the kitchen.

Sabine yanked at the ropes around her body trying to free herself before he returned. Minutes later, he came back with a tray of food. It'd smelled so delicious only minutes before, but now the thought of eating it made her want to vomit.

He placed cuts of parmesan chicken along with a side of mushroom risotto and glazed baby carrots artfully on the plates in front of the girls.

"Bon appetite, ladies."

"I'm not eating that, you psycho," Sabine said, turning her head away from the food.

"Oh, but you will, or I will cram it down your throat." He moved quickly to her and grabbed a piece of chicken, dangling it in front of her mouth. "Now open wide."

She reluctantly opened her mouth as he placed the chicken on her tongue. She chewed and swallowed, though it threatened to reappear as soon as she did.

"Good?"

She nodded as Lana sobbed beside her. Lana had bruises on her face and dried blood streaked on her skin. Thin lines that were now scabbed over marked her arms, and her clothes were in shambles. Sabine closed her eyes. Seeing Lana that way and knowing it was because of her was too painful. She couldn't believe the torture Lana had been enduring all that time. And for what? Why had Josh been so focused on her if it wasn't about her? Why would he want to hurt her so much by bringing her friend into it?

He sat down at the head of the table and watched as they shoveled the food into their faces, though it took a great effort for Lana. She could barely move from the abuse she'd suffered for weeks. Once they were finished, he cleaned the plates up and left them alone for nearly a half an hour while Sabine tried to free herself.

Sabine looked at Lana and mouthed, "I'm sorry." Lana could barely keep her eyes open and didn't seem to be aware of much.

Josh came back to the basement and smiled at the girls. He walked over to Sabine and yanked the ropes from her. Grabbing her around the waist, he threw her across the room and against the wall.

Her vision went black for a split second before everything slowly came back into focus. The feeling of warm water running over her head unnerved her. She immediately felt through her hair, only to pull back a blood covered mess on her hand. He was on her in an instant, sucking the blood from her wound. She scratched his face and punched him, which only made his grip on her tighten.

She managed to squeak out one word. "Why?"

"Jackson." He turned his attention to her neck and sunk his teeth deep into her throat.

Searing hot pain ripped through her flesh while a blood curdling scream erupted from her. She'd heard it echoing before she even realized it had come from her. His bite was the worst pain she ever experienced and just as bad as she always imagined it would be.

As she began to go light headed from him stealing her blood, all she could think of was Remy and how he had been right all along. She wished she'd listened to him and that he never stopped watching over her.

Josh disengaged his teeth from her throat and licked at the few stray drops of blood on his bottom lip. "He was my sire, and Remy took him from me. *You* were the only way I could hurt him."

She grasped at her bleeding neck as she struggled to find her words. "I'm nothing to him... You have it all wrong. He made me pretend to be with him to convince everyone there that day that I was his companion, but I'm not... You know he's not even around. Josh, I love you. Why are you doing this to me? I thought you loved me."

She didn't love him. The thrill of someone paying attention to her like he had and her desire to ignore Remy had clouded her judgement. But that didn't stop her from saying whatever she thought necessary to help her survive at that moment.

"Please let Lana go. I'll do whatever you want if you let her go."

"Not a chance. I'm going to make you watch me kill her, but first, we're going to have a little fun since that's what we had planned for dessert. It's a pity she's too out of it to watch," he said. Positioning his body over Sabine's, he leaned close to her face as he spoke. "It may have been all for show, but losing you will hurt him. I see it in him, even though he denies it. Bragging that I had you when he didn't will only make my revenge that much sweeter."

Pushing her skirt up, he forcefully parted her legs and lowered his head. He plunged his fangs into the delicate flesh of her inner thigh as she cried out again and started to lose consciousness.

He stopped abruptly and stood up. As he did, he pulled her to her feet, turning her around in the process. His arm wrapped around her throat and started to squeeze. The pressure on her neck began to lull her into unconsciousness.

"I wondered how long it would take you to show up."

Trying to clear the fog from her mind, she blinked her eyes, and saw Remy only a few feet away at the bottom of the stairs. His normally green eyes were as black as coal. He bared his fangs, and a guttural sound vibrated deep inside his chest.

"Let her go."

"No," Josh said, his voice wavering. "Stay where you are. I'll snap her neck like a twig before you can even hope to get to her. I'll break her just like you did Jackson. I promise you that."

Remy paced back and forth like a caged animal, knuckles cracking under the force of his hands balling into fists.

"Let her go, and I won't kill you."

"I'm not that stupid, Remy. There's no way you'll let me just walk out of here. This is what you deserve. You took Jackson away from me. You're not going to take killing her away from me, too. It's a shame I didn't get to fuck her first, but killing her will have to do."

I will get you out of this, Sabine. I swear to you on my life I will not let him harm you or your friend any further. Trust me. I love you. You have to hold on... please, hold on. The words echoed inside her head, but she didn't know if she was truly hearing him or if she was hallucinating. Her eyelids drooped as she fought to stay awake for him.

In a flash, she felt a great force pushing her to the ground as Remy crashed into Josh. She scrambled to

Lana and wrapped her arms around her as they watched the two immortals battle. Though Josh was younger, he had rage on his side and managed to land a blow to Remy that sent him stumbling back for a split second. Remy leapt at Josh and took him easily to the ground. Punching him over and over, Josh's skull cracked loudly with every blow. Remy thrashed him until there wasn't much left of his head but goo. Remy reached down, grasping Josh's spine in his bloodied hands and snapped it in two with one quick movement.

*

He was before the girls, and had Lana untied and on the floor in no time. Kneeling beside her, he assessed Lana's condition. Her body was bloodied and bruised. Her heart beat was weak and her breathing was shallow. Fearing she didn't have much time before death would grab hold of her, he bit his wrist and forced her to feed from him, though she didn't put up much of a fight.

Sabine collapsed to the floor beside Lana and retreated into herself as the realization of what happened sunk in. Remy reached over and grazed her cheek with his free hand. She trembled at his touch.

"Sabine? It's me. Don't be afraid. You know I would never hurt you." Her eyes glazed over as she stared past him, seemingly not hearing a word he said. He bit his other wrist, and offered it to her, though she didn't seem to notice.

"Sabine, you must drink," he said sternly through his teeth. "Let me help you. Don't slip away from me." He shook her gently, willing her to come back to him. She put her lips to the wound and lightly sucked the blood from his vein. He pulled his other arm from Lana, who'd already begun to heal, and cradled Sabine.

She looked up at him and smiled sweetly. "Thank you. I should have listened to you. I wouldn't have blamed you if you hadn't—"

"Shhh. Don't speak. I have to get you both out of here, so I can get rid of him, and you can heal."

He carried them to Sabine's car, and drove them both to Bastian's. Gretchen met them at the door and helped Lana to a room where she looked over her and willed her to sleep.

Carrying Sabine to his bed, Remy tucked her in before gently kissing her on the forehead. He turned to leave so he could take care of Josh's remains.

"Remy? Hurry back to me." Her eyes were heavy as she looked as if she were ready for the sweet relief of sleep.

Nodding, he left.

He sped back to the house where Josh's body lie, and searched the place looking for clues that Josh had any other plans, but found nothing. He opened a drawer with utility bills inside and flipped through them. It came as no surprise that not one was in Josh's name. He'd also found a closet full of framed photographs stacked in piles. The house belonged to someone else. He had to get the mess cleaned up and out of there before the owners of the home returned, provided Josh hadn't disposed of them altogether.

It took him little more than an hour to clean up all the blood and dispose of Josh's body in the woods. The ground was muddy and soft, allowing him to easily dig a hole to throw the rest of Josh in.

He returned to Willow Creek Manor at once, in search of Bastian. Throwing open the doors to Bastian's room, he found the feeble old woman who was Bastian's paired offering sleeping on the bed with him watching over her. His head jerked toward Remy with rage in his eyes, and motioned for him to leave. Bastian followed close behind.

Closing the door behind them, Bastian asked, "What is the meaning of this?"

"That arsehole violated not only Sabine, but her friend as well. He was Jackson's progeny and was after me all along. This attack is on *your* head, Bastian," he said, pointing his long index finger at Bastian. "I told you he couldn't be trusted." Remy trembled, trying to keep his anger at bay. He clenched his jaw so hard he thought he might break his teeth in anticipation of Bastian's response.

"It is not my fault. I had no control over him." Bastian waved a hand in Remy's direction.

"Maybe not, but you could have sent him away when I told you to. She is a broken mess in my bed right now, and I have to pick up the pieces."

"Then go to her," Bastian said, pointing down the hall toward Remy's room. "Take her now. Fix her. It seems to me that you made your bed when you chose to

187

kill Jackson, now you must lie in it. You might as well have some fun while you do."

Chapter 15

She awoke in a bed that she would come to know, but at the moment, was still foreign to her. The plush blankets comforted her, but she longed for comfort from Remy.

Where is he, and why hasn't he come back yet? Why did he bring me here instead of taking me home if he's going to go back to pretending I don't exist?

The muscles in her legs stretched, and it felt good. She sat up, wondering where Lana was and what she thought of being brought here of all places. Flipping the covers back, she looked down at her thighs, covered in dark, dried blood—her blood. Her fingers felt the skin of her inner thigh and found nothing but dried blood—no wounds or bite marks at all. She was completely healed.

She looked around the room and saw a full length mirror on the wall. Standing, she walked over to it, hesitating just before coming into view. She took a deep breath and stepped in front of the glass. A dark, bloodied mess moved into focus. She gasped as she viewed the person in the mirror looking back at her. Dark clumps of dried blood matted in her hair. Her clothes were stained and bloodied, as well as her neck, hands, and thighs. She sobbed at the sight of herself. She looked like a nightmare come to life.

I can't see Lana or go home like this. I have to get cleaned up first. Tears flowed like waterfalls over her cheeks. *I don't even have any clean clothes to put on even if I do manage to clean myself up.*

"Where the hell is Remy? I need him. Oh..." Had she really just admitted that to herself and worse yet, said it out loud?

The next moment, the door squeaked open, and she turned. There he stood, just as bloodied as her, but he was considerably dirtier with mud caking his boots and clothes, and his shirt was covered in blood splatters and brain matter. Blood dried in his dark hair and on his hands. His eyes became intense bright green as he licked at his bottom lip. He looked at her like he wanted to take her right there and then, blood, mud, brains, and all.

She wanted nothing more than to run to him and have him wrap his arms around her and convince her everything was okay, but she stepped back away from him when she saw the look in his eyes. They were the brightest shade of green she'd ever seen them be, and as beautiful as they were, the beast lurking behind them frightened her. He glanced away as he laid a tote bag on the chest of drawers and looked back at her. His eyes softened as he moved to stand just in front of her.

"I'm sorry I wasn't back sooner. Things took longer than expected, and then I had to see Bastian about what happened when I returned."

"Where's Lana?"

"She's down the hall sleeping. Gretchen has been looking after her." He moved closer to her, closing the small gap between them. Cradling her cheeks, he said, "I'm sorry, Sabine. I should've been there sooner."

"No, Remy. Don't... You saved my life and Lana's. Don't apologize."

"I've been keeping my distance, partly so he would think I backed off, but mostly because I doubted my instincts. After you and Bastian were both so adamant that he could be trusted, I discredited myself. This was the first time I was any real distance away from you. Bastian and I were taking care of a group of vampires sniffing around the other side of town down by the creek. I ran as fast as I could. I couldn't risk too much of my strength by teleporting."

"How did you know to come?" She reached up and brushed a strand of hair from his face.

"I heard you scream. I wouldn't normally be able to hear you as far away as I was, but a scream like that carries in the air." Rage flashed across his face briefly, and disappeared as he looked away from her and dropped his hands to his side. "You must have been terrified I wouldn't be able to save you from him."

"I didn't think you would come at first, but when you showed up... I believed you when you told me to trust you... and that you loved me." She bit her lip and looked down.

He furrowed his brow. "What are you talking about?" He grabbed her chin and tilted her face up to look at him.

"I heard you... in my head when he had me. You told me you would save me, and... you told me you love me."

He shook his head. "That did not happen. I was focused on him and how to get you away. I never said I loved you... It must have been the injury to your head."

191

She laughed nervously. "It must've been pretty bad if I made something like that up. But why did you look like you were going to fuck me when you just came in here if you don't feel anything at all for me?"

His hand dropped away from her face. Walking to the chest of drawers, he grabbed a stack of clothes out of the bag. "I grabbed you some clothes and those dreadful Chucks of yours. You can take a shower. There should be clean towels in there. I'll take you home when you're ready."

"You didn't answer me," she said, taking a step forward.

"I had a moment of weakness because of all the blood on you, if you must know. I wanted to eat you, not fuck you."

"Don't bother. I'll drive myself."

She went into the bathroom, slamming the door behind her and turned the water on. The clothes peeled off her skin and clung to her in places so much that she had to rip the fabric away from her body. She whimpered as the clothes, dried with blood pulled at her flesh.

A trash can sat beside the sink, and it seemed as good a place as any for the stained and tattered clothes. No matter how she tried to clean them, they'd never be wearable again. Her heart ached when she thought of how much she now hated the simple black sling-backs with the red soles she once loved. No way could she ever wear them again, even if she could clean them up. By the time she got undressed, the water was hot—almost too hot—but she didn't care. Let it scald away the memories of

Josh touching her and of the times they'd kissed for hours. *At least I didn't sleep with him.* It felt good to wash him away.

The door opened and Remy stepped into the bathroom with her. She knew he was there, even though he entered the room quietly.

"What do you want?"

"I was putting those clothes in here for you, and I wanted to see if you're hungry. I can have some food ready for you when you're finished."

"I just want to get Lana and go home." Her lip trembled. Tears poured down her face.

The shower door opened unexpectedly, and he stepped in behind her. The urge to cover herself came and went quickly. She knew he'd seen her before but she could still tell him to leave.

"Get out. I'm not finished, and I don't want you leering at me."

He said nothing and stepped into one of the streams of water. The shower was large and had three different shower heads. She kept her back to him as he rinsed his hair and washed his body. He picked up a bottle of shampoo, pouring some in his hand, and moved closer to her. His hands touched her hair gently, and began to work the blood out, careful not to pull her hair. He turned her around to face him and worked on the front of her hair. When he was satisfied her hair was lathered enough, he tilted her head back so the water could rinse everything out.

She closed her eyes, although she wanted to keep them open and look at him more than anything. She wanted to touch him… she envisioned herself touching him: his body, his lips, his hair, his face, his cock…

*

The water was deep crimson as it rushed down the drain, gradually turning clearer as the blood washed away. Turning her away from him, he washed her back thoroughly. He fought the urge to kiss her wet flesh, but couldn't keep his lips from briefly skimming her nape. Using all of his power, he prevented his fangs from extending. The last thing she needed was to fear him biting her after all she'd been through that day.

She swallowed deeply and spoke breathlessly. "Why, Remy? Why do you do this to me?"

"I'm sorry." His hands moved away from her body, and he was gone before she could follow.

* * *

"Are you okay?" Sabine sat next to Lana and stroked her hair.

"I am now, but I was beyond terrified. I thought I was dead and in hell."

"I'm so sorry I got you into this."

"It isn't your fault, Sabine. That guy was a psychopath."

"No… he was a vampire, and I never should have trusted him."

"I don't blame anyone but him."

"How long did he have you?"

"A few weeks, give or take, maybe a month. I don't even know for sure. I was supposed to go with my parents, right? Well, he got to them first and told them to go without me, and they did. I just don't understand why they would leave me like that, knowing I was in danger." Lana's eyes misted over as she fought the urge to cry.

"He influenced them. They didn't have a choice. They were forced."

"He made me call you so you wouldn't suspect anything. I wanted so badly to tell you or just blurt it all out, but I was so scared. He threatened to rip me apart and drink every last drop of my blood if I didn't do as he said." She broke down, laying her head on Sabine's shoulder. "I'm never going to be okay, am I? He ruined me." Her body jerked as she sobbed uncontrollably.

Sabine hugged Lana tightly, trying to calm her.

"I think I might be able to help you with that. If you could forget, would you?"

Lana leaned back with question in her eyes. "Yes." She wiped the tears away. "Absolutely, yes... but I don't understand how you can help with that."

"I can't, but Remy can. He could make you forget. Do you want me to see if he'll do that for you?"

Lana hesitated for a second while she thought of the possible consequences of allowing him or not allowing him. "Please?"

"I'm sure he'll do it. I haven't seen him since early this morning before we left," she said as the image of his wet body washing her flashed in her mind, "but I'll ask him as soon as I do."

"Can I stay here with you until then? I don't want to go home by myself."

"Yep."

Several hours went by, and there was no sign of Remy. Sabine didn't know whether to be thankful or worried. How would things be between them now?

It was a bright, warm day, and they were both thankful to be alive, so they decided to go out and enjoy the sunshine. They set up two lounge chairs in Sabine's back yard and tried not to think about much. They'd agreed the topic of Josh and his house of horror was off limits. Neither of them wanted to relive the experience, and Lana was anxious to forget it altogether.

Gretchen approached them from nowhere just before dusk. "How is my little patient?" She looked at Lana and gave her a genuine smile.

"I'm as good as I can be. Thank you for helping me."

Gretchen nodded and turned her gaze to Sabine.

"And you?"

"I'm fine."

"Good. Bastian sent me to check on you and to see if there is anything you need. He wanted me to tell you he is sorry he did not send Josh away when Remy urged him to and feels at fault. If there is anything you might want or need, now would be the time to ask. He doesn't feel remorse very often. He and Remy had a very heated discussion earlier that I believe has made Bastian recognize his own part in the situation."

"I don't blame him. Please tell him that. I don't blame anyone but Josh, but... why didn't Remy come instead of you? Not trying to sound rude, I'm just curious."

"Remy has... Well, he left several hours ago and has yet to return. He did not say where he was going. Bastian thought it best to give him a little time to himself in light of all that happened and has not summoned him."

Sabine pondered Gretchen's answer. "Okay. We do need something. Maybe you can help."

"I shall try."

"Lana wants to forget all that horrible bullshit that's happened to her over the past few weeks. Can you make that happen?"

Gretchen nodded and crouched in front of Lana. Her gaze met Lana's and she held her there for a few seconds before speaking, telling her to forget all the terrible things that had happened to her and to forget Josh ever existed. She told Lana that she had been hanging out at home and living a normal life from the time just before Josh kidnapped her.

Lana blinked and looked up at Gretchen. "Who is your friend, Sabine? I don't think we've met."

* * *

Sitting on the forest floor, he hung his head and stared at the ground. The scent of wood and dank earth clouded the air around him. A squirrel scurried up the tree Remy propped himself against, not really paying any mind to Remy at all. It would've been an easy meal had he been in the mood, but eating was the last thing on his mind.

How did she hear me? I didn't try to project my thoughts to her, and even if I'd tried, I have never been successful before. How could she possibly have heard? What the hell is wrong with me? I'm not supposed to have feelings for her. I never planned to fall in love with her. She doesn't even like me. There's no way she would return the love that I have reluctantly built for her. I haven't given her much reason to love me either. I've been an arse to her since the day I met her.

He thought back to seeing her a bloodied mess in his room and how she'd accused him of wanting to fuck her. *She was wrong... The look I had when I saw her was not one of lust. I didn't want to fuck her. I didn't even want to feed on her. I wanted to make love to her; more than anything, I wanted to lay her down and do everything in my power to pleasure her and erase the pain she felt. I wanted to taste her; not just her blood, but her body, her flesh. I wanted to be inside of her and fucking lose myself.*

I have to keep my distance from these feelings if I have any hope of surviving her. If I let my guard down to be with her, it'll only be a matter of time before someone kills me or her. I almost lost her this time. I foolishly left her alone with him, knowing he would try something at some point. The blood spilled was on my hands. Her blood was on my hands. I should have killed him as soon as I suspected him of being a threat. If I had, this never would've happened.*

Remembering Sabine's desire to visit every country in Europe, he came up with a way to make it up to her. *I might have to push my feelings aside, but I can give her some of the things she wants. I have the means to take her anywhere in the world she wants to go. Bastian will allow it if I swear we'll return by her birthday. I don't want her to miss out on the things she wants to do because of me or because of Bastian. It isn't fair to her. She deserves the chance to explore the world.*

He stood up quickly and ran, not stopping until he got back to Willow Creek.

Chapter 16

"I want to take her away, Bastian. I want to give her the chance to see the world before she's trapped here to rot for the rest of her life."

"Remy, Remy... Always the dramatic one. It is not so bad here. She will not rot until she dies."

"I suppose it's not horrible, but there are things she wants to see, things she wants to do. She mourns the loss of the opportunities and choices she once had. I want to give this back to her."

"Are you in love with her? Truthfully. I will know if you are lying."

"Yes."

"Does she return your love?"

"I do not know, my lord. I can only hope she will after I offer her this, though I don't expect her to."

"It is done. Take her soon. I trust you will return by her birthday to complete the ceremony. Do not make me regret this."

For the first time in as long as he could remember, he was a bundle of nerves. He moved quickly as to not waste any further time and packed a bag of a few necessities he always traveled with. Most things he needed, he picked up along the way.

He summoned one of the humans who worked for Bastian to drive them to the airport. After he loaded his bag into the trunk of his car, he raced to her house, leaving the car and the human driver behind. He wanted a few minutes to convince her to go before the car arrived to pick them up.

In an attempt to catch her off guard, he rang the doorbell. She'd never expect that from him. Anything other than him materializing out of thin air or popping in through the window would surprise her for sure. A long few seconds later, the door opened.

*

She opened the door and took a step back as she looked at him. "I have to say, I'm impressed. You actually used the door for once."

He stepped in and took her hands in his. "Go away with me, Sabine." His eyes showed an enthusiasm and brightness she had never seen from him before. The smile that had taken up residence on his face was genuine, not cocky at all.

"Go where? Back to New York?"

"No. Go away with me to wherever in the world you want to go."

She was speechless as she studied him. *Is he for real, or does he need me for some weird mission he's on again?*

"I don't understand. Why? Won't Bastian come after us if we leave?"

"I know the sacrifice you're making by being the chosen one, and I want to make some of your wishes come true. I know you want to visit all the countries in Europe and how you thought it was a silly dream, but I can give that to you."

"How do you know that?"

"Because I know more about you than you realize. I've been paying close attention to you all this time. I wasn't always trying to piss you off." He chuckled as a smile began to show itself on Sabine's lips.

"But, Bastian... Why would he ever let this happen?"

"I promised to return before your birthday. We have almost a year to explore this planet, to see all the wonders of the world, whatever you want. Please? Come with me?"

"If I go with you, I'll lose the time I have to spend with my family and friends. I don't know, Remy. I don't know if it's worth losing that."

"I will see to it that you are able to spend as much time with them as you want after you come to live with me. I have no desire to take you away from any of them."

"I don't even have a passport."

"You don't need one. I'll take care of any issues that arise. I can be quite convincing." He smiled slyly.

"Where would we go?"

"We can go to my place in London and plan from there... I've been a jerk to you too many times, and I understand your hesitation. I was wrong to be such an arse, Beanie. Let me do this for you."

"I need a minute to think."

"What is there to think about? Fulfill your dreams or stay here to wither away without ever truly living?"

Her breath caught in her throat as she thought about her fate. "Yes," she exclaimed with a grin.

He picked her up in his arms and swung her around excitedly. "Pack some things, and let's go. Someone will be here shortly to fetch us."

"Hold on a minute. There's something I need to do."

She walked into the living room where her parents were. The look in their eyes told her they heard everything, and wanted her to go. They both stood up and hugged her tightly.

Her mother said, "Go, Beanie. You deserve this. Just make sure you call me every day, and keep your heart guarded. He's still a vampire… and a very attractive man."

She nodded and hugged them back tightly.

He waited patiently for her outside while she packed. All kinds of thoughts ran through her head. Where would they go? What should she pack? Why was he really doing this?

His car arrived a few minutes later, and he called up to her. "Our ride is here. Don't worry about forgetting something. We can buy whatever we need once we arrive."

She rushed down the steps, and her parents hugged her once again, telling her they loved her. Shay reminded her to bring her back lots of souvenirs. She walked out the front door and stopped for a second. The surreal turn of events rushed to her head. She'd gone from being half-asleep while watching a movie with her family to getting ready to catch a plane to London. Taking a deep breath she walked toward the car.

Remy stood by the back passenger side door. He opened it for her and motioned for her to get in. She expected him to sit up front since it was his car, but she didn't mind it when he climbed into the backseat after her.

Not only did he sit in the back with her, but he sat close to her. His thigh brushed against hers. He turned to her and touched her cheek, pulling her face closer to his. "I want to make this time together everything you've ever wanted. Anything you want, you may have. All you need to do is tell me your desires."

She smiled at him and looked away. He held her hand as they traveled to the airport. Somewhere over the Atlantic, she dosed off, leaning against him with his arm around her. When she awoke, they were on the ground in London.

* * *

The time flew by as they explored Europe. They only stayed in London a few days, but his place was every bit as immaculate as the one in New York City. A deeper connection between them began to take root and grow. Her feelings for him intensified, and she dreamt of him more and more. Each dream happened in a different place, but every one ended the same: him making love to her with a passion so strong she often wondered if she'd really been dreaming. Every time she awakened, she expected him to be there beside her, and her heart ached each time he wasn't.

It got significantly harder to mask her feelings as he ushered her through the streets of Paris, where they spent the better part of the first month. They had no timeline, other than to be back by her twenty-first birthday, and no definitive plans. She didn't care if they never left Paris. She loved being there, but most of all, she loved being there with him.

They had gone to The Louvre the first full day they spent in Paris. It was everything she dreamed it would be. They spent many nights at the Eiffel Tower, looking out over the city, sparkling and twinkling below. Though he didn't really prefer to go out in the daylight, he would whisk her away to museums, or to the French countryside to leave their nights open to explore the city.

They killed more time by shopping at all the upscale designer boutiques. He lavished her with things she never could have imagined. He bought her so many beautiful things they had to start shipping the stuff back to Willow Creek so they could continue to travel without being encumbered, but what she cherished most were the times he would give her a simple rose or flower he picked for her from a garden.

The last day they spent in Paris, he took her to the Christian Louboutin boutique, and told her to pick out anything she wanted. He'd told her he remembered how much she loved those red-soled shoes. He knew how they had been ruined for her, not only physically but emotionally as well. She couldn't bring herself to put them on again after the horror she experienced with Josh. He convinced her to wear her new pair—shiny black, four inch stilettos with pointy toes—when he took her out to dinner every night.

Next, they traveled to Italy, where they visited Venice, Tuscany, the Leaning Tower of Pisa, Pompeii, and then on to Rome, where they saw the Coliseum, the Sistine Chapel, and the Vatican. Over the next several months, they explored every country in Europe, from Norway to Ireland and Sweden to Spain and then on to Eastern Europe and Moscow in Russia. Some places they stayed for days, others they stayed only a few hours. He was determined to give her the world, or at least Europe for now.

They spent a couple of weeks and their last night back in London before heading back to the States.

For close to ten months, they traveled. They shared so many details of one another's lives that the connection that had taken root early on in their travels now started to grow and blossomed into a beautiful flower. They were *friends*. Neither one of them would ever have believed it possible, but they were. Arguing between the two of them was long gone. The thought of living together once they returned home began to not seem as bad as they both imagined in the beginning.

Both of them secretly pined for the other one, while neither one of them had the courage to put their feelings on the line. Sabine settled down into her bed for the last night she would spend away from Willow Creek. Remy knocked softly on the door before entering.

"I trust you're all settled in? Do you need anything else before you sleep?"

"Just one thing… Will you stay with me tonight?"

If his heart beat at the same speed as a human, it would have skipped a beat just then. "Yes." He sat down beside her with his back against the ornate headboard.

"I know it might sound silly," she propped her head up on her hand and looked up at his lips, "but I think I might miss you when we get back."

"It isn't silly, love. I'll miss you, too."

"I know it'll only be a couple of weeks until I move in with you, but—"

"Sabine… stop talking." He bent down and kissed her hard, throwing his leg over her, straddling her body. His hands, gripping her wrists, raised her arms and pinned them above her head as he kissed her hard. Keeping her arms pinned with one hand, his other hand slid over her body and cupped her breast, teasing her bud with his thumb through the satiny material of her nightgown.

Her lips parted to allow his tongue access to hers as she kissed him back with more passion than she ever knew she could muster. She tried to free her hands so she could touch his body.

As if he sensed her desire, he let go of her arms. Her hands slid up the sides of his neck and fisted in his hair. As he pulled back to gaze into her eyes, she sought out the buttons of his shirt and tried to unfasten them quickly.

Sitting up, he ripped it away from his body and smashed his lips into hers once more. Shifting his weight, he settled between her legs as he sucked her bottom lip into his mouth.

She grinded against him, feeling the length of his erection through the denim of his jeans. Her hands gripped his hair as she pulled him closer to her. The smallest amount of space between was too much. She needed him inside of her as much as he needed to be there.

He kissed a trail down her neck and onto her breast. She bit back a moan as his teeth scraped against her erect nipple through her nightgown. His hands found the bottom of her gown and pushed it up, exposing her body. Nipping at her hip, his hand grazed her stomach as it found its way to her breast once again.

He began to kiss a line down her belly, stopping just at the top of her panties. She longed for him to keep going, but he planted soft kisses back up her abdomen, and pushed the nightgown the rest of the way up and pulled it over her head.

His eyes brightened as he spoke. "I've wanted you for so long, love," he said, raising her wrist to his mouth and kissing gently. "Do you know what you do to me? How much I crave you?"

He stared down hungrily at her milky white skin, at the mounds of her breasts moving up and down quickly with each breath. His head dipped down and gently sucked a nipple into his mouth. The intensity grew until his fangs descended and began to press into her skin. Just as the tips of his teeth were ready to pierce her flesh, he lifted his head and kissed her on the mouth again.

"Drink from me," she whispered against his lips. "I want you to."

"Not this time." He sat up on his knees and yanked her up to him. He held her close to him, wrapping his arms around her waist. "This is about both of us, love, not just me. I want you to feel *me* and all of the things I wish to do to you, not the false euphoria of my bite."

She pressed her hips against his and looked up at him through her lashes as her thumb hooked the top of her panties.

Reaching down between them, he tore off her panties with one quick yank, throwing the undergarment to the floor. He laid her back on the bed, his eyes traveling the length of her as he moved down her body. Draping one of her legs over his shoulder, he kissed the sensitive flesh of her inner thigh.

Her hips arched in anticipation. Closing her eyes, she waited for what seemed like an eternity as he nipped, kissed, and sucked at her inner thighs, hips, and belly. He hadn't touched her where she wanted to be touched, yet she felt as if she could go over the edge at any moment.

His tongue flicked out and licked the warm, wet mound of her sex. Her fingers tangled in his hair and pulled him closer to her. Pressure built inside as his tongue stroked her, slowly at first and increasing in an intensity that was almost un-humanlike. One of his hands gripped the inside of her thigh, so tightly he easily could have drawn blood with his nails.

Writhing in pleasure, her feet rested on his back as she arched hers. She screamed his name as she dissolved into pleasure, unable to hold on any longer. He smiled that cocky smile of his and licked her one more time for good measure before raising up to meet her face to face.

Her hands explored the space between them until she found what she was looking for. She ran her palm along the length of his cock and felt it grow harder. Somehow she managed to push him away from her so she could unbutton his pants and slide them down his hips.

In a quick movement too fast for her to see, his jeans were gone, and his body was heavy on top of her. He rested between her legs, and his lips ghosted across her neck. Grabbing one of her legs, he wrapped it around his body to rest on the small of his back. Supporting his weight with one arm, he gripped her hip with his other hand. Sliding his hand over her hip and to the apex of her legs, he looked deep into her. Reaching down to guide his cock into her, he hesitated at her entrance.

"You desire this?"

She nodded, never straying from his gaze.

"Tell me this is what you want," he breathed. "Tell me you want *me*. I need to hear you say it before I take you."

"I want you, Remy" she whispered. "I want you to make me yours. I want you to make love to me."

He kissed her, swirling his tongue around hers, and plunged himself deep inside, claiming her as his.

Remy paused, losing himself momentarily over the feeling of her around him. What he'd expected paled in comparison to how she actually felt as she cradled him inside her body. He closed his eyes and pressed his head against hers.

Forehead to forehead they moved in unison like they were meant to be together, like this was the choreographed dance they'd waited forever to perform.

Her hands slid down his back and gripped his ass as he thrust into her. He sat back on his haunches and pulled her up to him. She straddled him as she settled herself down over him. He grabbed her ass, helping her move up and down the length of his cock.

Fire pooled low in her abdomen as she rode him. Still holding onto her with one hand on her back, his other hand maneuvered between them, rubbing her in just the right place with his thumb. He felt her pulsate around him, and he relished the command he had over her body.

Just when she thought she couldn't move anymore, he laid her down and flipped her over to her stomach. Spreading her legs ever so gently, he entered her once more and kissed her back and shoulder as he made love to her. He pushed her hair aside, and sucked her ear lobe into his mouth. His hand held onto her hip as he pushed himself into her over and over again. It took everything he had not to bite her as her scent engulfed him, clouding his mind.

He was determined that this had to be about the passion they shared, not the false euphoria she would feel when he exerted his power over her. His fangs stayed securely in place, though he wanted to drop them and taste her sweet life force.

He pulled out of her and nudged her to her side, pulling one of her legs back to drape across him. He entered her once again. His hand slid over her belly and down to the v between her legs and stroked her again and again until she lost control once more and exploded with passion and pleasure.

He smelled her hair, and kissed the back of her neck. He couldn't keep his teeth at bay anymore and let them descend. His fangs scraped against the sensitive flesh behind her ear. He could take no more, grunting loudly, he lost himself completely to her. Kissing her neck, he whispered in her ear, "I love you."

Chapter 17

The room was pitch black, even though it was already mid-morning. The memory of the passion from the night before came washing over her. She felt around in the dark, desperate to touch him. She needed to be close to him, and, truth be told, she didn't mind the prospect of another go around with him before they traveled back to Willow Creek.

She loved him. There was no doubt in her mind. It took them finally being together for her to admit it to herself, but deep down, she'd always known she did. Though she desperately tried to keep him out of her heart, he'd managed to sneak his way in anyway. Once he told her he loved her, it had sealed the deal in her mind, and she was no longer afraid of how he would react. So many times she worried that his reaction would be cruel or mean if she confessed her true feelings. The threat of rejection was gone now that he'd confessed, allowing her to imagine what it could be like between them.

She rolled to the middle of the bed, expecting to crash into him. She felt nothing but empty sheets as her eyes struggled to adjust to the darkness. The room had no windows and the door was shut tight, allowing no natural light in. Finally, she was able to find the lamp on the nightstand, and flipped it on. The light blinded her momentarily.

She smiled as she turned toward the far side of the bed. Surely he had just rolled over to the edge of the humongous bed, and she hadn't quite reached him in the dark, but he wasn't there. Frowning, she lay back and started to notice her body. The familiar ache of her muscles after a night of hot sex was lacking. She expected to feel sensitive, if not a bit sore, down below after the previous night's activities, but she felt normal. She couldn't smell his exotic scent on her skin, and her lips didn't ache like they should after so many passionate kisses.

It was just another dream.

* * *

I've done it again. I revealed too much to her last night.

He sat alone in an empty room, desiring to go back to that place where he could enjoy her body and she could enjoy his with no repercussions. There was no furniture except the chair he sat on. This room was one he could never quite figure out what to do with. He had enough bedrooms, there was plenty of living space, and he had other rooms that housed his possessions. Maybe he could turn it into a library or art studio for her like he'd done at Bastian's. He pushed that thought away immediately because he knew she would grow to hate him once she knew the truth and would never return here, even if Bastian allowed it.

His hair hung in his face as he stared down at the floor. *How could I lose control like that? How could I tell her I loved her… again?*

The night she was attacked, he inadvertently let her know his true feelings, though he didn't realize it at the time. He couldn't figure out how she heard his thoughts because he hadn't tried to connect with her mentally. It was only later that he figured out they had a connection that had apparently presented itself for the first time that night.

Since then, he was able to hear her thoughts if he chose to do so. All he had to do was focus on her. He even figured out that if he let down his guard, he could speak to her without ever opening his mouth, and she, in turn, could invade his mind. He had been careful not to let her again. It was bad enough he slipped once, and he had no desire to do it again. Thankfully, he'd convinced her it was the bump to her head that had caused her to think she'd heard him.

Using his power, he'd influenced her dreams so many times over the years since he'd first met her that he lost count of just how many times he'd done it. He started out doing it as a way to get under her skin, and only had her dream of him without him really taking part in the act. He let her imagination take them where she wanted because he didn't really want to put out the energy it took to control her dreams. Planting himself was far easier.

It was only after he admitted to himself he had feelings for her that he took control, always careful not to reveal too much of how he really felt. The only reason he took the chance at these times was because she was sound asleep and couldn't poke around in his head.

It was a sick and twisted way to be with her, he knew that, and he felt like a sexual predator afterward, no better than the rapist she believed at times he might be. Still, he continued to plant himself time after time right up until he agreed to leave her alone to be with Josh. He continued controlling her dreams during their time in Europe, though he tried not to do it more than a few times a week. He contemplated telling her what he had done, but was terrified she would hate him.

Her feelings for him had grown exponentially during their time together in Europe. He felt exactly what she felt every time he went to her in her sleep or listened in on her thoughts. What if she only had feelings for him because of those dreams? The same dreams she wouldn't have had without him... What if he only started feeling again because of the interludes they had and how she reacted to him?

He buried his face in his hands in shame. How could he fix this? How could he make her look past the dreams, and see that he did really love her? Would she feel the same way once he told her the truth?

It didn't matter to him why he loved her or what had caused him to love her, whether it was of his own accord or her desire for him. He loved her regardless, and that was all that mattered. The only way to pay for his pervy act, as she would say, was to make her future something worth living for, something that wasn't inherently linked to him.

He wanted everything for her that she wanted, even if that meant giving her up. As soon as they returned to Willow Creek, he would do whatever it took to release her... to set her free.

His phone buzzed. The car that would be taking them to the airport would be there for them soon. He moved swiftly to her room.

"Sabine? Are you about ready to go?" he asked softly as he inched open the door and peeked in.

"I will be in just a few minutes. Could you take the two suitcases I have packed already downstairs? I have one more bag I need to throw my bathroom stuff in, and I'll be done packing."

He entered the room to retrieve the bags, noticing the door standing open to the master bathroom. Her reflection beamed at him from the mirror on the wall. She had no clue he could see her. Stopping in his tracks to stare at her, he was mesmerized by her body. He shook his head as if to shake the image out of his mind and turned his back to her.

"The car will be here for us in about thirty minutes."

*

"K!" She continued to shuffle around the bathroom as she got dressed.

She headed downstairs twenty minutes later to meet him. As she descended the staircase with one small bag, she found him standing as upright and rigid as a statue by the door. He looked lost in deep thought like he was in some sort of a trance. Those green eyes of his were the doorway to his soul, and she wanted nothing more at that moment than to look deep into them to see what he was thinking.

"Something wrong?"

He blinked and came out of the trance like state. "No. I was just thinking... You had a good night last night?"

"Yes." *What an odd question. As far as he knows, I fell asleep pretty early.* "You?"

*

He nodded and looked away. "Would you like to eat something quickly before we go?"

"I'll get something at the airport. I feel kind of weird this morning. Not really hungry."

"Oh? Are you ill?" It was only a formality. He *knew* why she felt weird.

"I don't think so. I just had a dream that is really sticking with me and fucking with my mind a little."

His face gave nothing away. "I hardly ever dream, so I don't understand why it would have such an impact on you. What happened in the dream?" It wasn't entirely true that he rarely dreamed now, but he didn't want to get into it right then.

"Doesn't matter. How much longer until the car gets here?"

"Should be here in a few minutes." He took her bags outside and waited. The confession weighed on the tip of his tongue, and he feared she would not return home with him if he told her now. He couldn't face losing her and the wrath of Bastian all in the same day.

* * *

Sitting nowhere near as close as they had all those months earlier on the way to the airport, they sat in the backseat of Remy's car, traveling back to Willow Creek.

218

Their time together had been beyond anything Sabine could have ever imagined. She was grateful that he had given her so much, but now she wondered if she did something to upset him.

He was distant from the time they left London until now, and barely spoke to her at all. He sat with his arms crossed the whole time on the plane. She wanted to lean on him and have him put his arm around her like they'd done so many times when they traveled by air, but he was shut off to her, and she didn't know how to open him back up.

She turned her head so she could see him out of the corner of her eye. He watched the scenery go by like he was looking through it. *What's wrong with him? Why is he ignoring me now?*

"Hey?" She turned to him and touched his thigh.

"Yes?" He continued to stare out the window, seemingly not noticing that she was touching him.

"Did I do something to piss you off?"

"No."

She didn't believe him. Why wouldn't he look at her if he wasn't pissed off? "I don't know why you won't talk to me."

He faced her. "I'm sorry. My mind is elsewhere."

"Yeah, I see that." She barely shook her head, and looked away.

He scooted closer to her and held her hand. "I need to tell you something."

She shifted her weight nervously in anticipation.

"Okay. Should I be worried?"

219

"No… Yes. I mean, I don't know. What I have to tell you may change the way you see me, and I'm terrified of losing our friendship or that you'll hate me."

"Um, can we pull over? I don't want to have this kind of conversation in a confined space like this. I have a feeling I'm going to need some air."

"Yes… Pull the car over." He barely raised his voice, but the driver did as he was instructed.

The car veered off the road to a wide spot where not much was around. He got out and spoke to the driver as Sabine exited the car. As Remy walked over to where she stood, the car drove away.

"Wait! What the hell is going on? Why is he leaving?"

"I told him to. I'll get you home safely after we talk. I know you've been dreaming of me since we first met, and it's my fault."

"What do you mean?"

"I used my power to influence your dreams."

"Why would you do that?"

"At first, I wanted to ruffle your feathers. I thought it would be entertaining for me to know you were having provocative dreams of me while you pretended to hate me or that I might scare you after the first one you had."

"Ok, it's kind of weird, but it isn't the worst thing to happen to me."

"There's more… After the night you were attacked, it went further. I started taking part in those dreams, and I shared them with you. Before that, I was only there and able to see what you dreamt. To me, we have made love numerous times even though you thought you were only dreaming."

"Wait. You mean you had sex with me against my will?"

"Not exactly," he interjected, though she didn't seem to hear him.

"While I was unconscious? How could you do that?" Her eyes misted over with tears as disgust for him ran through her entire body. Her stomach churned as she fought the urge to dry heave.

"We did nothing physically. I understand if you never want to speak to me again, and I intend to do everything in my power to release you from the hell you were sentenced to with me."

"But… if we didn't really do anything, and it was all in a dream, then why would you think I would hate you? It's kind of pervy of you, but I can't complain. Those dreams have made my nights pretty awesome." She chuckled and kicked at the dirt beneath her feet.

Both of his eyebrows raised briefly as relief washed over his face. "You don't hate me?"

"No. At one time, I would have, but I've grown to know and care about. I know things between us started out badly—mostly your fault by the way—but I owe my life to you. I would have died if you hadn't saved me."

*

"I may have saved you, but you wouldn't have been in that position if it weren't for me." The realization that she would most likely always be in danger as long as she was linked to him crashed into him like a tidal wave.

How many countless enemies had he made over the years that might feel the need to attack her in order to get back at him just like Josh had done? As long as she was paired with him, the only safe place she could be was at the manor, which was not the life she deserved. In addition to the life she'd wanted to live being stripped away from her, she might lose her life for real because of him.

"I also wouldn't have seen any of the things you've shown me. I'd be getting ready to move into a house full of vampires, thinking I'd missed out on everything in my life. I feel almost okay with the whole thing because of you."

"I will free you. It's not right. I don't wish you a life of slavery."

"Slavery? Don't you think you're over doing it a little?"

He shook his head. "If you are not free, you are a slave. If you are forced to do things you wouldn't normally do for another, you are a slave. If you have no free will, you are a slave. Trust me on this."

"Did you own slaves? Is that why you were so offended when I would call you 'master'?"

"No, I didn't," he said, dragging his hand through his hair.

"Then, tell me what's up. I saw you stiffen every time I called you that. I see how serious you get when you talk about anything even remotely close to slavery."

He shook his head defiantly. "No."

"So, let me get this straight. You can invade my sleep, make me dream of you, harass me for years just because you feel like it, but when I ask to know about your past so I can try to know and understand you better, you can't give me that? That's pretty shitty, Remy. I thought we were friends now. I guess I was wrong."

"*I* was a slave." He wrung his hands and paced back and forth. "My father tried to force me into another arranged marriage less than a year after my wife died. He wanted me to marry the daughter of a man he barely knew. He thought it would advance him socially and expand the lands of his estate. I refused. I could never see myself with another woman, especially so soon after her death. When he finally realized I would not budge on my decision, he beat me nearly to death. He disowned me, took everything away from me, chained me up in a barn, and ordered me to hard labor on the estate." He stopped pacing and stood before her with his head hung low.

*

He moved closer to her, wrapping his arms around her. The space around them began to distort, and she felt nauseated. She closed her eyes to try to clear her vision, and when she opened them, they stood by her bed in her room.

She hugged him tightly. "I'm so sorry that happened to you."

"I don't want to talk about it anymore," Remy said as he stepped away, removing her arms from his body.

She nodded, and said, "Thank you for telling me."

"Shall I stay away until it is time?" He looked around the room, eyes landing anywhere but on her.

"You don't have to, unless you want to. Shit... You're probably going to get tired of me pretty fast, so I totally understand if you don't want to see me right now."

"At one time, I thought I would tire of you in the first hour. Now, I think it may take closer to two hours."

He smiled that cocky grin at her, and she picked up a pillow to crack him in the face with it. As she swung, he stepped aside, and she fell on the bed.

"I must go now. This is far too tempting to me." He gestured toward her lying on the bed.

He left her in her room and exited through the front door for once. Sabine mulled over everything he'd told her, from messing with her dreams to his past life as a human.

I feel like I should be more upset by his confession of making me have sex dreams about him. Maybe I enjoyed it a little too much to actually be pissed. So many times I woke up wanting it to be real. That must've started happening when he started controlling what happened. I don't think I've ever had a dream of him that I didn't end up having sex with him, other than the very first dream I had the night after I met him, so how could I be mad when my own mind made us do the same things?

The last one was amazing. She could feel her body warming him. His skin, his body—it was all too real to have been just a dream, though she knew it was. The telltale signs of post-sex were gone, and she couldn't feel his essence on her body. There was no soreness in her muscles or any other indication to prove it really happened.

She could only imagine how good sex could be with him if he controlled everything in the dream. It drove her crazy thinking about it.

As she reminisced about the physical things they'd shared in the dream, she had an epiphany.

He told me he loved me.

Chapter 18

The time had come. Her twenty-first birthday had arrived. Most young adults spent their twenty-first drinking and partying, readying themselves for life on their own as an adult. Had she gone to college, she'd have been ready to graduate soon and move out into the world to make a life for herself. Instead, she was packing all of her things to move across town and into a life of seclusion.

She was to arrive at Willow Creek Manor by 8pm, which thankfully gave her family enough time to do their usual birthday celebration of pizza and cupcakes. It was a bittersweet event. She loved what her family did for her every year, but this would be the last. Never again would she get some random gift from Shay while pizza baked in the oven with the smell of cupcakes in the air.

The time for her to become food for Remy was officially here. She didn't know if she should be excited or distressed. Distressing to lose her free will, but exhilarating to spend the rest of her life with him... If only it could be like their time together in Europe had been, instead of cooped up in a big house in Willow Creek with nothing to do.

Her hands shook as she threw item after item into suitcases and boxes. Packing was a tiresome chore she always had a bad habit of putting off until the last minute. Remy had taken it upon himself to pack for her during most of their time traveling because he could do it faster than her, and he knew she would wait until the last minute. Maybe she should have called him to come pack for her this time, too.

Someone from her new home was to come later and pick up what she couldn't pack into the car that would take her to her destiny. *How the hell do I decide what to take with me now? I don't want to leave any of my stuff behind. I don't want to have to leave any of it behind.*

Her mind strayed from the task at hand. How would Remy treat her now that they were forced into close quarters indefinitely? Would he treat her as a friend like he had during their time in Europe, or would the lack of excitement cause him to act like he hated her again? One thought stayed just in the back of her mind. She tried not to notice, but it was there. *Does he really love me?*

* * *

He reluctantly stayed away from her for two weeks. Every thought he had eventually led to her and how he could make this all go away. Running was out. Bastian would find them with very little effort in no time at all, and would she really want to go on the run with him anyway? How would that be any better? She would still be isolated from everyone but him.

He considered bargaining with Bastian, but that wasn't likely either. Once Bastian's mind was made up, it was no easy task getting him to change it. It could take decades before he would even consider thinking about it, and it could be too late for her by then.

Refusing might be the only viable option. If he refused, Bastian, theoretically, couldn't go through with it because there would be no one to pair her with. There were only a handful of actual residents at Willow Creek Manor, and they were already paired off. Bastian would never risk taking in a stray now that Josh slipped under his radar. He'd already been more careful about who he even let visit the estate and the town.

There were very specific rules to a vampire wedding, and one of them was there could be no influence involved. He didn't have to worry that Bastian would order him to complete the ritual because Bastian was a stickler for rules.

The worst that would happen to him for refusing would be nothing worse than what he'd already lived through as a human. Even if Bastian decided to kill him, which he was certain would not happen because Bastian would feel his death, it would be worth it for her to be free.

Looking at the clock, he noticed it was almost time to fetch Sabine. He hadn't seen her since the night they returned from their trek through Europe. She wouldn't run now, he knew, and Bastian had allowed him to back off from watching her almost a year ago. Her privacy and time to herself was the only thing he could give her right then. He'd been vigilant about making sure no outsiders got through the borders. It was the only way he could think of to keep her safe without being close to her. No more dreams either. He had refrained from doing that now that she knew the truth.

He briefly contemplated telling her of his plan, but didn't want to involve her in the event Bastian would punish her for conspiring against him. Walking outside, he got in his car and sped off to pick her up.

* * *

"So what happens now?" Sabine sat on the floor amongst piles of clothes and assorted boxes.

"There will be a ceremony so it will be publicly known to the vampire community that you belong to me and no one else may claim you or harm you, or they risk death." Remy leaned against her chest of drawers.

"I have never felt more like a piece of meat in my entire life."

"You're not a piece of meat. Why do you say that?"

"Pretty sure you used to view me that way. I mean, apparently, I'm less than a vampire because I'm human and if I'm 'yours'. I'm nothing but a possession, and you're going to be treating me like your own personal food bank. So, yeah, I feel kind of like a piece of meat."

"I promise you things won't be so bad. You're not a possession to me. I care about you. I didn't always, but I do now."

"I really do trust you, but you have to stop saying I'm yours. It freaks me out a little."

"Done... unless, of course, you're in some sort of grave danger; then you're 'mine'."

She shook her head and laughed softly. "Can you help me get this stuff in the car?"

"Yes, but I have something I want to give you before we go." He reached into his pocket and pulled out a small silk pouch and moved closer to her. He sat down beside her on the floor and handed the gift to her. "Happy birthday, love."

She took the pouch from his hand; the cool silk caressed her fingers. Smiling at him, she opened it up and turned it upside down in her palm. A tiny charm shaped like the Eiffel Tower dropped into her hand. "I love this, Remy. Thank you so much." She closed her fingers around the charm and reached out to hug him.

He smoothed the hair on the back of her head with his hand and inhaled her scent, knowing he was choosing to let her go and that their time together might be coming to an end within hours.

Pulling away from her, he spoke. "You're welcome. I picked that up in Paris while you were sleeping. I thought you might like it as a reminder of our time together."

"I really appreciate this, and I have the perfect chain to put it on. Let me fish it out and we can start taking things out to the car." She turned to her jewelry box, and he saw her reflection in the mirror as she smiled to herself.

"Why don't you just take a couple bags for now? We can get more once you're settled."

"Whatever. I'm having a hard enough time deciding what to take. Grab that suitcase and box over by the door. I'll just take that for now."

He took her things and loaded them into the car, watching her through the living room window for a few seconds. Her parents hugged one another with tears in their eyes. They grieved the loss of her, though she would only be a few miles away. If things worked out like he hoped, she would be back in no time. If it didn't work, he would make sure she could see them whenever she wanted. It was stupid to be cut off when they were so close.

And, if things did go as he planned, would he be able to simply leave her alone to live her life? He loved her. Would it be so easy to let her go? Or would he watch over her to make sure she was okay and taken care of, never knowing he was so close? So many decisions to make, so little time.

She made her way down the stairs holding her sister's hand to where her parents waited. He tried not to watch to give her a moment of privacy but couldn't tear his gaze away. He saw the emotions so evident on her face and the faces of her family. Tears slid down her cheeks, and he wanted nothing more than to kiss them away. He wanted to tell her it was all going to be alright and to just give him some time to make everything right.

He waited patiently by the car until she came out. As they got settled in the car, he looked at her tenderly and brushed a lingering tear away from her cheek. "Are you ready to go?"

"Not really." She looked away from him and stared at the window to her bedroom.

He patted her on the knee, put the car in gear, and pulled away from the curb.

* * *

A chill passed through his spine just after he'd brought Sabine to his—their—room. "I have been summoned by Bastian. Please, make yourself at home. Get settled, and I should be back shortly to help you unpack. I cleared out the whole right side of the closet for you."

He raced down the hallway to Bastian's room. Even the few seconds he stayed with Sabine instead of immediately going to Bastian hurt him clear to the bone.

"Yes, my lord?"

Bastian sat at a small table, sipping a small glass of blood. "You must not feed on Sabine tonight. You cannot feed on her until the ritual tomorrow night. I trust you have not fed from her before now since it was forbidden for you to do so."

"I haven't tasted her, but I thought the ceremony was tonight. Why has it changed?"

"If you're hungry, go out to the woods or to the creek to catch something."

"I'm not hungry. I just thought we were doing this tonight."

"So anxious for her to be yours? You amaze me more and more every day. We are performing the ceremony tomorrow because not all of my guests have arrived."

He rolled his eyes. "We do not need guests."

"You know how this is done. There must always be an audience to any vampire affair so there are plenty of witnesses, especially when it is a wedding. It is not every day that my favorite progeny marries. Let us celebrate. Does she know you will be married as far as vampires are concerned?"

"I have not mentioned that to her, my lord, other than in jest, but I think she understands."

"Good. Make sure she dresses in the finest dress she has. If she has nothing suitable, she may borrow something from the guest closets. I will say the words, and you will feed on her in front of the others to consummate the union."

He nodded, knowing his plan to refuse to feed on her at the wedding would keep the promise he made to her so long ago. He wouldn't feed on her until she was ready, and she never indicated to him that she was. At least, not outside of a dream. That was a promise he didn't intend to break.

Remy took his leave from Bastian and went back to Sabine. He entered quietly to find her sitting on the floor, legs crossed and reading a book. Her eyes did not shift from the page as he walked in. Finding her there in his room like that was one of the most beautiful sights he had ever seen.

"Sorry to interrupt your reading. I wanted to let you know that we will be going through the ceremony tomorrow night. We have to pick something for you to wear."

"I didn't realize there was a dress code."

"I'm afraid so. I have to tell you something, and I don't know how you'll feel, but there's nothing that can be done about it."

She looked up from her book and watched him as he fidgeted and looked away from her.

"You will officially be my wife after tomorrow night. The dress you wear will be your wedding gown."

"Oh, geez." She swallowed hard. "I know you said you were to treat me like I was your wife. I just didn't think that meant that I would *actually* be your wife."

"Only to other vampires. It would not mean that in your human laws."

"So, what? I have to pledge to love and obey you for the rest of my life? Till death do we part?"

"Obey... love is not acknowledged."

"Sounds like a dream marriage to me." She rolled her eyes and crossed her arms in front her. "So much for me not being a slave."

"Sabine, please don't."

"Fine. What am I supposed to wear? I don't have anything anywhere near as nice as a wedding gown. Does it have to be white, too?" Sarcasm dripped from her words.

"No, it doesn't. Come with me. We'll find you something appropriate."

She followed him down the hallway to a part of the house she hadn't seen before. He opened a large black door adorned with intricate carvings. Behind the door was a walk-in closet that was every bit as big as a large bedroom with racks upon racks, and shelves upon shelves holding rich, luscious garments of all colors, sizes, and styles. There were corsets, ball gowns, medieval gowns, cocktail dresses, suits, and tuxedos as well as casual, every day clothes.

Her jaw dropped and her eyes widened as she stepped into the room. "My God. I have never seen anything like this in my entire life. Does that dress have diamonds on the neckline?"

"It more than likely does... Pick what you like."

"I don't know if I can, Remy! This is too much!" Her face lit up with a huge smile.

"Would you like me to help you? This sort of reminds me of our little trip to Barneys last year, except you're not in such a pissy mood this time."

She playfully smacked his arm. "I'll have to try on some stuff, too. Isn't it bad luck for the groom to see the bride in her gown, or to see the gown at all?"

"I don't know. Sounds silly to me."

"You honestly have never heard about it being bad luck to see a bride in her gown?"

"No. Why would I care?"

"Never mind. Just help me. We can pick something, and I'll try it on later."

They spent the better part of an hour searching through the closet before deciding on a purple corset with a matching floor length skirt that had a short train trailing behind it. She left him behind to pick out his own clothes as she went to try on the dress.

She made sure to lock the bathroom door behind her. It wouldn't keep him out if he was determined to follow her, but it gave her some peace of mind. Her luck was already shitty, and there was no need to add anything bad to it. She felt beautiful and sexy when she tried the garments on, though she couldn't tighten the corset very much on her own so she wouldn't get the full affect until the next day.

* * *

Remy quickly picked out a white shirt and a long, black and dark green court coat while she tried on her dress. He loved all the modern conveniences and advances in technology, but he did miss the style of dress from years past. This was the perfect opportunity to revisit those days of old.

They met back in the bedroom—their bedroom—once he was sure she'd had enough time to try on her dress. Of course he'd heard it was bad luck for a man to see a bride in her dress before the ceremony, but he liked acting like he was above those sorts of things.

"I think I'm going to go to bed soon. I just feel like sleeping. If I stay up, I'm going to keep worrying about tomorrow."

"What is there to worry about? You don't have to do much but agree and stand there looking pretty."

"I know, but I'm a little nervous about being around so many vampires. I'm guessing I'll be the only human. I don't like being the only morsel of food at a banquet."

"Don't worry yourself, love. You will be protected. No one can touch you, and you won't be the only human. Bastian employs many of the townspeople, and there will be others who have human companions as well."

"What makes you so sure no one will hurt me? Who's to say there won't be some rogue vampire or group of vampires who would attack me just to cause problems?"

"That won't happen here. It's hard to explain, but rules that govern us are something vampires view as almost sacred. It is death to anyone who defies them. Death is something that most of us do not desire, otherwise we wouldn't have chosen immortality."

"It's all so much to take in. Vampires can be murderous monsters, yet they won't break a rule. Weird."

"It isn't so hard to understand if you think about it. Humans can also be murderous monsters and still uphold traditions and customs. Not much difference, now, is there?"

"Touché." She pulled the covers back, and slid down into the bed. "What are your plans for the rest of the night?"

He shrugged, and said, "I'll probably read or something."

"Okay, could you do me a favor?"

"Maybe. Depends on what you're asking."

"Could you make me dream of something nice?"

"We don't have to dream for that to happen." He zipped over to her side, and stood by the bed with a big grin on his face. "We can shag right now if you're up for it."

"I didn't mean that kind of dream," she exclaimed, pulling the blanket up over her face.

"Oh... My mistake."

Lowering the blanket to look at him, she said, "I thought maybe you could make me dream of something nice so I won't have a bad night. Take me to Paris?" She toyed with the Eiffel Tower charm that still hung from her neck.

He got into the bed with her, covering himself up and pulling her to his chest. "Relax, and I will do what I can."

She closed her eyes as he stroked her hair and rubbed her arm lightly. Within a few minutes, her breathing and heart rate slowed as she drifted off to sleep. He kissed her head softly and closed his eyes as he concentrated on her. Sending out his influence, he gently touched her mind with his presence.

* * *

She found herself walking down a Parisian street past museums, cafes, restaurants, and shops. She peered in windows at things she couldn't afford and smelled fresh croissant baking at a nearby café. Looking around at the city passing her by, she sat on a concrete wall lining a park, trying to decide what to do and where to go.

A hand gently touched her shoulder. She turned to see who had touched her, only to find Remy standing behind her. He sat down on the wall next to her, looking at people walking by.

"Is this how you wish to spend your time, or would you like to do something else? We could go for a walk."

"I'm fine either way."

"You don't sound fine. Is there something else you want?"

"It's just that I was thinking it might be nice to go back to New York. It's silly since I wanted you to bring me here, but now that I'm here, I just want to go back to

Central Park. I loved looking out the bedroom window in your apartment down at the park."

"Whatever you wish, love. Close your eyes for a second."

When she re-opened her eyes, they sat on a bench located near the zoo in Central Park.

"Thank you." It was chillier than she expected, nowhere near as warm as it should've been for that time of year. She was amazed by even the tiniest details he was able to include; the smell of a nearby pretzel cart, the chill in the air, the sound of people chattering and traffic racing down nearby streets...

"At least you can whisk me away to any place in the world I want to go, even if it isn't real."

"Hmm." He smiled slightly and nodded

She looked at him as he sat beside her, unable to tear her gaze away, despite the beautiful scenery around them.

"What now? Why do you stare at me like that?"

"I think I love you, Remy," she blurted out.

He shook his head. "You don't."

"How would you know if I do or don't? You told me you loved me, and I believed you."

Glancing down at the ground he quietly said, "I never told you I loved you."

"You did. In a dream that you controlled, just like this one. You said it when Josh had me, too. You denied it, but I know what I heard."

"So what if I do?" The piercing gaze of his eyes landed on her. "You won't be with me for long anyway," he said as he stared off into the distance.

"What?" she asked, reaching out to his face to make him look at her. "What do you mean I won't be with you for long?"

His hand waved her off as he moved out of her grip. "Nothing. I was only seeing if you were paying attention."

"Don't lie to me. You know I'll remember this when I wake up."

"Only if I allow you to remember."

"Then what's the big deal? Tell me what you're talking about."

*

He hesitated and couldn't look at her. Telling her of his plan would hurt them both too much and he couldn't bear to see it on her face.

"I am going to refuse our union. It's the only way I can see to get you out of this arrangement and back to your life."

"Oh... I guess I was a fool to think you really loved me."

"I do love you, Sabine." He turned to her with burning desire in his eyes, and touched her cheek. "This is why I want you to be free. Once I succeed, I will leave you to your life. You won't hear from me again, and you'll be able to live your life however you wish. I will set up a fund for you that will keep you until you die, and you can have my apartment here in Manhattan if you like. You'll need to be somewhere with real culture in order to succeed. I only desire to take care of you, and I want you to live life to the fullest. You are a beautiful artist, but

240

artists like you don't always gain the recognition they deserve. This, in turn, leads to you having to get some menial job that takes you away from your true passion, and I don't want that for you. Not when I can provide for you comfortably for the rest of your life."

"But I won't have you."

"No... I will only hold you back. I'll make you forget about me if it'll make it easier for you."

"Bullshit, Remy! I don't want to forget about you! You say you don't want to take me away from my passion, but what if my true passion is you? How could your presence hold me back from anything?"

"Children. I can't give you that. You must find a man who will love you and give them to you."

"What if I don't want children?"

"Don't be ridiculous. I know you do. I've seen it in your dreams, and I've heard you talk about it with your friends."

"Okay, so what if I do? There are other means of having children. Artificial insemination is a thing, you know?"

"I don't want some bugger's sperm inside you if you're mine. I don't care how it gets there."

"Now it's your turn to stop being ridiculous, and there you go again with that 'mine' shit... I'll adopt."

"What kind of father could I really be? I don't possess *human* emotions or form bonds like that."

"But you do! You love me! That *is* an emotion and a bond. What's the difference?"

"The difference is that I don't *want* a child. I don't want a reminder of what I lost."

*

"And that's the real reason you can't be with me, isn't it?" His silence was all the answer she needed. "You don't want me as a reminder either. I love you, and if I'm not good enough for you then so be it. I'll not try to live up to a ghost. Leave me alone."

"Sabine…"

"Leave. And don't you dare make me forget this either."

He stood up to walk away from her. Looking back over his shoulder, he said, "You would never know…"

Chapter 19

She awoke the next afternoon to see him sitting in the chair across the room, asleep. That was odd. He'd been in bed with her when she fell asleep and hadn't hesitated to sleep beside her at other times. Why did he move? She studied him as the memories of her dream came flooding back to her, though she felt there were holes or gaps in her memory.

Paris, Central Park, talking about children, that was all there, but there were places that were black scattered throughout and what she could remember didn't match up.

What else was said? I know there had to be more to it than he wished I could be free so I could have kids. It seemed like we left on bad terms. What am I missing?

"Remy! Wake up!"

His eyes shot open, sitting straight up in the chair.

"What's the matter? Are you okay?"

"Why can I not remember all of what happened between us in that dream?"

Relaxing back into the chair, he asked, "Do you always remember every detail of every dream you've ever had?"

"No, but when I dream about you, I do. Every last detail stays with me. So, why not now? What happened that you don't want me to remember?"

"Nothing. You just forgot."

"Tell me what you remember to jog my memory."

"You got mad because I told you I didn't want children, and it ended there."

"Well, I've just caught you. I don't remember being mad at you for that. Why would it matter to me if you didn't want kids?"

"I don't have time for this. I have to prepare for the ceremony. It's starting in a few hours." He stood up and walked out of the room, closing the door behind him.

Think, Sabine, think. What happened? Why did our conversation get so heated? Why does it matter if he doesn't want kids? Unless we were discussing having children together. That has to be it. Maybe Gretchen can help.

She walked four doors down the hallway and gently tapped on the door. "Gretchen? It's Sabine. Can I talk to you for a minute?"

A muffled voice came from the other side of the door. "Yes. Come in."

She walked through the door. Gretchen sat at a chair in front of a large vanity, applying make up to her fair skin. Why she needed make up, Sabine didn't know. She was flawless and one of the most beautiful creatures she'd ever seen.

"I know this might sound weird, but if a vampire made me forget something, could you make me remember?"

"Possibly. It all depends on how willing the victim is to give up the information they've been told to forget and how powerful the vampire is."

"Well, I guess I'm the victim in this case, and I want to know."

"I'm guessing Remy has done something to you against your will?"

"Not exactly. He made me dream of us in Central Park after I asked him to, and I know he erased some of it from my memory. He's never done that before, and I want to know what went wrong this time. I need to know what he's hiding from me."

"Very well. Come to me." Sabine did as she was told and stood in front of the blonde vampire. Gretchen's cold eyes looked her up and down. "Kneel before me." Sabine kneeled, looking up at Gretchen. "Close your eyes, and I'll see what I can see."

She placed her thin fingers upon Sabine's temples and closed her eyes. Sabine felt an odd sensation running through her mind, like she wasn't alone with her thoughts.

She dropped her hands and gasped as Sabine opened her eyes.

"What? What did you see?"

"I didn't see anything about your dream. It was locked away too deep to find."

"Then why did you gasp like you were shocked. What did you see?"

"I saw... Remy. He loves you deeply... and you love him. I can see it in his actions. I didn't know it was possible."

"Vampires never fall in love with humans?"

"It's not that. That actually happens more than you would think. I just didn't know *he* was capable of love."

"What else can you tell me?"

"Nothing. All I saw were things you already know. It's been right there in front of you since you went to New York together last year. You honestly didn't know?"

"I suspected. He told me as much during times I felt we were connected, but he denied it."

"Now you know. Do with the information what you will. You're lucky to be marrying a vampire who loves you. He would die for you. I would die for you. Remy is like my brother, and you will be my sister. If he loves you this much, then so do I."

"Okay, well thanks."

She had to get the hell out of that room. Gretchen seemed almost crazy at the revelation of Remy's feelings.

Sabine had to start preparing for the ceremony, and needed to leave herself plenty of time to shower, fix her hair and apply her make up.

She stepped into the shower a little while later, relishing the warm water flowing over her body. Her mind wandered to the last time she'd been in that particular shower. Remy washing her hair was one of the most erotic things she'd ever experienced. She wished he was there with her again.

She wrapped herself in a big fluffy towel a little while later and went to the bedroom. Two women she'd never laid eyes on stood before her.

"We're here to help you get ready. My name is Marlene, and I'll help you with your hair. This is Claire.

She'll do your makeup, and we'll both help you into your dress. Have you picked out shoes yet? We saw the dress, but no stockings, undergarments, or shoes."

"I haven't picked out shoes yet. I can't believe I didn't think about them at all. And just what kind of undergarments do I need? Bra and underwear aren't good enough?"

"Yes, of course, that'll be fine, though you won't really need a bra. I wasn't sure if you would be wearing a petticoat or slip of some kind. I brought you an assortment of shoes Remy picked for you that might complement your dress. They're just inside the closet door if you'd like to try them on."

"I'll go ahead and pick now before we get started with the rest." She walked over to the closet, careful not to let her towel drop. At least fifteen pairs of shoes were lined up in rows for her to choose from. She looked them over carefully. Her dress was a little long, so she needed to go with heels. That eliminated about five pairs of flats. She always loved higher heels, and thought about how tall Remy was before choosing. He was easily 6'3", so she could get away with any height. She chose a pair of royal purple, strappy sandals with a 5" inch heel. They had a hidden platform, which would help her balance herself better on such a high heel.

She looked down at her feet and frowned.

Claire noticed and asked, "Is there something wrong? Do you need other shoes to choose from?"

"These are wonderful. I like them very much, but my toes are a bit plain. I like having them polished when I wear open-toed shoes."

"Not a problem. Sit down and I'll give you a quick pedicure."

She sat back down at the little table where make-up and hair products were laid out. Marlene straightened and blow dried her hair. She went to work manipulating and sculpting Sabine's hair into an elaborate "S" design on the back of her head while Claire worked on her feet.

Claire moved on to Sabine's face next. She plucked Sabine's brows and slathered on different moisturizers and primers before starting on her make up. She blended a foundation that matched her porcelain skin perfectly and finished it up with some powder and a setting spray. Her eyes were lined with black kohl and lids coated with a silvery powder before mascara was swooped over her lashes, making them look twice as long as normal. Her lips were dabbed with a bit of red lipstick before a clear gloss was applied, giving her lip just the right amount of sheen.

She stepped into the long skirt, and Claire zipped it up for her. They slid the corset down over her head and bare chest. Both of them worked behind her for what seemed like forever. They tugged and pulled to the point that she thought she might go light-headed from her breath being forced from her body. When they finally finished, she peered at herself in the mirror.

The woman she saw looking back at her, wasn't her. It couldn't be. This woman was far too elegant and beautiful to be Sabine Crowley. As she looked closer, her own familiar eyes stared back at her. She looked at her body and determined it was worth the temporary light headedness to look as good as she did. She stepped away from the mirror and into her shoes. Walking around the room, she had more confidence than she ever knew she possessed.

She couldn't wait for Remy to see her. If Gretchen was wrong and Remy didn't love her already, how could he not fall hopelessly in love once he saw her?

"It's time," Claire said. "Follow us. We'll escort you to the ballroom."

She followed the two women out the door, down the stairs, and into a large room where guests milled about. She only caught a glimpse of this room once, the first time she visited. The double doors were made of platinum and accented with diamonds and jewels of all colors. The floors were marble and the walls were lavishly decorated. Many tables were set up all around, leaving a wide carpeted path down the middle.

A hundred or more faces stared back at her as she entered the ballroom. Bastian stood on a platform at the top of a short stair case. Smiling warmly at her as she entered, he descended the staircase and met her in a flash. He offered his arm to her, and she in turn wrapped her arm around his.

"You look lovely, Miss Crowley. I look forward to your time here with us, and I hope that you will never hesitate to come to me with any concern or problem you may have, even if it is about Remy. I know he can be strong-willed and difficult at times."

"Thank you, Bastian, but I can handle Remy. He isn't so bad."

"He really has fallen for you. I never would have believed it if I did not see it with my own two eyes. He must be eager for this union to take place. There is nothing more intimate than a vampire who loves the one he feeds from."

Neither of them said anything else as they walked up the short stairs to the raised platform. She scanned the crowd for any sign of Remy, but she could not find him. *He better not leave me hanging. I will be so pissed at him if he doesn't show up.*

Bastian placed his hand on the one that gripped his arm. *He will not leave you here alone. He is on his way now. Do not worry that he will do this to you.*

Sorry. I didn't mean to think so loudly. She smiled nervously at Bastian as he nodded once to her.

The doors opened once more, and Remy stood there wearing the fanciest clothes she'd ever seen a man wear. He wore black breeches and a black and green court coat with a white shirt underneath that didn't look the least bit modern. He looked like he was on a royal court from the seventeenth century. His hair was tied back in a low ponytail, accentuating the sharp cut of his jaw. His face was hard, mouth set in a straight line, and his eyes were fierce as his gaze landed on her. If she didn't know him before, she would have passed out and died right then. Aside from the clothes he wore, he was menacing to say the least, but the look of him made her body ache to be taken by him.

*

Remy stood frozen in place as he looked at his would-be bride. She was the most beautiful creature he'd seen in over four hundred years, and he realized in that moment that he loved her more than he ever thought possible. Though he loved his wife with all he had at the time, what he felt for Sabine was stronger. It pained him to look at her, knowing he had to give her up. He regained his composure and tore his gaze away from her.

Bastian put up a hand as if he were telling Remy to stay where he was and turned to Sabine

"It is time. Are you ready to begin?" Bastian asked.

She took a shallow breath and exhaled, the flesh of her cheeks flushing crimson. "As ready as I'm ever gonna be."

His voice grew louder and echoed through the ballroom. "Welcome my brothers and sisters." Voices hushed and everyone focused on Bastian. "You have all been invited here this evening to witness the union of my progeny to his human companion. Most of you in attendance know by now that I have an arrangement with the inhabitants of Willow Creek. Sabine has been sent to us to fulfill this arrangement. Remy, please come forward."

Remy stepped forward, taking long strides to meet Bastian and Sabine. His back was perfectly straight, lengthening him to his full height. As he stood at the bottom of the steps in front of them, he bowed. "My lord."

"Remy. Step up, and take Sabine's hand."

Remy moved to stand beside her, and turned her to face him. He took both of her hands in his, kissing her right hand before lowering them.

"Sabine, do you promise to obey Remy no matter what his intention may be so long as he protects you and provides for you?"

She hesitated for just a moment before answering. Remy could hear her reservations about making such a harsh vow as he listened in on her thoughts.

"Yes."

"From the moment of this union, let it be known that no vampire shall ever try to claim Sabine Crowley. No vampire may ever lift a finger to harm Sabine. She belongs wholly to Remington Bludworth. Anyone violating this union will be put to death. It is time, my child. Feed from your bride."

*

Remy looked deep into Sabine's eyes. She saw a hint of something. Sorrow? Fear? She couldn't quite put her finger on it. As he leaned in to kiss her, she expected to feel the euphoria take over her mind and body, but it wasn't there. His lips explored hers fervently as if it were the last time he'd ever kiss her. Her body threatened to go limp in his arms from the sweet pressure of his kiss and the lack oxygen in her lungs. After only a few seconds, he pulled away, turning to Bastian.

"I will not feed from her." He walked several paces away from Sabine as a collective gasp came from the audience.

"What is this?" A hint of anger flashed on Bastian's face.

"I will not feed on her. I love her, and I wish for her to be free and not tied to me or this fucking town."

"I suggest you take a moment to collect yourself and rethink this decision."

"I will not. It is forbidden for you to use your power to force me to do this, and I refuse. Since there are no other free vampires living amongst us in our home, you will be forced to let her go."

"Need I remind you that *I* make the rules here? And even if I choose not to force you, much has changed while you were gone. There are free vampires living here and even if there were not, there are numerous vampires here who would step in to take your place. Look around you. Do you see the faces that desire her? Do you see those who hunger for her as we speak? You are foolish if you throw this one away. She will not be free."

*

Remy stiffened, hands fisting at his sides. This was all happening too fast. The thought of another possessing her royally pissed him off, but he was so stubborn, he wasn't yet ready to abandon his plan.

Bastian spoke again. "Now, the choice is yours. *Feed on her or let her belong to another*!"

Bastian's voice commanded Remy to choose. His body stiffened, and he fought himself with every step he took toward her. He willed his legs to stop moving, but he had no control. His actions were ruled by his desire for her. Bastian had commanded him to make a choice, and his primal need for her made the decision for him.

*

He turned to her with hunger in his eyes. His fangs, fully extended, flashed at her from behind his sweet lips. A low growl emanated from his throat. He moved closer to her as if he were stalking her. He was a hunter, and she was his prey.

This was not the Remy she knew and loved. Her Remy was hidden away behind the eyes of the beast stalking her. In a split second, she made a decision. She put her hands lightly on his chest. He stopped, grabbing her hands, as if he wanted to push them away. She spoke softly as she looked him deep in the eyes. Her words were meant only for him, and she didn't care that almost every pair of ears in the ballroom could probably hear her.

"Remy..." she whispered. "Look at me. Listen to what I'm saying to you. I want to spend my life with you, and I can't stand the thought of living one day without you. You've shown me the world, and I have no doubt you'll show it to me again. I love you, Remy."

She brushed the few stray strands of hair away from her neck, and tilted her head to expose her throat to him.

His eyes burned with desire for her, and his body relaxed as he leaned closer to her. A familiar warmth started to consume her, starting at the point where his teeth gently touched her flesh. The points of his fangs pierced her skin as waves of passion washed over her body, threatening to send her falling to the floor.

*

He held her tight as his fangs plunged deep into her neck, drinking her down. The blood was warm and sweet like honey against his tongue. He savored her taste, and knew then that he would never desire another. The flavor of love and its ambrosial lusciousness lingered as he stopped drinking. His skin warmed as her blood nourished him.

He pulled his fangs out and held her tight. A bloody tear ran down his cheek and dripped onto her shoulder. He quickly healed her wounds and awaited Bastian's finishing words.

Bastian spoke. "It is done." He raised his hands into the air as the room erupted in applause.

Remy scooped Sabine up and rushed her to their bedroom, laying her softly on the bed.

"Are you alright?"

She looked up at him in a daze and began to giggle. "Your last name is Bludworth. You're a vampire and your name is Bludworth." She now laughed hysterically. "No wonder you never told me what it was."

"Yes, Sabine. My name is Bludworth. You're the first one in over four centuries to ever point that out. You are so clever. How did I ever manage to get along without your wit before now?"

She stopped laughing abruptly. "I love you." Two tears formed and dripped from her eyes.

"And… I love you." He bent down and gently kissed her lips. Pulling her upright, he positioned himself behind her. He yanked and worked the ribbons lacing up her back until she was free. She took a deep breath, the first since she'd gotten into the garment. He raised her arms above her head and slid the corset up over her body. Taking her hands in his, he lowered them and his lips skimmed her nape. His hands moved over her shoulders, down her back and around her ribs, finally settling on her bare breasts. He licked and nipped at the spot he'd bitten only a few minutes before.

"Do it again. Drink from me," she whispered breathlessly, tilting her head to further expose her neck to him. "Let me nourish you."

"There's another spot I'd rather taste. One I've been fantasizing about for the last year…"

"Go for it, then." She angled her head to brush her cheek against him.

"Why rush? The payoff is far greater when you have to work for it."

His thumbs teased her nipples, coaxing them to harden and stand erect. He grasped her left breast firmly while he rolled the bud of the other between his forefinger and thumb. Turning her around, he pulled her onto his lap. She hiked up her skirt as far as it would go before straddling him. His heart began to beat faster as his shaft swelled beneath her. Her hands caressed his chest, and she gasped as she felt the drum of his heart beneath her fingers.

"I thought your heart didn't beat."

"I lied, love."

He kissed her breasts, flicking his tongue hungrily at her nipples. She bit back a moan. The sensation of his tongue on her sent ripples of pleasure throughout her body.

His fingers gripped her sides and gently rocked her against himself before pushing her away from him to help her stand beside the bed. He turned her around and unzipped her skirt, slipping it down over her hips as his hands rounded her curves.

Sitting back, he gazed at her perfect ass before reaching over and pushing her panties down to her feet. His fingers dug into her hips as he yanked her back to his lap.

She kicked her shoes off and turned to wrap her arms around his neck. She placed her legs on either side of him and settled on top of his erection. She grinded against him. The friction of their bodies rubbing together consumed her as she became slick with desire.

She unbuttoned his coat, sliding it off his shoulders and arms. Her hands searched his chest and down to his waist before finding the bottom of the shirt. She pushed it up over his head and tossed it to the floor. Her fingers slipped just inside of the waistband of his breeches as she lifted herself off him. He raised his hips, allowing her to pull them off. His cock stood erect and exposed as the material slid down his body.

Her hand enveloped him, sliding up and down the length of his manhood. He kissed her again as his hips bucked beneath her. Tracing her lip with his tongue, he gently took her bottom lip between his teeth before kissing her deeply.

He gripped her back as he rolled them over. He settled himself between her legs as his fingers skimmed over her body. Feathering kisses down her belly, he worked his way over to her thigh. Pushing her thighs far apart, he found the artery he had so longed to drink from running up the length of her leg.

The thump of her quickening heart beat filled his ears. He reached out with his power and caressed her mind, preparing her for the bite. His fangs extended and his mouth watered thinking about how she would taste. As his teeth sunk into her warm flesh, she cried out, enraptured by his touch. Pulling his teeth free from her flesh, he swallowed the last bit of blood in his mouth before healing the two tiny puncture wounds.

Her scent made him ache with desire to taste the soft flesh of her sex. His finger swirled around her throbbing nub, just before he parted her and licked gently.

His tongue worked her enthusiastically as he applied more pressure. One finger slipped inside and eased in and out. Darts of pleasure jolted her body at the touch of his tongue and the feel of his finger inside her. Her body tensed as she prepared for the sweet release of orgasm.

"Please..." she begged. "I need you inside me, Remy. Please? I can't take it anymore."

He moved up to look into her eyes.

"Maybe I should make you wait a bit. Wouldn't that be fun?"

"I've waited long enough." She nipped at his chin.

He positioned the head of his cock at her dewy entrance, and slid himself slowly inside of her, watching her face as her body adjusted to him before pulling out again. He rocked his hips rhythmically, slowly at first, gaining speed with time. He bent down and kissed her breast, tongue flicking at her nipple.

Her legs hugged his hips as he picked up speed and pounded into her. She frantically grabbed at the flesh on his back, urging him closer. His lips grazed her throat as he blew cool air onto her skin. He took one of her hands and kissed her palm before pinning it against the pillow, wrapping his fingers around hers.

The love she felt for him invaded his body and pierced his heart. He had no doubt that they were meant for one another, and that she was his destiny. In that moment, they were of one flesh and body. Their minds opened to one another as love washed over them. He made sweet love to her and fucked her hard at the same time.

She'd never been fucked so good in her life, or felt the emotions he emitted for her in that moment.

He continued to pump his cock into her, reaching down to stroke her so she would come again. After she moaned loudly over her climax, the palm of his hand slammed into the head board, cracking it as he tried to restrain himself from devouring every last drop of blood in her body.

He ran his tongue along her neck as his teeth elongated once again. Sucking gently at her skin, he plunged his fangs into her once more. She was so high on him that he didn't need to use much power to keep her from feeling pain. He drank her sweet blood as he thrust harder and faster, finding his release while his fangs lingered in her flesh.

Sweat beaded on her forehead as she cried out in pleasure, but he wasn't done. No, he had to make her know she was his one more time. He would never be satisfied that he'd made her come enough times. His hand felt for her clit, and he went to work. He looked her deep in the eyes as he stroked her until she exploded hard and fast one more time.

She screamed his name as her back arched. Breasts heaving, she breathed heavily trying to catch her breath. He collapsed beside her and pulled her onto his chest and into his arms. He'd given his heart wholly to her, and he would never let her go.

Epilogue

"Are we ever leaving this bed or this bedroom? We haven't been on the other side of that door or out of our little sanctuary here for over a week."

"No." He kissed her passionately. "Do you have something better to do, wife?"

"No, husband." Her arms wrapped around his neck and pulled him closer.

He kissed her nose and looked down at her. "Are you hungry?"

"A little. You?" She smiled up at him and cocked her head to the side so he could get a good view of her neck.

"I'm always hungry for you, love. If you're offering, I'm biting, but we need to get you some food first so you don't lose your strength. You haven't eaten since yesterday. Shall I ring the kitchen and have something brought to you, or do you want to leave our quarters?"

"Just call down. Nothing fancy, though. Maybe a BLT or something easy like that."

He smirked at her as he sat up and reached for his phone. "I never would have thought you'd be so eager to stay cooped up here with me in this place; after all that whining you did."

She tossed a pillow at his head. "Quiet, you. If I seem to recall, you weren't exactly thrilled about it all either, so shut your trap."

Remy sat the phone down and turned to playfully tackle Sabine when a shiver as cold as ice ran down his spine. "Bugger! Bastian has called me. I should've known he'd interrupt our fun sooner or later. Call down and get something to eat. I'll be back shortly."

He was at Bastian's side momentarily. "Are you enjoying your honeymoon, my boy?"

"Yes, of course. I'd like to get back to it, actually. Why did you summon me?"

"I had not seen you in a week, though I have heard you more than I cared to. By the sounds of it, I thought maybe you had killed the poor girl at one point with all the whimpering and moaning from her and the growling from you."

"She lives, I assure you."

"Excellent. I am glad this has been a successful pairing and that you made the right choice. Now, I have some things I will need your assistance with. I hear there is a large pack not far from here, maybe twenty miles or so. I need you to come with me to scout out the situation. I must find out if they mean us harm, or are just passing by."

"Bastian, I beg you, please take someone else. You know you are going to kill them. You always do. So why pretend you might leave them be? I'm in the mood for love right now, not death."

"Do not forget your role here. I am happy you have found love in your blood mate, but your personal relationship with her does not supersede your duties to me. The fact remains, she is here merely for sustenance no matter what you feel for her. Now, get dressed and return to me quickly."

Remy nodded and returned to Sabine. "I must go, love. Apparently it's imperative I accompany Bastian to slaughter a group outside of town that may or may not be a threat."

"How long will you be gone?"

"Not long. Go ahead and enjoy your meal when it arrives. I should be back by the time you're finished."

"Question. Why kill them if they're not a threat? I mean, I know they're vampires, and death to them all," she smirked at him as he narrowed his eyes at her, "but what's the point?"

"I don't believe it's vampires this time, and honestly... I don't know. I've never understood Bastian's need to kill those who sniff around, and I can't fathom why anyone would be drawn to this place."

"Not vampires? Then what?"

"Don't worry about it, love. The less you know, the better."

"You're scaring me."

"No need for that. I'm not worried, and you shouldn't be either." He slipped on a shirt and bent down to kiss her gently on the forehead.

"If you say so."

"Just to be safe, stay here. I know you must be eager to visit your friends and family, and now would be a good time since we're being forced out of bed, but please wait until I return."

"I'll wait. I do want to see them, but I'd be just as happy to spend the next month with you in bed."

He arched an eyebrow and flashed her a sexy grin. "I must go now before Bastian has my head for defying him. We'll have plenty of fun when I get back, but I think it's time I look into the secrets of Willow Creek." He walked swiftly toward the door and left Sabine hungering for him.

The End... for now.

About Stephanie Summers

Stephanie Summers is a wife and mother of two. She recently graduated from West Virginia University with a degree in accounting, though writing is her true passion. Stephanie seemed to always have a story or two or ten running around in her mind. At the ripe old age of 30, she finally decided it was time to put aside the thought that she didn't have what it took to write a novel and began writing her first story.

Works by Stephanie Summers:

The Willow Creek Vampires Series
Craving
Haunting
Awakening
The Bludworth Chronicles: Origin (A short companion story to The Willow Creek Vampires Series)

Take Me Series
Take Me On
Take Me Home (Coming Soon)

Short Stories
Saved by the Bear (An Erotic Short Story)
Love Forgotten (Published in the anthology Stardust: A Futuristic Romance Collection)

Links to check out:

www.facebook.com/authorstephaniesummers -
Check out my Facebook page for teaser chapters,
contests, and to keep up-to-date on my latest projects.
www.authorstephaniesummers.com
www.twitter.com/authorsasummers
http://eepurl.com/PWB0P - Sign up for my
newsletter to keep up to date with new releases and
appearances.

Would you like to see the characters in The Willow
Creek Vampires Series come to life on your television or
a movie screen? Then, consider supporting Craving! The
more supporters it has, the better chance it has of being
noticed.   Thanks   so   much!
http://iflist.com/stories/craving#

Enjoy a free preview of Take Me On (Part one in the two part Take Me Series)!

PROLOGUE

The deep, somber voice of the man I gave my whole heart to fills the air around me. Lyrics of the lost love of his life assault my mind, pulling me back to a time when we were inseparable. Standing frozen in place, I know undoubtedly those words are meant for no one but me as I see him for the first time in over a year. The stage where he stands is less than fifty feet away, but his presence is felt in every corner of the room.

As his lyrics wash over the chaos of the crowd, he takes control of them, bidding them to feel the emotion pouring from his voice. His gaze seeks me out though I know he can't possibly see me. His eyes close and everything else but the two of us disappears.

His voice finds its way to me, forcing everything else to melt into the background as it wraps around me much like his arms used to. Each word escaping his lips is like a hammer smashing to bits the wall I've built around my heart. Try as I might to repress them, plump tears form at the corners of my eyes as I think back to what he did for me and how much he cared when no one else seemed to even notice I was broken.

I thought I would be okay seeing him from afar, but I'm not. I want to run up on that stage like a mad woman, drop to my knees, and beg him to take me home and make the pain stop for both of us. I have to get out of here now... before I do something stupid... before the man I'm here with notices my heart still belongs to Ash London.

10 days earlier...

Looking down the tracks for a glimpse of the train, like that action alone will make it appear sooner, I shift my weight back and forth impatiently. Sadly, patience is a virtue I no longer possess, though I never had much to begin with. I've had enough of the stench of urine and rats scurrying about on the tracks below. I'm ready to get above ground once more so I can get to a brunch date with my best friend, Tori Tabor. Just my fucking luck, the train is running late when I have somewhere important to be. Isn't that how it always is?

Finally, the train arrives, and I push my way on, but give up my potential seat to an elderly lady who needs it more than I do. More and more people crowd on, and I'm starting to feel like a canned sardine. The guy next to me, with his unkempt hair and mouth hanging agape, leers at me with a dead-behind-the-eyes stare the entire trip. I inch away from him as best I can, but it just seems like every time I look up, he's that much closer. Why do I always attract the attention of weirdos? I sometimes wonder if I have a sign on my forehead that says, "Hey! You there, nut job! Pay attention to me!"

As the train nears my destination, I'm ready to disembark and get to the restaurant. The train slows, grinding to a halt, as a throng of people try to exit while narrowly avoiding those cramming their way on. Chaos ensues, and I barely make it off the train in time.

I rush up the steps, making sure I have left Mr. Weirdo far behind. The warm summer air greets me as I emerge and hurry toward my destination. I have several blocks to go, and as I finally approach the home stretch, I rush down 9th Avenue and to the restaurant where I'm meeting Tori.

Glancing into the restaurant window as I get closer to the door, I spot Tori sitting just inside. Waving to her, I enter and squeeze past a small group of people crowding the aisle.

"I'm so sorry I'm late. The train was held up. Have you been here long?"

"Just got here. I was afraid I had left you waiting."

"Oh, good, so we were both late. No harm, no foul," I say, plopping myself down on the chair.

A tall thirty-something waiter casually strolls over to our table. He takes our drink orders and gives us a few minutes to look over the menu.

"He was a cutie. Maybe you should give him your number," Tori says with a twinkle in her eye.

"Yeah, and maybe a monkey will fly out of my ass. Oh, look…" I say, pointing at nothing, "there goes a pig flying by, too."

Tori laughs, rolling her eyes at me in the process. She always tries to get me to hit on some guy, and I never do. Seriously, she's done this since high school. Some things never change.

She glances toward the floor. "Let me see the shoes. Did you go shopping?" Tori and I have shared a major shoe addiction for years.

"No, I didn't. I've had these for a year or so." One foot adorned with a black Giuseppe Zanotti strappy sandal with a three inch heel emerges from underneath the table. I fail to remind her that I very rarely ever go shoe shopping anymore, despite the rush it used to give me. It's just one of the many parts of myself I entangled with him that no longer gives me the joy it once did.

"They're quite lovely, Lila," Tori says as she admires them like the shoe junkie she is. "Did you get the invitation to the opening yet?" Her raised eyebrows and wide eyes give away her excitement. She's been working hard for months to open up her own rock and roll nightclub.

"I did, and can I just say that it looked fabulous? It really captured the feel you're going for."

"Thank you! I designed it myself..." Drumming her fingers on the menu, her eyes dart to the floor and back up at me. "So?"

"So, what?" Did I miss something? She's looking at me like I have.

"So... please, Lila? I really want you to go... It's my grand opening and I want my best friend there by my side. It could be your last big hurrah in New York if you decide to move, too."

"I'll be there," I say with a sigh. "I'd be the shittiest friend alive if I didn't show up to support you." God only knows, she's been there for me more times than I can count. I owe it to her to support her on her big day.

"Not gonna lie, I was gonna say that next to guilt you into it if I had to."

"I wouldn't do it for anyone else," I say as I lean closer, winking at her.

"I know." Tori smiles brightly. "It's because I'm awesome and you love me."

We look over our menus in silence for a moment. I know exactly where this conversation is going, and the bad part about it is, I'm the one who's going to steer it that way. I can't help myself. I'm a glutton for punishment.

"I haven't laid eyes on him in over a year, and I don't know that I want to now." My stomach does somersaults at the thought of running into him, much like the night we met at a very similar event organized by Tori. "I've moved on, and I don't want him to think otherwise. I avoid walking by his house even though it's the shortest way to the subway just because I can't stand the thought of seeing him face-to-face. Shit, I even bought a car to avoid the whole thing. It just sucks that I can never find a good place to park so I end up taking the train anyway. And you know yourself that I decline invitations, even ones from you, all the time when I think he might be there."

"I know it'll be rough for you being in such close proximity, but why don't you bring that guy you met the other day? Shane, was it? Maybe it won't be so awkward for you if you're there with a date."

I'd met Shane through no effort of my own. I sat with an empty chair beside me in a crowded pizzeria one afternoon a few weeks back, and he asked if he could sit down. What was I supposed to do? Be a bitch and brush him off? No, my grandmother didn't raise me like that, so I smiled and said, "Of course." He sat down. We chatted. He asked me for my number, and here we are at that awkward are we or aren't we dating phase.

"I thought about doing that. We've hung out a couple of times now, but how do you invite your potential love interest to an event featuring your larger-than-life beast of an ex-boyfriend, who might want to kill the new guy just for the hell of it, and said ex's band?"

"Try to avoid him. It'll be hard, but I think you can do it. I doubt he would approach you when you're there with someone anyway, no matter how he felt about it. He still respects you. Hell, he's still in love with you if you want my honest opinion. He wouldn't do anything to cause you any further grief. Have you told him who your ex is?"

"No, he doesn't know."

"You really don't have to tell the dude Ash is your ex if you don't want to."

"I know, but I feel kind of guilty if I don't tell him. I mean we haven't really had the whole 'ex' conversation. I'm just worried that someone will say something to me while I'm there that will give it away, and then I look like the asshole who is trying to flaunt the new guy in front of the old guy. I don't want to be an asshole. And with possibly moving soon, I don't know that there's even a point to having that conversation anyway." I gaze out the window at a couple passing by who seem lost in each other's words and briefly reflect on my own romantic past to a time when I could've easily been part of a couple doing the same exact thing. The feeling of nostalgia quickly passes as the pain begins to settle in once again.

"That's understandable, but I don't think anyone would be that stupid to say anything, and you are *not* an asshole."

I turn my gaze back to Tori and grin. "You're underestimating the general stupidity running rampant at any given moment around those guys." We share a hearty laugh over the general dumbassery of a good chunk of the band's entourage.

"Okay, so please don't throat punch me when I ask what I'm about to ask. You know I have to or I wouldn't... Is there still a chance of a future for you two?"

I narrow my eyes at Tori and purse my lips together. "You're lucky I love you or I'd so bust you right now... I'm over him. Us together just won't work. I don't trust him anymore, and you know once that's gone with me, it's gone. There's no going back."

Tori nods and glances away. "I'm just glad you're going." A wide, toothy smile overtakes her face as her gaze lands back on me. "I have worked so hard on opening this place, and it wouldn't be the same without my best friend," she says as she reaches across the table and places her hand on mine. "I really hope you decide to stay in New York. I know it's selfish of me, but I really do cherish our friendship, and I will miss you tremendously if you go. I prefer meeting with my accountant face to face instead of through emails," she says as she grins at me, pulling her hand away.

"I'll miss you, too. If I move, I can always visit and you can come and visit me, too. It's only an hour flight and an hour drive once you land. We can discuss your financial information then." A smile flashes back at her despite the feeling of sadness creeping over me.

"Well, this baby is going to need an awesome aunt so you better visit us!"

Tori is just shy of five months along and her fair skin and strawberry blonde hair possess the radiant glow of pregnancy. She is just beginning to really look pregnant with the cutest little bump on her petite frame.

"I can't wait for your ultrasound so I can start buying cute outfits! I hope it's a girl so I can buy her shoes," I say excitedly. Even if the feeling of glee over buying myself a pair of shoes has been ruined, I can revel in buying them for someone else.

"Yeah, she'll have two shoe addicts in her life."

"A little shoe junkie in training." I laugh. It feels good to have something as positive as the birth of a child to look forward to. Being an only child, I never really thought about having a niece or nephew, but I am really excited at the possibility of hearing "Aunt Lila" come out of a small child's mouth.

The waiter returns to take our order, and we both opt for pancakes and a side of fruit. I splurge and have a mimosa as well. I need it badly. I've never been much of a drinker aside from the occasional indulgence or need to escape, but sometimes you just need something to take the edge off.

"I'm so proud of you, Tori. This new club of yours really is going to be a huge success. You know you can get Ferrum to play anytime, and pretty much any other bands they have connections with. It's going to be the biggest thing to hit this city in years."

"Being married to a famous musician does have its perks."

"That it does. Oh, wait... I wouldn't know about that one."

"Oh, come on, hun! You claim you haven't been hung up on him in like six months. Don't let seeing him get you down. You could run into him at any time, ya know, and I'm actually surprised you haven't since you live so close to each other. You're just spazzing because it's been so long. After it's over with, you won't even remember why you were worried."

"I hope you're right."

I truly do hope Tori is right. I haven't seen or spoken to Ash in almost thirteen months. Leaving him ranks pretty high on the list of hardest decisions I've ever had to make. He was the first and only man I absolutely loved in every sense of the word. I thought I knew what love felt like before him, but was wrong—terribly wrong. I fell for him harder and faster than I ever thought possible. He taught me what it was like to really be in love and have those feelings reciprocated.

I hate to admit it, but I miss that feeling. I miss being beside him. I miss his smell, the feel of his skin, and the deep blue of his eyes. I miss how he used to wake me up with a kiss to the forehead when we'd slept in late. I miss how safe I felt with him—like no matter what, he'd keep the vile and evil things in life at bay. I miss how he would call me in the middle of the night when he was on tour just to say goodnight and that he loved me. I miss it all... I miss him. And there it is. Will I ever be able to truly say goodbye to him in my heart?

The past year has been a roller coaster of emotions for me, and I only recently have become a bit more emotionally stable, though I still falter more than I'd like. Of course, I've tried hard to convince Tori, along with everyone else I know, that I got over him a long time ago. As far as he knows, I was over him immediately. I never let on otherwise.

That's a secret I have to keep locked away. If I admit out loud that I'm not over him, then I end up fighting a war within myself to stay away from him. I have always prided myself on being strong, and I feel like I have to put on a façade to keep my emotions in check. My secret and my heart must continue to be guarded.

275

When I first left, I had to practically lock myself in my bedroom to keep from running back to him. I cut myself off from the world, my business suffered, and I lost people who I thought for sure were truly my friends. The pain I felt was unbearable. Every day felt like a knife pushing further and further into my gut. It twisted and inched deeper and deeper, finally delving so deep that it sliced open my soul. Little bits of me escaped into nothingness as I lost myself to depression and anger.

He wouldn't just let me go, either, which didn't help things at all. Every time he would show up at my door or call, another piece of my heart would break, and I would question if it was all worth it or not. I dreamed of going back to him, but knew what our life had become and knew it would never go back to the way it was, not without both of us fighting for our love, and not without the trust that had long left the relationship. He had changed and so had I. There was no going back for us.

I'm no longer the optimistic girl who believes love is all you need to survive once you find the person you're meant to be with. I'm not the girl who went through some of the worst things that could ever happen to a person or a relationship, but still managed to hold out hope that I would find my Prince Charming someday.

I have no faith in love anymore. I don't believe everyone is entitled to a happily-ever-after, and I know in my heart that I won't get one. I'm forced to put on a show to reassure those around me that I'm a strong, optimistic woman and that I'm just fine and ready to love again. It's only when I'm alone that I'm able to remove my mask and accept my fate.

I desperately wish I could go back to being the girl I once was, but that girl is gone, and she's never coming back.

CHAPTER 1 – LILA STEPHENS

The sunlight broke through the curtains, warming my skin as I slept. A light, morning breeze blew through the window, leaving me feeling refreshed when I awoke, which was drastically different than how I'd been for months. Losing my grandmother, Edie, had really taken its toll on me since she passed earlier in the year. Once I made it through the numbness and depression began to set in, I knew I had to get away. I had to change things up if I didn't want to sink down into the hole I had worked so hard to crawl out of only a few years before when my life had last spiraled out of control. The second morning in my new home left me feeling optimistic for what the future might hold.

Stretching my arms and legs, I sat up and threw my legs over the edge of the bed and took a deep breath. Letting it out, I pondered what to do for the day. I was a little obsessive about getting familiar with my new surroundings and decided it was time to go out and explore. After showering, I pulled on my distressed denim capris, a deconstructed Black Sabbath T-shirt, and a comfy pair of walking shoes. I tied back my dyed black cherry hair into a high ponytail and grabbed my purple Coach sunglasses. I hooked a leash on my old beagle dog, Manny, who'd been going a little stir crazy while I unpacked, and headed out to get to know my new neighborhood.

I stepped out into the unseasonably warm early-October afternoon. It would be getting colder soon as the warm air of summer blew away, leaving the cold winter wind to take its place. I was determined to make the most of the warmth while I still could because the forecast had indicated that these were the last couple of days before heading into a cold snap that could bring freezing rain and ice.

As I walked down the street, I soaked up every bit of the neighborhood. My mind raced, frantically trying to take in everything I encountered. It would take me ages to remember where anything was, but I was up to the challenge, and I had the rest of my life ahead of me.

Manny and I continued on our journey to who knows where when several blocks from my house, I stumbled upon one of the greatest sights known to woman kind—the elusive man beast. You know, those men who are ridiculously tall, ridiculously built, ridiculously good looking, and also ridiculously hard to find outside of a movie screen or television show. This one happened to be trimming some hedges along a house that sort of resembled mine.

His skin, covering long, lean muscles, glistened as loose burgundy athletic pants sat dangerously low on his hips, exposing the top of a perfectly defined "v." He was the most mouthwatering thing I'd seen in all of my life. His dark chestnut hair, gathered at his nape, hung just below his shoulders. He was one of the tallest men I'd ever seen, well over six feet. Christ, he was a real beast of a man. I felt myself gawking at him and tried to look away before he caught me. I was sure he would probably think I was some kind of a freak with a staring problem.

From across the street, I remember thinking how he kind of looked like the lead singer of Tori's husband's band Ferrum, but she hadn't mentioned him living in the neighborhood when she was helping me find a place to live. It just never really occurred to me that it could actually be him. I assumed with the amount of people living in the whole of New York City, it was more likely that I'd just found his clone. I wondered to myself if rock stars even did their own yard work. *Note to self: this is the way to go when I want to go... well... anywhere.*

Though I might have internalized it, I was never one to put on a show by acting all giddy over an attractive man, so we quickly moved on. Manny and I eventually found a nice dog park where I was able to let him run off leash for a bit. I loved watching him forget how old he was and revert back to a state of puppyhood. I could swear he was smiling beneath the grey hairs that had begun to sprout around his muzzle.

Scanning the large park, I finally found an empty wooden bench to sit on while he frolicked with the other dogs. It wasn't that I didn't want to meet anyone —I did—but I was enjoying the time to myself. I tended to be a loner for the most part, never easily letting others in. I found it hard to trust people I didn't really know because of things that had happened to me over the years. This was why I developed such a close bond with Manny.

The day I found him seemed like it happened just weeks before, though in reality it had been several years. Gone was the little puppy in a box with a "free" sign outside of the grocery store, and in his place was the aging dog I knew and loved. As close as my best childhood friend Paige and I had been over the years, it paled in comparison to the bond I shared with him. He was still the only one I could ever truly be myself around. He knew my deepest, darkest secrets, and he never judged me for them. We had a connection I couldn't really explain. If you're a dog person, you understand already. If you're not, then there just aren't any words I can use to convey the strength of that bond.

I developed my addiction to shoes by the time he came into my life, and I chose to name him Manolo, or Manny for short, after one of my favorite shoe designers. I didn't actually own any Manolo's back then, but that's beside the point. I'd had him for close to nine years when I moved to New York, and I couldn't imagine my life without him.

My great Aunt Nora, Edie's sister, offered to take him to live with her in Ohio when I made the decision to move, but there was no way in hell I was going to let that happen. He was the closest remaining family I had, and I didn't know how much time I had left with him. Besides that, Nora was older than dirt, and I didn't know how long she'd really be able to care for him. Then where would he be? Probably with me in New York anyway.

The sound of Manny barking and growling snapped me back to reality. A Jack Russell attacked him playfully, and he was having none of it. I forced myself to stop reminiscing about the past and collect him before he got into too much trouble. That was all I needed, an angry mob of fur baby parents after me and my crotchety old dog. He wasn't really crotchety, though. He just had a little less tolerance for younger dogs than he used to.

As we left the dog park, my thoughts turned toward the greatest sight of all, and I wondered if he would still be outside. I made up my mind that I would have to check out the situation because I was definitely going to walk back by there. After all, I didn't want to risk getting lost on my way home, and I knew that street would lead me right to my front door. It'd be silly to go any other way, right?

Grey rain clouds invaded the sky that had been so blue just a few moments before and thunder rumbled through the sky in the distance. I hoped I could make it home before it started to pour the rain down. I hustled as fast as I could get Manny's little legs to go.

My palms began to sweat a little as I gripped Manny's leash, and my heart thudded hard against my chest as I walked back up the street in anticipation of what I might see. Luckily for me, Mr. Elusive Man Beast was still outside. He sat leaning back on the front steps with his long legs stretched out in front of him. His head tilted up toward the sky with his eyes closed. The sun peeking through the clouds kissed his pale skin, and his chest glistened. Fucking hell, I never thought sweat could be so sexy. Before I could stop myself, I pictured climbing him like a mountain and having my way with his body. I hadn't had any desire to be with a man in a very long time, but at least I knew I wasn't completely dead inside. He stirred up something deep down that hadn't been aroused in ages.

I tried to avert my eyes before he caught me gawking at him, but found it difficult. My brain shouted for me to look away, but I was too busy savoring the eye candy before me. Lowering his head, he looked in my direction as he started to stand. I sucked in a breath and held it there, just as our eyes met and held each other briefly. I mentally cursed the rain clouds for forcing me to take off my sunglasses. At least I could've hidden behind them if I still had them on. *How am I going to get out of this without looking like a complete doofus?* I didn't know whether to smile, wave, or run away flailing my arms like a lunatic.

He cocked an eyebrow and smirked at me. Yes, *smirked* at me. I can't recall a smirk ever making much of a good impression on me... not until that one anyway. They always seemed so obnoxious, but his sure as hell wasn't. Smiling back at him, I quickly glanced away and exhaled. My eyes scanned the ground for a large rock to climb under, but, alas, there were none big enough to be found. Thankfully, I was too far away for him to notice my skin as it flushed bright red, or so I hoped anyway. I just needed to breathe and forget about it. How often did I get a sexy smile from a gorgeous man who just happened to look like a famous rock star? Enjoy the moment and move on.

CHAPTER 2 – ASH LONDON

I cranked up the A/C and sat down on the hardwood floor by the vent in my living room. Sweat dripped from my neck and trickled down my back. I was in desperate need of a shower, but would have to wait to cool down first. I liked my balls far too much to subject them to an icy cold shower, and I felt like I might die of a heat stroke if I got under hot water.

Every time I forced myself out of the sanctity of my home to go for a run, I found something that needed done outside when I got back. I hardly ever left when I wasn't touring, so when I did, all the things I neglected to do around the house just drove me fucking nuts when I noticed them. Instead of coming in and cooling down, I would inevitably end up outside puttering around. It wasn't like me to leave things unattended, other than when I shut myself off from the outside world from time to time.

I pondered, like I always did when I finished up some tedious task outside, about hiring someone next time; maybe the same guys who took care of this stuff when I was touring. I certainly could afford it, but would never actually do it. I never hired anyone for that kind of stuff when I was home no matter how much I thought about it because the boring and mundane had a way of making me feel like a regular dude instead of the headliner at a freak show. I felt like I could really be Ash Volkov for a minute instead of Ash London.

This time around, was different, though. I didn't feel like putting energy into anything other than lying around on my ass and staring at the TV or sleeping. Ferrum's last tour had ended three months before, and I became a recluse, using the excuse that I was writing so I'd be left alone. Every day that went by dragged me deeper into seclusion and loneliness. I only kept up with my workouts because I had a public image to maintain, and if I turned into a slob, we'd more than likely lose a good chunk of our female fans or, at the very least, I'd be ridiculed by the anonymous masses online for letting myself go to shit.

I lowered myself down to lie on the floor and closed my eyes for a few minutes. As soon as they were shut, an image of the girl with the nice ass from outside was all I could see. Gawking from girls was nothing new, but for some reason she caught my attention for the time being. She was probably just a fan who had managed to catch me outside, which did happen more than I liked. The idea of moving to some secluded place with no neighbors for miles was one I thought about more than once or twice. As much as I tried over the years to keep my personal life private, including where I lived and my real name, there were always those few who were determined to figure out where I lived that eventually succeeded. The ones who found me were usually more aggressive than she was. It wasn't unusual for people like that to march right up to me and demand my attention. I didn't get that vibe from her at all. In the brief moment she caught my eye, she looked uneasy, like she wanted to run.

There was something about her I found sexy as hell, but I couldn't quite put my finger on it. Maybe it was the Black Sabbath shirt she wore, which somehow managed to cling to her body in just the right places. Her taste in music definitely added to the hotness factor in my book. The fact that she had a nice back side I'd noticed the first time she walked up the street only added to the fascination I suppose. I didn't even know what she looked like up close, but I knew I wanted to see more of her.

If I ever got the chance to get close enough to her, maybe I would talk to her and pull myself out of the miserable funk I'd found myself in. I was good at making the first move, although I hadn't always been. I reluctantly let my stage persona, the loud, foul-mouthed dick who took shit from no one and had no problems saying what he thought, take over my life for the most part. I found it difficult at times to shed him, no matter how badly I wanted to.

I was only able to be my true self when I was away from the music scene, but very few ever saw that side of me. It was easier to bury myself and be what people expected of me when I was in the public eye than to constantly answer why I was being so quiet or why I seemed distant. Was I sick? Why was I not being the life of the party? Why was I pissed off? It got old fast.

Growing up, I had a lot of friends who I knew were there because they liked me for who I was and what I had to offer. I met my two bandmates in high school, and we always knew we wanted to be rock stars. As I grew older and became a prominent part of the music industry, I found I could trust very few people, even the friends I'd made early on in life. Someone always wanted something from me whether it was exposure, money, or just flat out sex. I'd been taken advantage of by friends, family, acquaintances, and especially women too many times to count. I was at a point in my life where I didn't trust most of the people I met and was even skeptical of my own bandmates at times.

And speaking of flat out sex, I was much more of a man whore than I ever thought I could be when I first dreamt of being in a band back in high school. Back then I was lucky to get a girl to smile at me, let alone go anywhere near my cock. My life as the front man for Ferrum was your typical rock and roll rollercoaster. Sex, alcohol, drugs... you name it, I had access to it. Now that didn't mean I indulged in everything offered, but I had a hard time turning down an attractive woman offering herself to me.

For all the ass I got once I made it, I'd only had one serious relationship in my life. It started back before Ferrum really broke onto the scene, and we were together for a couple of years. We tried to make it work, but in the end, it was all for nothing. I've met plenty of women who claimed they could handle me and the spotlight, but no one ever lasted more than a couple of weeks before they showed their true colors, which usually consisted of greed, selfishness, jealousy, and immaturity.

I was finally at a point in my life where I wanted to meet someone and settle down, and I was hopeful I could find an honest woman who didn't give two shits about who I was. Unfortunately, Ash London's reputation had made that impossible for me to do.